"Ashdowne,  distr

Georgiana explained.

At her words, he threw back his head and burst into laughter, making her wonder if insanity ran in his family.

"I beg your pardon, but you're just so deuced... unpredictable," he finally said.

It hardly seemed a compliment, so Georgiana tossed her curls in pique. "I could say the same of you!"

"Really? How delightful," he murmured, and Georgiana felt the familiar sensation of surrender as he stepped toward her.

"No!" she said, holding up a hand to fend him off. "I haven't been able to think at all during supper. You are simply too unnerving."

Ashdowne's smile was slow and provocative. "Unnerving, am I?" he purred, taking another step forward. Georgiana moved away, only to come up against the wall of the house at her back.

"I like being unnerving...."

Dear Reader,

Welcome to Harlequin Historicals, Harlequin/Silhouette's *only* historical romance line! We offer four unforgettable love stories each month, in a range of time periods, settings and sensuality. And they're written by some of the best writers in the field!

The ever-popular Deborah Simmons is one of those writers. Best known for her medieval novels that feature the mighty de Burgh and de Laci families, Deb is a writer with an amazing range of talent and storytelling. Her newest, a Regency titled *The Gentleman Thief,* will put you under the spell of the charming Johnathon Saxton, Marquis of Ashdowne. In this story, a beautiful bluestocking stirs up trouble during a season at Bath when she investigates a jewel theft and finds herself closely scrutinizing—and falling for—the irresistible marquis.

Carolyn Davidson returns with *The Bachelor Tax,* a darling tale about a least-likely-to-marry "bad boy" rancher who tries to avoid a local bachelor tax by proposing to the one woman he's *sure* will turn him down—the prim preacher's daughter.... *My Lady Reluctant,* a terrific new medieval novel by Laurie Grant, is a true knight-in-shining-armor story filled with edge-of-your-seat intrigue and loads of passion.

Rounding out the month is *The Outlaw's Bride* by Liz Ireland, a rising talent who also writes contemporary romances for Harlequin. In this kidnapped bride story, a reputed Texas outlaw and a headstrong "nurse" fall in love—despite the odds against them. Don't miss it!

Enjoy! And come back again next month for four more choices of the best in historical romance.

Sincerely,

Tracy Farrell
Senior Editor

Deborah Simmons

THE GENTLEMAN THIEF

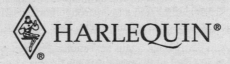

HARLEQUIN®

TORONTO • NEW YORK • LONDON
AMSTERDAM • PARIS • SYDNEY • HAMBURG
STOCKHOLM • ATHENS • TOKYO • MILAN • MADRID
PRAGUE • WARSAW • BUDAPEST • AUCKLAND

ISBN 0-373-29095-0

THE GENTLEMAN THIEF

Copyright © 2000 by Deborah Siegenthal

Printed in U.S.A.

Please address questions and book requests to:
Harlequin Reader Service
U.S.: 3010 Walden Ave., P.O. Box 1325, Buffalo, NY 14269
Canadian: P.O. Box 609, Fort Erie, Ont. L2A 5X3

For David Robert

Chapter One

No one took Georgiana Bellewether seriously.

To her utter dismay, she had been cursed with the lush curves of a cyprian, sprightly blond curls and big blue eyes that had often been compared to limpid pools. People took one look at her and decided that she didn't have a brain in her head. Of course, most men didn't think women intelligent anyway, but in her case they could conceive her to be nothing except a goosecap.

It was mortifying.

Her mother was a dear, rather flighty character, her father a genial, rotund squire, and Georgiana had no doubt that she would be happier had she taken after them. Unfortunately, of the four Bellewether progeny, she was the sole child to have inherited the characteristics of her great-uncle Morcombe, a noted scholar with a keen mind. Since her first toddling steps, Georgiana had devoured all manner of study, surpassing the skills of the family governess, the local academy for young ladies and her brother's tutor with equal fervor.

Her own particular talents leaned toward the solving of mysteries, and she often cursed the female form that kept her from life as a Bow Street Runner. Instead of following clues and daringly capturing criminals, she was forced to content herself with voracious reading and the unraveling of small puzzles that were presented to her in Chatham's Corner, the hamlet where her father reigned jovially as both squire and sheriff.

But this year, she vowed, it would be different. Her family had repaired to Bath for the summer, and Georgiana intended to make the most of her new location. Surely, in the famous resort town she would come upon at least one poser worthy of her skills! And certainly the wide and varied populace must be possessed of a more discerning nature than the rural inhabitants to whom she was accustomed.

Unfortunately, after a week spent visiting the Pump Room and strolling the avenues at the most fashionable hours, Georgiana was forced to admit her disappointment. Although she had enjoyed exploring, thus far she had met the same sort of genteel types with whom she was already familiar. Worse, not a single conundrum had she come across.

With a sigh, Georgiana glanced about the reception rooms of Lady Culpepper's lavish town house, eager for a diversion at the first real ball she had attended, but she saw only the usual assortment of dowagers and gouty gentlemen who populated Bath. Several misses, younger than herself, were there with doting mamas, hoping to snare a husband among the resort's visitors. Unfortunately, Georgiana had yet to meet one with more on her mind than marriage.

She dismissed them all only to have her gaze arrested by an elegant figure dressed entirely in black. Now there was a puzzle, Georgiana thought, her eyes narrowing. It didn't take someone of her particular talents to realize that the appearance of the Marquis of Ashdowne was most unusual, for the haut ton no longer favored Bath as they had a half century ago. Handsome, charming noblemen of Ashdowne's ilk stayed in London or followed the Prince Regent to Brighton. Or, Georgiana speculated, they spent their time at scandalous parties held in their huge, elegant country homes.

Not for the first time since she had heard of his visit, Georgiana thought Ashdowne's sudden interest in Bath was decidedly odd. She would have liked to find out why he was here but had yet to wrangle an introduction. He had arrived just a few days ago, sending all the young unmarried ladies, including her sisters, into a flutter of excitement, and it was difficult to see him through the crowd of women who surrounded him.

He had let one of the fashionable houses in Camden Place, and this was the first the general populace had seen of him. He was here supposedly to take the waters, but Georgiana found the idea absurd, for he was not quite thirty and not reputed to be ailing. Make that *definitely not* ailing, Georgiana amended, as the group parted, affording her a good view of the man.

He was the very picture of health. Indeed, the Marquis of Ashdowne might well be the healthiest man Georgiana had ever seen, she decided, with a swift intake of breath. He was tall, probably six feet in height, and slender. Not skinny, mind you, but broad shouldered and muscular, though not in a bulky sort of way. All in all, the marquis possessed a grace and bearing Georgiana had not expected in one of the overfed, debauched members of the ton.

Lithe. That was the word that struck her as her attention traveled up the elegant, expensive clothing to his face. His hair was dark and sleek, his eyes a startling blue, and his mouth was... Georgiana could muster no description for it, with its lush curves and a small indentation above his

upper lip. Ashdowne, she realized, swallowing abruptly,
was handsome beyond belief.

And awake on every suit.

The knowledge came to her with a shock, for although
Georgiana was all too aware of the misjudgments to be
made based upon outward appearance, she assumed that
someone that rich and powerful and beautiful could not
possibly be blessed with brains, too. But she was wrong,
for just as she blinked in amazement at his features, the
Marquis of Ashdowne met her gaze with his own, bright
with intelligence. Had Georgiana been the fanciful sort,
she might have thought him aware of her scrutiny, for it
seemed as though he had singled her out of the crowd
most particularly.

Georgiana drew back, ashamed to be staring, and when
one of Ashdowne's dark brows lifted in response, she colored. Fanning herself, she deliberately looked away. She
had only been studying the man, as she would anyone
else, and she grimaced in annoyance at his intimate
glance. Ashdowne probably thought her just another one
of the smitten females who practically swooned at his
charm.

Whirling around, Georgiana was nearly halfway across
the airy reception room when she realized that she had
missed a golden opportunity for an introduction. Botheration! She snapped her fan in disgust, for she knew better
than to let her personal feelings interfere with an investigation. She could hardly imagine a Bow Street Runner
abandoning his case because one of his suspects eyed him
with too much familiarity.

With a small sound of irritation, Georgiana turned back
toward the way she had come, but already her place had
been filled by other women, both young and old. Then
her mama appeared, cajoling her to dance with a young

man, and Georgiana, from long experience, knew better than to argue.

Mr. Nichols, Georgiana soon discovered, was a nice enough fellow, here with his family from Kent, but as he spoke haltingly on such bland topics as the weather and the society of Bath, Georgiana's attention wandered. Although she kept craning her neck in an effort to see Ashdowne, when she finally spied the marquis, he was heading out to the garden with a young widow who apparently had abandoned her mourning most precipitously.

Georgiana frowned as Mr. Nichols met with her again during the dance, and she nodded absently at his questions. She really had no time for such inanities! Unfortunately, she recognized all too well the dazed expression on her partner's face. If focused, it would no doubt rest upon her curls or her white throat, or worse yet, the alarming expanse of pale breast that her mother insisted she expose as fashionable.

He paid no attention to what she was saying, of course, and at times like these, Georgiana was often tempted to whisper of insurrection or confess to a murder, in an effort to jolt her audience into awareness. Her admirers usually fell into two camps: those who paid no heed whatsoever to what she said, and those who hung on her every word.

Unfortunately, the latter were of no more use to her than the former, for she always failed to engage them in any kind of meaningful discourse. The sapskulls agreed with everything she said! She supposed she ought to be used to it by now, but nevertheless, Georgiana felt a twinge of disappointment.

Her mother was always extolling the virtues of marriage and parenthood, but how could Georgiana even entertain the notion of a life spent with a man such as this? Yet how was she, in her small venue, to acquaint herself with anyone else? Education among the gentry was a haphazard business at best, and even those with a modicum of schooling seemed to be struck dumb by her appearance.

It was the curse of her existence. And so she discouraged them all, much to her mother's disappointment, and resigned herself to a life of spinsterhood, where she might have the freedom to finally dress and act as she wished, providing her great-uncle Morcombe left her the stipend he had promised. Not that she wished him to pass on in the near future.

It was with much relief that Georgiana realized the set was coming to an end, and she sent Mr. Nichols happily off to fetch her an ice, which granted her a slight but much desired reprieve from his company.

"Isn't he wonderful?" her mother gushed into her ear. "I have it on good authority that he will come into a lovely piece of land in Yorkshire from his grandfather, which ought to provide him with a thousand pounds a year!"

The earnestness in her dear mother's face prevented Georgiana from dashing the woman's hopes with a scathing reply. If not Mr. Nichols, then some other gentleman would be forced upon her, so she simply nodded absently while searching the room for Ashdowne. To her surprise, he had joined in the dancing, moving with a grace that caused a fluttering sensation in the pit of her stomach.

"Please, excuse me," she said, moving away from her mother with a distracted air.

"But Mr. Nichols…"

Ignoring her mother's protest, Georgiana slipped into the crowd. Although she lost sight of Ashdowne, she was pleased to be free of both her dear mama and Mr. Nichols, and so she made her way slowly through the press of people, watching and listening. It was one of her favorite pastimes, for there was always the chance she might over-hear information that could come in handy. Not gossip, of course, but something pertinent to her investigation.

In this case, talk about Ashdowne.

Unfortunately, she didn't hear much of use, only that he was so dashing and charming, etcetera, ad nauseam. He had been a younger son, coming into the title after the death of his brother a year ago. He appeared to have set-tled into the title quite nicely, according to one knowing matron, and did not hold himself above the rest of the world, as evidenced by his most gracious manner. Etcet-era. Ad nauseam. The conversations were much the same. All the gushing over Ashdowne became positively annoy-ing, and, perversely, she became even more determined to find the man guilty of something.

"Ah, Georgie!" Stifling a groan, Georgiana turned to find her father standing beside her with a sober-looking gentleman. Another potential suitor for her, she surmised, fighting the urge to run screaming from the room.

"Mr. Hawkins, here she is, my eldest daughter! Lovely girl, just as I told you, and such a clever thing. I'm sure you will find her most interested in your scholarship!"

Georgiana, knowing her dear father all too well, gath-ered that *he* was not, and was eager to pass his new ac-quaintance on to herself.

"Georgie, love, this is Mr. Hawkins. He's newly ar-rived at Bath, too, and hoping to find a living here, as he's a vicar and very learned."

Georgiana pasted a smile on her face and managed to greet Mr. Hawkins with a modicum of civility. He was attractive in a rather severe way, but something in his gray eyes told her that he was not the kind of gentle, unassum-ing soul as was their own Vicar Marshfield.

"A pleasure, of course, Miss Bellewether," the man

said. "But a lady such as yourself could hardly be expected to understand the intricacies of philosophy. Indeed, I suspect that most men would be hard-pressed to match my knowledge, since I have devoted my life to its study."

Before Georgiana could argue that she was a devotee of Plato, who had, after all, founded the science of logic, Mr. Hawkins went on. "And, I must admit that Rousseau has fallen out of favor, what with the unpleasantness in France. However, I cannot see how he can be blamed for what befell the unfortunates there."

"So you believe that—" Georgiana began, but Mr. Hawkins cut her off with a sniff.

"But, then, the most enlightened men have often suffered for their genius," he declared.

It didn't take Georgiana's keen faculties to determine that the pompous vicar counted himself among the persecuted academics, and Georgiana's spark of interest was immediately and firmly doused. She would find no intellectual stimulation here, for Mr. Hawkins obviously was in the habit of expounding—not conversing.

Stifling a yawn, she stood there while he tossed off long words and theories in a strange mix that left her certain he understood very little of what he was spouting. No wonder her father had been so eager to be rid of the man! Georgiana was rapidly reaching her limits of endurance, too.

"Ah, there is our hostess!" she said, in an effort to break away, but Mr. Hawkins would not let her go so easily.

"Humph! I am surprised that she has opened her home to so many of her social inferiors, for it has been my experience that those of her rank are rarely cordial to the less fortunate."

Although Lady Culpepper was prone to the condescending air of the nobility, Georgiana did not find her any worse than most. "I admit that she could be more gracious, but—"

"Gracious?" Mr. Hawkins cut Georgiana off with an unbecoming scoff, an odd vehemence in his voice. "The lady and her kind are not known for their courtesy to others, but lord their wealth and power over the rest of us. I find them frivolous beings with no concerns except their own selfish caprices!"

Mr. Hawkins's sudden venom surprised Georgiana, but then, as swiftly as it had come over him, the mood was gone, replaced by a rather bland expression. "However, a man in my position must do his best to mingle with society," he added, as if begrudging his chosen career.

"I would think it your vocation to convince people to be more charitable," Georgiana noted idly.

Mr. Hawkins responded with a patronizing smile that made her bristle. "It is to your credit that you would think of such things, but I can hardly expect such a beautiful lady to understand the complexities of my position," he said, and Georgiana was tempted to boot him into a new position with a good swift kick. "Indeed, I vow that you, Miss Bellewether, are the saving grace to a tedious evening spent in ill company."

If Georgiana had thought the man too full of himself to have noticed her presence, she was sadly mistaken, for even as he spoke warmly of her, his gaze drifted tellingly to her bosom. And for a religious man, he was studying her a little too avidly for her taste. "You must excuse me," she said abruptly, and hurried off into the crowd before he could launch into another lengthy discourse.

After slipping through the assemblage, keeping her eyes and ears attuned to anything of interest, Georgiana halted behind a tall potted plant, a large fern of some sort, where she listened to several conversations, all of them exceedingly dull. At last, growing restless, she was about to depart when there was a shuffling nearby and the sound of whispered voices, which, as everyone knew, invariably signaled something interesting.

Moving unobtrusively closer, Georgiana peered through the greenery in an effort to catch a glimpse of the speakers. She saw a rather sturdy looking gentleman with a sadly receding hairline whom she immediately recognized at Lord Whalsey, a middle-aged viscount. Rumor had it that he was dangling for a rich wife among those who came to Bath, and, indeed, he was a popular one with the ladies, if a bit full of himself. As she peeked under a particularly large leaf, Georgiana could see him hunched next to a younger man with a rather pinched face, and the two appeared terribly serious. She leaned closer.

"Well? Do you have it?" Whalsey asked, his voice betraying an agitation that immediately seized Georgiana's attention.

"Er, not exactly," the other man hedged.

"What the devil? I thought you were going to get it tonight! Demn, Cheever, you swore you could manage this, you—"

"Hold on there," the man called Cheever said in a placating tone. "You shall have it all right. There's been a complication, that's all."

"What kind of complication?" Whalsey spat. "And it better not cost me more!"

"Well, I've run into a bit of difficulty locating it."

"What do you mean?" Whalsey cried. "You know very well where it is! That's why we came to this deadly dull backwater!"

"Of course, it's here, but it's not lying about in plain view, now is it? I've got to make a search for it, and I haven't had a chance because some bloody idiot's always around!''

Forgetting about Ashdowne, Georgiana held her breath and stuck her head right into the foliage.

''Who?'' Whalsey asked.

''The servants!''

''Well, tonight's your chance, you dolt! What are you doing standing here?''

''I might as well enjoy a bit of the evening while I'm out, mightn't I?'' Cheever said smoothly. ''It hardly seems fair that you're dancing and frolicking while I'm doing the dirty work!''

Whalsey's face turned florid, and he opened his mouth as if to shout, but, to Georgiana's disappointment, he appeared to recover himself, lowering his voice until she had to strain to hear. ''If you're angling for more money, I told you I haven't a penny to—''

Frustrated by the inaudible words, Georgiana leaned forward a little too far. The plant, berthed in an elegant urn, tipped slightly and, caught in its growth, she too swayed precariously. With a low gasp, she reached for a heavy leaf, hoping to right both the shrub and herself, but lost her balance. For one moment, Georgiana seemed to hang in the air, staring at the horrified faces of Lord Whalsey and Cheever.

So intent was she upon the fleeing twosome as they hurried away that Georgiana did not see the other man approaching. Only after she veered violently in the other direction in an attempt to regain her footing did she glimpse him. And then, of course, it was too late. Both she and the wretched plant toppled directly into him, sending all three of them to the floor in a heap.

Vaguely Georgiana heard startled gasps from around her as she struggled to separate herself from the thick leaves. She was on the carpet, her legs all tangled up with those of the man who lay beneath her, and her gown had risen scandalously to expose her ankles. Worst of all, she had missed hearing more about the nefarious plot she was certain the two men were hatching. Botheration!

Blowing away a fat curl, Georgiana pushed off the floor in an effort to sit, only to hear a pained grunt from below as her knee connected with a certain portion of male anatomy. With a cry of dismay, Georgiana jerked upward, but she was stopped by her twisted skirts and fell forward once more.

More gasps went up from around her and then Georgiana felt firm hands upon her waist as she lifted her head only to recoil in horror at the face that came into view. Dark brows were no longer raised in arrogance but lowered in a disturbing manner that made the elegant features below them appear rather fierce, while that compelling mouth twisted into something resembling a snarl. "For God's sake, stop wiggling!" he said.

"Ashdowne!" Georgiana breathed. She had a moment to blink in alarm before the hands at her waist lifted her effortlessly upward and then they were both upright, the marquis setting her on her feet. She took a faltering step backward, but he held on to her, and Georgiana suddenly became aware of the heat generated by his touch. Like fire, it burned through the thin silk she wore, igniting her skin and sending warmth rushing throughout her body.

Curious. Georgiana glanced at her companion and stared, transfixed. He was just that much more beautiful up close, his eyes so blue as to make her own seem insipid instead of limpid, and Georgiana felt an odd dipping sensation in the pit of her stomach. As she gaped, he released her and stepped back, his handsome face wearing an expression of extreme annoyance as he raised one slender hand to brush a smattering of dirt from his elegant silk waistcoat. To her dismay, the marquis was looking at her as if she were an irritating bug he would like to squash— or at least be rid of.

Jolted from her stupor by the realization, Georgiana muttered her apologies in a hushed whisper that sounded like the breathless nonsense of a swooning admirer. And then, Georgiana, who thought herself past the age of blushes, felt a fiery stain rise in her cheeks as embarrassment claimed her. She was *not* one of those marriage-mad misses, and she desperately sought the words to convey that to his lordship. But her halting excuse was cut short by the arrival of her mother, along with two servants, who hurried to clean up the spilled soil.

"Georgie!" Wincing at the sound of her pet name called out loudly, Georgiana did not hear Ashdowne's murmured platitude. And before she could question him, he tilted his head and moved away, as if all too relieved to quit her company. To her dismay, Georgiana found herself surrounded by her mother and her sisters, while he disappeared into the crowd.

"Georgie! What on earth were you doing—inspecting the shrubbery?" her mama asked, eyeing the nearby plant as if it ought to explain itself. When it did not, she turned to her daughter.

"Lovely girl, but not too graceful, I fear." Her father's booming voice made Georgiana grimace, as did the titters of her sisters. Must her whole family make so much of this?

"Are you all right, Miss Bellewether?" As if things were not bad enough, Mr. Nichols had found her again. And how could he not, considering the spectacle she had made of herself? "I say, one can hardly move in this dreadful squeeze, and to clutter the floor with obstacles..." He shook his head, his gaze drifting down her wrinkled clothes to her ankle. Hastily Georgiana smoothed her gown and sighed as her mother urged her to a nearby chair and Mr. Nichols forced upon her the ice that was now sadly warm.

While they fussed, Georgiana fought the urge to leap to her feet and flee their attentions. Worse yet, she felt as if all eyes in the room were upon her—a terrible prospect for someone who was trying to be unobtrusive. She had bungled royally—and just when she was finally hearing something interesting.

Scowling with exasperation, Georgiana waved her mother away and searched the crowd for any sign of Lord Whalsey and his cohort, but all she saw was Ashdowne. Although he appeared to be speaking with the hostess, his eyes were on her, his mouth curved in condemnation as if he held her entirely responsible for the recent debacle.

Botheration! She had not asked for his help, nor had she even seen him tendering it, so he could hardly blame her if his efforts went awry. She would have done better without him, she thought, her cheeks flaming, and she had a notion to tell him so, but her opportunity for dialogue had once again slipped away. And it was all her own fault!

A Bow Street Runner would not have gaped like a schoolroom miss at a pretty visage, but would have made the most of the chance encounter, asking Ashdowne what he was doing in Bath, judging his answers and slyly maneuvering him into an admission of...something. Georgiana wasn't sure what exactly, but she was determined to find out.

She glanced toward the subject of her musings and nearly started in surprise, for he was gone once again, Lady Culpepper now being deep in conversation with a turbaned matron. Amazed, Georgiana blew out a breath, disturbing one of her curls, and shook her head. The man seemed to appear and disappear in an instant, and she decided it was a good thing she was not given to whimsy, or she might suspect him of preternatural abilities.

"...like limpid pools." The sound of Mr. Nichols's voice brought her attention back to him, and, pasting a smile upon her face, Georgiana tried to show more forbearance than was her wont. She managed the task for a few minutes before abandoning her efforts and excusing herself.

Telling her mother that she needed to freshen up after the mishap, Georgiana instead roamed the room looking for Whalsey and Cheever, to no avail. When she caught a glimpse of Mr. Hawkins bearing down upon her with grim intent, she fled out into the garden, where she breathed a deep sigh of relief.

The night air was scented with the spring flowers that lined secluded walkways, lit only by the glorious display of stars overhead. Another young lady might have found magic in the evening, but not Georgiana. She wondered who was out there in the darkness. Had Whalsey and his cohort adjourned to a more private location to discuss their suspicious business? Only Georgiana's innate good sense prevented her from indulging her curiosity and slipping onto the paths herself.

With a sigh, she cursed the gender that made her prey to the designs of men and subject to the confining strictures of society. A Bow Street Runner could easily go wherever he wanted, whether a midnight garden or the seediest neighborhood in London. Ah, what a wonderful life, she thought, never pausing to wonder how such a fellow would manage to gain entry to a party such as this one. She spent long, delightful minutes enjoying the illustrious career that could have been hers, if only she had been born a man.

Georgiana might have remained there forever, lost in pleasant musings, if not for a loud giggle that erupted behind one of the nearby shrubs. With a sigh, she decided it was time to return to the party before she saw the kind of assignation that was of no interest to her—the romantic sort. No doubt her mother was searching for her, for it was growing late, and the rather staid Bellewether party would be heading home soon.

With one last glance at the dark lawn, Georgiana turned and slipped through the French doors into the reception room, prepared to find her family, when a bloodcurdling scream rent the air. Stunned, she turned toward the sound and caught sight of the hostess, Lady Culpepper, rushing down the main staircase, accompanied by the turbaned matron she had seen earlier.

Both women looked distraught, and Georgiana hurried forward. She reached the bottom of the steps just in time to hear the turbaned woman babble something about a necklace, and then the cry went up, carried through the crowd faster than any wildfire: *"Lady Culpepper's famous emeralds have been stolen."*

As news of the theft flew through the reception room, the rest of the house and, presumably, all of Bath, Georgiana, who had refused to budge until she heard the whole of it, was privy to the first breathless report of the turbaned woman she later identified as Mrs. Higgott.

Weeding through the babbling to the bare facts of the matter, Georgiana learned that the two women had been discussing Lady Culpepper's jewelry when Mrs. Higgott expressed admiration for the emerald necklace, well-known among the ton as the pride of her collection. Lady Culpepper, either graciously or vainly, offered to show off the piece and the two went to her bedroom, where they found the jewel case open upon the bed, the piece in question gone and the window open.

Since a servant had been stationed in the hall outside the door all evening, it was assumed that the thief somehow managed to scale the side of the building, a feat that engendered nearly as much talk as the burglary itself. Although Georgiana forced her brother Bertrand to accompany her on a tour of the grounds afterward, there was nothing to be seen in the darkness, and all her efforts to question the two women were turned aside. Indeed, the party quickly broke up out of consideration for Lady Culpepper's terrible loss, with everyone expressing shock at the commission of such a crime in quiet Bath.

Everyone, that is, except Georgiana.

Chapter Two

Thrilled at the first true challenge to her abilities, Georgiana rose early the morning after the incident and seated herself at the rosewood writing desk in the drawing room, where she put to paper every detail she could recall of the evening and the company. Unfortunately, she had been unable to view the scene or question the principles, but she was very thankful to have been present during the actual theft.

The mystery itself was a positively splendid one, not your average crime, but obviously a well thought out and daring perpetration, and Georgiana smiled absently as she made note of that which she deemed important. The time, of course, was of interest. When had Lady Culpepper last been in the room before returning with Mrs. Higgott? And what of the servant outside the room? Had he heard nothing? Was he truly there all night, or had he left his post?

And what of the room itself? Did it open onto any others? Georgiana would dearly love to look for any clues the thief had left behind, including the jewel case itself. From what she could understand from the two women's ramblings, the container had been left behind, despite the gems that remained inside it.

Georgiana frowned. Why steal just the necklace? Had the thief been pressed for time, or hindered by what he could carry with him? A man who scaled the exterior wall could not be hampered with a bulky parcel, but Georgiana found it difficult to believe that someone had gone to such lengths to gain entry. Perhaps the fellow had tossed up a rope, she thought. Uncertain of the logistics of that sort of thing, she vowed to ask Bertrand. And she fully intended to view the building in the daylight.

If only she could see the room itself! Something about the open jewel box sounded familiar, but, unable to place the memory, Georgiana made a quick note of it and then pulled out another sheet of foolscap upon which to name her suspects. Her hand nearly trembled with the force of her excitement, for here not only was a challenge to her skills, but an opportunity. If she could solve this puzzle and present the culprit's name to the authorities, she might finally receive the respect she craved.

Resting her chin on a hand, Georgiana smiled dreamily as she imagined the accolades due her, especially if she managed to recover the stolen jewels! More important than praise, however, was the possibility that she could make a name for herself, and she enthusiastically pictured a future filled with investigations as people from all over the country came to consult her, Georgiana Bellewether.

Heaving a sigh of delight at such pleasant fantasies, Georgiana nevertheless turned her attention back to the task at hand, for she must first determine the identity of the man who had taken Lady Culpepper's necklace. Although the burglar might be someone unknown to her, a member of the criminal community who had lain in wait for his chance, logic argued against it. No common cutpurse would rob a house on a night when it was filled to brimming with guests and servants.

Whoever had done the deed did not waste time ransacking other rooms, but knew just where to go to find his prize. Georgiana abruptly dropped her hand and lifted her chin as the conversation she had overheard behind the plant came to mind. She had known from their whispers that Lord Whalsey and Mr. Cheever were plotting something nefarious, but little did she imagine the two men capable of a crime of such epic proportions!

With a grim expression, Georgiana tried to copy down everything the two had said, including Mr. Cheever's complaint that he was hampered in his efforts to ''get it'' by the presence of servants. Oh, it was really all too simple, Georgiana thought, and as visions of acclaim once more rose to mind, she placed Mr. Cheever and the man who hired him first upon her list.

But, as promising as the two men were, Georgiana still intended to consider all possibilities, and so she wondered just who else at the house that night might be responsible. The culprit could be a servant, she thought, though such instances were rare, and who among them during the busy party would have found time to scale the building? She wished that she might question those in Lady Culpepper's employ in order to obtain all pertinent information.

As to the guests, Georgiana found it difficult to name too many candidates among the genteel inhabitants of Bath. Most she deemed not clever enough to pull off such a scheme, while others were too honest and bland to suddenly take up a life of crime. But as she thought of all those simple faces, Georgiana suddenly remembered the vicar and his vocal contempt for the wealthy. Frowning, she wondered if the good cleric could have managed to steal the necklace. The venom in his words had disturbed her and, without hesitation, she counted him as her second suspect.

Once more, considering everyone she had seen, Georgiana easily dismissed the dowagers, the gouty old men and the young ladies as incapable of entering and escaping through the window. No, the culprit was definitely someone agile, slender but with the strength to climb, graceful undoubtedly, and…dressed all in black?

Georgiana's eyes narrowed as an image of Ashdowne, dark and elegant, filled her mind. Ashdowne, who seemingly appeared and disappeared at will, certainly looked as if he could do anything, including scale the side of a building, and his strength had been evident in the way he lifted her with ease off his prone body. The memory made Georgiana flush with an unwelcome heat, as did the knowledge that the handsome nobleman had reduced her to a yammering ninny.

Georgiana scowled, angry with herself and at the man who was so carelessly capable of rendering her speechless. He was up to something, and she knew it! He was far too…healthy to need the waters. Of course, his presence in Bath might well be due to a lady, Georgiana realized with an odd surge of disappointment. All too often, gentlemen of the ton dallied with wives, widows and other available females. But somehow Georgiana had expected more from the possessor of those startlingly intelligent eyes.

And as she considered the women who had been in attendance last night, Georgiana was hard-pressed to come up with viable candidates. To her mind, the ladies present did not look worth the effort, but she was not a man, and everyone knew that their thoughts were unpredictable, at best. Georgiana had seen Ashdowne with the widow, but she had gone on to dance with others, while he was nowhere to be seen. As usual. And in the end, it was his unexplained disappearances that convinced Georgiana to add his name to the list of suspects with a flourish.

Although she had no liking for Mr. Nichols or any of her other admirers, in all good conscience, Georgiana could not include them, for none seemed to possess the wherewithal for so daring a burglary. And even should she have misjudged them, according to Bertrand, the young bucks were congregated in the card room during the time of the robbery, engaged in some sort of wagering. She had questioned her brother thoroughly and accounted for those few young men who might have the necessary agility.

Which left very few suspects. Of course, it was possible that the burglar was someone outside the party, abetted by a knowledgeable insider, a prospect that Georgiana found most frustrating. She was simply going to have to obtain the names of all the guests and talk to the servants—and to Lady Culpepper herself.

Putting aside her list of suspects, Georgiana swiftly penned a note to the lady, begging to call upon her as soon as possible concerning a matter of gravest importance. She decided to send a servant round this very morning with the message, for the sooner she gathered her information, the better the chance of retrieving the stolen gems.

Although the theft had been brilliantly executed, Georgiana did not doubt her own abilities, and she envisioned a swift resolution to the mystery. Mr. Cheever's pinched features rose in her mind only to dangle there uncertainly, for somehow he did not appear capable of such cleverness. Indeed, as much as she tried to fight it, Georgiana felt an unwitting admiration for the culprit. Here, at last, was someone worthy of her own talents. She sighed and sank her chin onto one hand.

It was simply her ill luck that he was a criminal.

* * *

After waiting impatiently throughout the morning, Georgiana finally received a response to her missive, and, hurrying off to avoid her sisters, she arrived at Lady Culpepper's elegant home shortly after noon. There she was shown into a salon, where the hostess was seated upon an elegant wing chair, a luncheon tray on the table beside her.

"Come in, young lady!" the older woman called in a shrill voice, and Georgiana stepped forward into the lavishly appointed room, with its carved white marble chimneypiece and cut-glass chandelier. The furnishings looked much as they had last night, but Lady Culpepper appeared far older in the daylight that streamed in through the tall windows.

Georgiana felt the noblewoman's assessing gaze upon her as she took a seat. "Thank you for seeing me, my lady," she began politely, only to be met with a sour expression.

"And well you should be grateful," Lady Culpepper said. "I have refused all callers today, as befitting my distraught condition. So tell me, what is this matter of grave importance you have to discuss? Do you know anything about my necklace?" Georgiana nodded, and the older woman leaned forward, one bony hand clutching the mahogany edge of the chair. Her eyes glittered shrewdly, and Georgiana realized that Lady Culpepper was no fool.

"Well?" she asked impatiently.

"I have reviewed the incident with the information at my disposal and have narrowed down the suspects to a likely few," Georgiana answered. At Lady Culpepper's odd look, she added, "I consider myself most adept at the solving of mysteries and hope to come to a definite conclusion soon. However, I would like to speak with the servants, if I may, and ask you a few questions.''

"Who are you?" Lady Culpepper demanded.

"Georgiana Bellewether, my lady," she answered, wondering if the woman was forgetful. If so, that might put a different slant on the case, making it more difficult to ascertain the time of the theft.

"A nobody!" Lady Culpepper said in an imperious tone. "Just what makes you think you can barge in here—"

"But you invited me, my lady," Georgiana protested, earning a rebuking glance for her interruption.

"You, young lady, are impertinent! I agreed to see you because I thought you knew something about my stolen necklace!"

"But I do!" Georgiana said. "I can help you, if—"

"Bah! The help of a silly girl who thinks she knows more than her superiors!"

"I assure you that my abilities are quite well-known at home, though here in Bath—"

"Home! A tiny village of no importance, I am sure!" Lady Culpepper sniffed, and Georgiana decided another tack was called for at once.

"What have you to lose, my lady?" she asked. "I want no reward, but only wish to assist you as well as I may."

A look of avarice flashed in the older woman's eyes at the mention of a reward. "And you will most certainly have none," she confirmed. A moment passed in which Georgiana met her glare impassively, and finally Lady Culpepper sniffed, her chin held high. "Very well. Ask your questions, but quickly, for I have more important matters demanding my attention than to indulge the whims of every silly girl in Bath."

In the few minutes that Lady Culpepper allotted her,

Georgiana discovered that the jewel case had been found open, its other contents left intact. The door was locked, and the servant stationed to watch it swore that none had entered.

"And why did you set the servant to guard your room? Does he do so at all times or only during entertainments at your home?" Georgiana asked.

Lady Culpepper appeared startled by the question, then she lifted her chin to look down her nose at Georgiana. "That, young lady, is none of your affair. Enough of these questions!"

"But, my lady!" Georgian protested. Unfortunately, all her efforts to see the premises were met with haughty refusals, as were her requests to talk to the servants, while Lady Culpepper grew increasingly short-tempered.

For her part, Georgiana was unimpressed with the noblewoman. The more she spoke, the more Lady Culpepper resembled a fishwife, and Georgiana wondered about her antecedents. Biting back a sigh, she persevered as best she could. "Can you think of any servant or guest at the party who would do such a thing?" Georgiana asked.

"Certainly not!" Lady Culpepper answered. "One hopes that none of one's acquaintances is a foul criminal! Of course, this is Bath, not London, and it is no less than what I deserve for opening my home to the ill-bred rabble that frequent this city. I assure you that as soon as I have my jewels back, I will be returning to London, where I am far more selective in my invitations."

Georgiana refrained from mentioning the higher incidence of theft in the more notorious city, but nodded in a placating manner before continuing. "You have no enemies or those who might seek to target you in particular?"

Georgiana noted the sudden paling of the older

woman's face with interest. Whether Lady Culpepper was angered by the very suggestion of malice or by the truth of it, Georgiana could not tell. "Begone with you, child! I have wasted enough of my time with this nonsense!" she said, her tone brooking no opposition.

With a wave of dismissal, Lady Culpepper called for the butler to show Georgiana out, and there was nothing to do but thank the ungracious woman for her time. As Georgiana took her leave, she could not help feeling dissatisfied. She was struck by the uncharitable notion that the obnoxious woman deserved to have her jewels stolen, but firmly quelled such thoughts, for it would not do to let emotions color her investigation.

Once outside, Georgiana told the startled butler that she was going to have a look around the grounds and walked into her ladyship's garden without a qualm, leaving him sputtering on the doorstep. She made her way slowly to the rear of the building, where she stood staring up at the reported locations of the bedroom windows. The view was much better in the daylight, and Georgiana noticed an arched pediment that curved above them—as well as upon the windows below.

Blinking at the sight, she wondered if, instead of scaling the side of the building, the culprit had simply slipped into another room and out onto the pediment to climb inside Lady Culpepper's bedroom. The footing for such a feat looked quite precarious, and Georgiana's heart began hammering fitfully at the idea, for she did not like heights in the slightest. However, an agile man who was unafraid and trained in such dexterous movements might well—

"Harrying the plants again?"

Georgiana was so lost in thought that the abrupt sound of a caustic voice close by startled her and she whirled around, sending her reticule swinging wildly. It connected quite firmly with the form of a man she had not realized had come to stand behind her.

"Oomph!" he said, laying a hand upon his patterned silk waistcoat. "What do you have in there, rocks?"

Georgiana's gaze flew from the slender gloved fingers to the handsome face, where one black eyebrow climbed upward, and she blinked in horror. "Ashdowne! I mean, my lord! I beg your pardon!"

The marquis's beautiful mouth turned down at the corners as he smoothed the elegant material, drawing Georgiana's attention across his broad shoulders and wide chest to his flat abdomen. The sight seemed to make her own far more rounded stomach dip and pitch, and with effort, Georgiana tore her gaze away and back to his face. "What are you doing here?" she asked suspiciously.

The black brow lifted again, above eyes brimming with distaste. It was a look Georgiana recognized from the night before, and once more she felt like an insect that the marquis found particularly annoying. While she stared, he tilted his head to the side as if to better study the strange specimen that was she.

"I've come to offer Lady Culpepper my condolences, of course," he said, his tone implying that his movements and their cause were none of her business. "And you?" he asked, glancing rather pointedly toward the side of the building that had so occupied her interest.

"Yes, I was just doing that myself," she muttered, trying to marshal her wits. If Ashdowne had been attractive at night, dressed all in black and moving at one with the shadows, he was startlingly so in the daylight, the sun catching the even contours of his face and glinting upon his golden skin. His dark lashes were thick and lustrous, his blue eyes so vivid that they stole Georgiana's breath, and that mouth...

When she found her gaze lingering, Georgiana wrenched it away to look down at her toes. If the simple sight of the man wrought such havoc with her senses, then she would do better to inspect the ground at her feet, she decided with some aggravation.

"Ah," Ashdowne said in a voice that told her he did not believe her explanation for an instant but was too much of a gentleman to argue. "I don't believe we've been properly introduced, Miss—"

"Bellewether," Georgiana said, relieved to find speech much easier when she had no real view of the marquis. "I, uh, should beg your pardon for, uh, knocking you down last night."

"I must say, I think a potted plant hardly the place for an assignation," Ashdowne said, and Georgiana's gaze flew to his face.

"Oh! I was not…" As the words left her mouth, Georgiana realized her mistake. Just one glance at those lips and already she was becoming stupid! Fighting back a snort of disgust, she turned toward the flowering shrubs that carved pathways through the rear of the property and lifted her chin.

"I was not meeting anyone," Georgiana declared. When silence met her protest, she frowned. "Actually, I was listening and learning, a habit of mine, you might say, for you never know what interesting things you can discover."

"Ah, gossip," Ashdowne said in a tone of dismissal.

Georgiana stared at his neck cloth, determined to be able to speak to the man without swooning. "I am not concerned with rumor or innuendo, but facts only—facts, in this case, pertinent to the events of last night," she said. "You see, I have a knack for solving mysteries, my lord, and I intend to lend my talents to the resolution of the theft that occurred here yesterday evening.''

Georgiana looked up in challenge, but Ashdowne's expression was unreadable. He neither scoffed at her declaration, nor did he appear particularly threatened, and she had to stifle a surge of disappointment that her bold words did not result in his immediate confession to any number of misdeeds. He only tilted his head, as if to study her in that way of his which she found vastly insulting.

''And just how do you intend to do that?'' he asked. His lovely lips curled wryly, and Georgiana suspected he was laughing at her. Unfortunately, it was an attitude with which she was more than familiar.

It was the curse of her appearance. If only she looked like Hortense Bingley, the spinster who haunted the lending library at Upwick, or Miss Mucklebone, a bluestocking who wore thick glasses and was known to brandish her cane at tart-tongued youngsters. Once, during her schoolroom years, Georgiana had borrowed a pair of spectacles from a classmate in an effort to be taken more seriously, but her parents had put a stop to that immediately upon her return home. And so she had to bear the scorn of those who took her at face value, including, apparently, the marquis.

''I intend to discover the culprit through simple reasoning, my lord,'' Georgiana said, tossing her curls. She was so annoyed that she managed to eye him directly without feeling anything except contempt. ''By studying the facts, eliminating all but the most probable of possibilities, and drawing a conclusion.'' With a curt nod, Georgiana begin moving. ''And now, if you will excuse me, I must be on my way. Good day, my lord.''

''Don't hurry away,'' Ashdowne said, and to Georgiana's consternation, he fell into step beside her. "I find your comments most fascinating. Please tell me more."

A sidelong glance at his restrained expression told Georgiana that he did not believe her capable of doing what she claimed. Few men did, but somehow his skepticism riled her more than usual. If he had so little faith in her abilities, why was he pretending interest? Georgiana scowled suspiciously. "I hardly think so," she murmured, keeping to her pace.

"But I find these methods you spoke of most interesting," he said. His blue eyes were suddenly intense as they met her own. To Georgiana's relief, they had reached the front of house, where Ashdowne presumably was headed to make his call, and she seized the opportunity to escape that intent scrutiny.

"I fear I must be on my way, my lord. Perhaps another time," she murmured, her hand trembling as it found the gate. And then, aware that she was acting rather rudely, but resentful of the way he seemed to be toying with her, Georgiana slipped away without a backward glance. As she hurried onto the street, she heard no steps behind her to indicate the marquis's entrance into the house, and it took all of her will not to turn around to verify the speculative gaze she sensed was upon her.

It was only when she had reached the corner that Georgiana realized she had once more let pass a golden opportunity to question the man. Fast upon the heels of that discovery came self-censure. Never before had she behaved like such a pea-goose with someone! Ashdowne, it seemed, had a most peculiar effect upon her.

The knowledge was decidedly lowering.

Georgiana stood in the Pump Room surveying the crowd and leaning on one foot in an effort to rouse her weary limbs. She felt as though she had been waiting here forever, hoping to catch a glimpse of Lord Whalsey, who usually made an afternoon visit. Indeed, everyone appeared at the social hub of the city sooner or later, on a daily basis, more often than not.

At least that's what Georgiana told herself to strengthen a resolve that was sadly slipping. Although Whalsey would be wise to conduct himself in his accustomed manner, she knew that he might even now be racing toward London with his booty. It was a discouraging thought, for how was she to follow? Again Georgiana cursed the limits of her gender, which prevented her from pursuing her prime suspect wherever he might go.

Unfortunately, she could only look for him in the Pump Room, and she had to admit that she was becoming weary of her watch. Her sisters had long ago left for a walk in the Crescent and her other acquaintances dispersed to hillside climbs or carriage rides. Only Bertrand, content to do nothing, lounged in a corner chatting to a couple of young men she had tried her best to discourage.

Georgiana was able to turn them aside more easily than usual today because they, along with everyone else, were occupied with discussion of the theft, including wild conjectures as to the culprit. She had listened to the speculation with some impatience, for rumors were growing apace. Most of the dowagers were certain a group of ruffians had moved to Bath to terrorize the town, and it was all Georgiana could do not to scream in exasperation at such nonsense.

The theft was not the work of a gang, but one man alone, Georgiana thought, shifting to her other foot. A vision of Ashdowne as he had been last night, all in black, swam before her, and she dismissed it. Although he was certainly suspicious, she was here to concentrate on Whalsey and his cohort, who were the most likely candidates.

Blinking, she searched the room once again, and her hours of vigilance were rewarded when she caught a glimpse of the viscount. He moved through the crowd, greeting his favorites among the middle-aged widows, before finally settling down with a serving of the odoriferous water for which Bath was famous.

"Lord Whalsey! Good afternoon!" Georgiana said, stepping forward boldly. They had been introduced briefly a few days before, but she saw no recognition in his eyes, only a spark of interest as they focused eagerly on her bosom. Hiding her annoyance, Georgiana forced a smile. "I did not see you leave the ball last night. Did you depart early?"

The inquiry, innocent though it was, made Whalsey start, and his gaze moved up to her face in what could only be described as a most anxious manner. Georgiana felt a surge of triumph rush through her, though she held it firmly in check. "And what of the fellow who was with you? Mr. Cheever, wasn't it?"

Whalsey, his mouth working silently, looked guilty as sin, and Georgiana wondered just how swiftly she could bring him to justice. "Look here, Miss…Miss…"

"Bellewether," Georgiana answered with a confident smile. "You two seemed to be discussing something frightfully important, and I was wondering if—"

He cut her off with a choked sound, his face growing red and mottled. "I hardly think—"

"Did you accomplish all that you intended?"

With an alarmed expression, Whalsey rose to his feet. So eager was he to escape her probing that his hand swung from his side, knocking over the cup and sending the contents splashing up the front of Georgiana's muslin gown. Shocked by the dash of hot water, she stepped back only to come up against a stand used by the orchestra.

For a brief moment, Georgiana teetered there before losing her balance entirely and crashing backward, taking the support with her. It struck the violinist, who fell into one of his fellows, and before long the musicians were all collapsing into each other like a set of dominoes. After a series of loud, wailing screechcs that accompanied their downfall, the music came to an abrupt halt and silence descended as every head in the Pump Room turned toward Georgiana.

Her skirts entangled with the stand and one arm stuck through the bow of the violinist, Georgiana watched dejectedly as Lord Whalsey made a hasty escape. Blowing out a breath to dislodge the curl that had fallen across her face, she blinked when a gloved hand appcared before her. Glancing upward, she felt an odd sense of disorientation at the sight of Ashdowne, tall and handsome and collected, leaning over her.

"You, Miss Bellewether, are dangerous," hc said with a wary scowl. Nonetheless, he pulled hcr to her feet just as easily as he had the other night, and one look from him had the musicians rising without complaint to continue their concert. As if by decree, the other visitors turned back to their conversations, and Georgiana could only gape in wonder at a man who could wield such heady influence.

"Thank you. Again," Georgiana mumbled as he led her away from the orchestra. "You have come to my rescue more than once."

"I admit, Miss Bellewether, that you appear to have a penchant for mishaps, and I count it my ill fortune to be in the vicinity," he noted with a wry grimace.

Was that an insult? Georgiana wondered as she struggled to discreetly pull the wet material of her bodice away from her chest. Although dampened muslin was rumored to be all the rage among the more daring London ladies, she had no desire to display her body so unerringly beneath the clinging fabric.

From somewhere, Ashdowne produced a shawl, which he dropped over her shoulders, but not before his blue gaze traveled the length of the front of her in a rather stimulating perusal that caused the tips of her breasts to stiffen in response. Curious. Plenty of other men had stared at her bosom without causing such a reaction, Georgiana thought, wrapping the shawl around her tightly.

It was a measure of her own flustered state that she did not note where Ashdowne had obtained the garment or that she did not find his rather intimate study annoying. Indeed, she knew a strange sort of thrill to have attracted his attention in that manner, which was only fair considering that the very sight of him usually reduced her to an unparalleled state of idiocy.

Ashdowne, however, looked none the worse for his brief display of interest. His expression was that of a man wearied beyond endurance, and Georgiana began feeling like a bug again. If only she could actually sprout wings and fly away...

"I suspect these disasters are all part and parcel of your unusual...pursuits, but I'm beginning to think that you need someone to keep you out of mischief," he said.

Georgiana blinked. Surely a marquis would not bother himself to complain to her father about her? Nor, as far as she knew, were there any laws against accidents such as the one that had just taken place.

What could the man possibly do to her? Georgiana wondered. But then he smiled, his elegant lips moving into a positively decadent curve that well answered her question. *Anything he wants,* she thought with the last of her wits.

"And since I seem to be the one most affected by your antics, perhaps I should apply for that position," he said, stunning her speechless.

Chapter Three

Johnathon Everett Saxton, fifth Marquis of Ashdowne, lifted one dark brow in surprise at the expression on his companion's face. Over the years, he had received a wide variety of looks from the ladies, but never had one eyed him with anything bordering on alarm. As usual, Miss Georgiana Bellewether's reaction was far from ordinary.

Perhaps his offer to act as a sort of keeper for the errant young woman was none too flattering, but her obvious dismay was not exactly what he had anticipated. The Saxon good looks and a certain rakish charm had assured Ashdowne of more than his share of the fair sex, while now, as marquis, he received far too much attention for his taste. Somehow the thought of being sought only for his title put a damper on his previous enthusiasm.

But Miss Bellewether could hardly be accused of chasing after his name, Ashdowne mused. Although the chit ought to be grateful for his attention, she appeared flustered, irritated and nearly panicked, as if she found him objectionable in some way. Apparently it was his misfortune that the only woman who was not inclined to be his marchioness was some kind of lunatic. A *dangerous* lunatic, he qualified grimly.

He had not suspected as much at first. Upon sighting her at Lady Culpepper's ball, Ashdowne had been momentarily taken with the young lady, as would any normal male, for Georgiana Bellewether had a body that might cause a lesser man to drool into his neck cloth. With those lush curves, that mop of blond curls and the delicate oval face of an angel, she would have been toasted as a diamond of the first water in London, with offers flying at her head, despite her simple background. Or she could have reigned over the demimonde as the most sought after of cyprians.

Of course, all that success was dependant upon her silence—and her stillness, Ashdowne thought. Unfortunately, once Georgiana Bellewether began moving, all hell was inclined to break loose, for she was probably the clumsiest creature in all of Christendom. A veritable accident in the making, she had managed to knock him to the floor last night, an ignominious experience that still stung. Luckily the tumble hadn't hurt anything except his pride, or else the evening might have gone awry in more ways than one.

But that episode was the least of it. Since then, she had hit him with the world's heaviest reticule and single-handedly brought down an entire orchestra. Ashdowne would never view the words *strike up the band* in quite the same light again.

Not only was she disaster prone, but the young woman fancied herself some sort of investigator! Although nearly every man at the ball had a theory about the Culpepper robbery, few would claim themselves capable of catching the thief, and certainly no lady would admit interest in such things! Ashdowne didn't know whether to laugh or ship her off to Bedlam.

And so he did neither, but watched her carefully. Long

ago, he had learned to listen to his instincts, which were buzzing and hissing most alarmingly in connection with Miss Bellewether. Perhaps it was the physical danger she represented to anyone fool enough to get close to her, or something else. Ashdowne didn't know.

He had to admit to some curiosity as to what disaster would next follow in her wake, so possibly his interest amounted to nothing more than the same bizarre fascination that drew people to public hangings. It was only human nature to want to witness calamity, and despite the past stifling year, Ashdowne still called himself human. Whatever the reason, like a man flirting with his own doom, he could not seem to ignore Miss Georgiana Bellewether.

She was diverting, to say the least, and barring the recent trouble with his sister-in-law, Ashdowne could not remember when he had last been so intrigued. It was startling to realize just how mundane his life had become since assuming the title. He had not set out to embrace a life of boredom. Far from it, for he had always held his stolid, conservative brother somewhat in contempt.

It was only after that gentleman had keeled over from apoplexy and the title had been thrust upon him that Ashdowne had realized what a tiresome business it all was. Of course, he could have refused the responsibilities that fell to him, but too many people, from farm tenants to servants staffing the family seat, depended upon him now. And so he had immersed himself in the business of being Ashdowne, and although he didn't regret it, he felt as if he had been swimming for some time and had just now come up for air. Only to find himself in a fog induced by the young lady at his side.

"This, uh, really isn't necessary," Miss Bellewether said. She spoke in a breathless voice, as though she had barely recovered after her misadventure in the Pump Room, and certainly a dousing with Bath water could steal your breath away. Ashdowne knew his had been sadly short after just looking at her, especially when the wet muslin had clung so delightfully to her pert nipples.

He forced his thoughts in a different direction. Gad, he must have been too long without a woman if he could be stirred by this wretched female! "Let me at least see you home," he said, smoothly stifling his wayward lust. "Where are you staying?"

Ashdowne listened with approval to her mumbled direction, though he knew her address already. He made it his business to learn everything that might impact upon him and his plans, and he had discovered all that he could about the bothersome Miss Bellewether, Lady Culpepper having proven quite helpful in that regard.

The outraged matron had complained at length about the impertinent young woman who invited herself in only to claim that she was going to solve the theft. And all through Lady Culpepper's shrill diatribe, Ashdowne had struggled with his own incredulity. He knew that common citizens rarely bothered to intervene in a criminal case, let alone a genteel female. What was the chit about?

Ashdowne's gaze traveled to the lady in question, though he found it difficult to equate the self-proclaimed investigator with those bobbing blond curls. He shook his head in wonder. Obviously Miss Bellewether had recovered herself, for she no longer clung fiercely to the shawl he had borrowed from a matron, but neither did she seem at ease. She was staring straight ahead, her chin lifted, as if prepared to make some pronouncement, and Ashdowne found himself leaning close to hear her next inanity.

"I appreciate your assistance, my lord, but I assure you that I am not singling you out for any sort of..."

"Torture?" Ashdowne suggested wryly.

Although he had not thought her capable of it, the little miss made a face that evidenced some backbone behind that beribboned and beruffled exterior. Tossing her gorgeous curls, Miss Bellewether gave him a mutinous expression that Ashdowne found oddly charming. He must be truly desperate for diversion. "But, tell me, how is the investigation going?" he asked, to deflect her wrath.

Miss Bellewether, however, did not look appeased. "It is going quite well!" she answered, as if daring him to dispute her. "In fact, I am quite certain of the identities of the perpetrators."

"Perpetrators?" Ashdowne asked. "Then there is more than one?"

To his surprise, she slid him a suspicious glance, and Ashdowne wondered what she saw when she looked at him. Apparently, it was something that nobody else noticed, and the thought sent a shiver up his spine, as if someone were walking on his grave. Unnerved, he rolled his shoulders beneath his fine tailored coat as he awaited her answer.

But when it came, it was as astonishing as anything else she had ever said. "I do not feel at liberty to discuss the case," she muttered, refusing to look at him.

Uttered with all seriousness, her words stunned Ashdowne from his pose of practiced charm into a startled stare. Who did this mop-haired minx think she was? For a moment, he didn't know whether to laugh or to strangle her. Unfortunately, they were in full view of several others who were strolling the streets, so the latter was not really an option, and the former would not further his cause.

With an effort, Ashdowne forced himself to swallow the sharp retort that came to his lips while he tried to appear humble. But since the pretense was not part of his usual repertoire, he was not too successful. "Well, I certainly wouldn't want to interfere with your investigation," he said smoothly. "Quite the contrary, in fact. Perhaps if I were to offer my help to you, as an assistant of sorts, you might feel comfortable speaking more...freely."

His companion gave him a sharp look that told him she thought he was teasing her, but Ashdowne waited expectantly.

"Oh! I've never considered..." she began, only to trail off.

Ashdowne remained impassive as her blue eyes studied him, though it was a trifle difficult when he really wanted to get his hands on her neck—or perhaps lower, where an expanse of luscious white breast peeked above the edge of the shawl.

"That is, I have always worked alone," she mumbled, gazing down at her toes.

It was a habit she had when with him. Although Ashdowne was not certain what it signified, he did not believe it had anything to do with modesty or deference, much to his regret. "Ah, but perhaps, as a man, I could be of some use," he suggested.

She glanced up at him with a startled expression, a flush staining her cheeks, and Ashdowne felt an echoing interest in his breeches, along with an absurd sense of triumph. At least the chit was not wholly indifferent to him, if she thought he had offered to accommodate her in a purely personal fashion.

"I meant that I might be able to move easier than yourself amongst the male members of society, in places where you, for all your wherewithal, cannot be expected to go," Ashdowne qualified. She stared up at him, and for a moment he felt transfixed by those blue eyes. They had stopped before her residence, and he stepped closer, an odd sort of anticipation buzzing in his veins.

It had been a long while since his last intimate encounter. Too long. And the young lady before him was a scrumptious delight for the senses, with her flushed skin and bright hair and mouth made for kissing.

"Georgie!" The call came from inside the house, destroying the moment between them and making Miss Bellewether wince. Was it the nickname that dismayed her, or the long minute they had spent mulling over the possibilities between them? Ashdowne had to admit that he was fairly dismayed himself to be attracted to the disastrous Miss Bellewether, no matter how briefly.

"I will consider your kind offer," she said in what could be nothing but a dismissal. And then, as if she feared to look upon his face, she turned and fled, hurrying toward the house and leaving him standing outside like a tradesman.

At the sound of the door closing behind her, Ashdowne shook himself. He could not remember the last time he had been so summarily dismissed. Even as a younger son, he had moved in the first circles, his looks and charm and ready money assuring him a place at every party.

Rolling his shoulders, Ashdowne set off down the street. He was certain that more than mere shyness had sent her running inside, and the knowledge left him bemused. Although no angel, he was hardly the type of rake to instill terror in the hearts of young virgins. What, then, drove her away from him?

Ashdowne had an idea, but he planned to find out for sure. His instincts were twitching, and he had no intention of letting Miss Georgiana Bellewether do anything to disrupt his life more than she had already.

* * *

Lord Whalsey was nowhere to be seen! Georgiana stifled a groan of frustration. She had joined her family in attending this rout in the hope of cornering him again, but both he and Mr. Cheever were conspicuously absent. What was she to do now? Whalsey might very well be at the Pump Room or a concert, or worse yet, headed to London to sell the necklace!

Georgiana's shoulders slumped as she wondered what course to take. She could present her observations to the magistrate, but experience told her that gentlemen on the whole were extremely dubious of her talents. Her evidence of an overheard conversation and a guilty reaction probably would not convince him, and then Lord Whalsey would escape with his ill-gotten gains!

Blowing away a curl that had plopped over her forehead, Georgiana leaned back against the balustrade behind the elegant town house. She had pleaded a headache when asked to dance and made her escape onto the balcony that overlooked the tiny garden. Here in the silence, she tried to concentrate on her next course of action, but her thoughts were interrupted all too soon.

"Ah, Miss Bellewether. What new disaster are you contemplating?" The question was spoken in a deep, familiar voice that made Georgiana whirl around in surprise.

Stifling a gasp, she blinked at the shadows near the doors, where she could dimly make out Ashdowne's tall form. How long had he been there? It was rather frightening to think that, for all her skills, she had not noticed his presence, and Georgiana shivered, for the marquis was not the typical nobleman. He was unlike any man she had ever known.

"I..." Words failed her when he moved into the pale moonlight, all in black again, his handsome features cloaked in mystery. Georgiana's stomach dipped, her pulse raced and her skin tingled. Lifting her hands to her arms, she rubbed the prickling flesh in hopes of warding away the feeling, but to her dismay, the brisk motion did not help, and Ashdowne stepped closer.

"I hope you've been thinking about me," he said softly, and Georgiana's eyes widened. She had imagined herself immune to the charms of the male gender, but she was rapidly learning differently with Ashdowne. Like a lingering illness, he disturbed her senses and stayed upon her mind, despite her efforts to banish him, and now, standing before her with a smug smile, he totally flustered her. However, Georgiana wasn't about to admit as much to the arrogant marquis, so she lifted her chin and frowned at his neck cloth.

He chuckled, apparently amused by her obstinateness. "No? Well, then, I've come to convince you."

He purred, almost like a cat, and Georgiana shivered, for here was no tame tabby. She cleared her throat. "Convince me, of, uh, what?" she asked, still refusing to look at him.

"To take me on…"

Georgiana drew a sharp breath.

"…as your assistant," he added, and she exhaled slowly. "I'm offering my services to you, to aid in your pursuit of justice. What say you, Miss Bellewether?"

Georgiana hesitated, daring to slant a quick glance at him. At first she had thought Ashdowne much like any other man in respect to her abilities, a scoffer so certain of his own superiority that he would not even listen to her theories. But now he appeared to be in earnest. He no longer wore the aloof expression that made her feel like an insect he would prefer to be rid of—and soon. Instead, his features reflected a rather benign interest.

Georgiana blinked, uncertain, but it appeared that for

once in her life, a man was actually seeking her opinion, and not in the idiotic manner of one of her swains, either. Ashdowne's eyes were not glazed over, but were as alert as ever. They glittered faintly, with a rather predatory gleam that made her stomach pitch. Although he said nothing, Georgiana could almost feel the expectancy shimmering in the air. Or at least that's what she thought it was, for she felt all tingly and alive, as if poised upon the brink of solving one of her mysteries.

Looking away before she became befuddled, Georgiana clutched the balustrade tightly. She tried not to envision what it would be like to be able to speak to someone— *anyone*—about her investigation, let alone bask in the glow of this handsome man's attention. The temptation was great, but did she really want to give away any information to one of her suspects? The very notion made her shiver, though more with excitement than dismay.

Then again, she had just been wondering what to do about Mr. Cheever and Lord Whalsey. In the face of their obvious guilt, it seemed foolish to worry about Ashdowne. No, Georgiana amended as her gaze slid over his dark figure. It would never be foolish to remain cautious around the marquis, for here in the moonlight he exuded danger in a manner that Whalsey and Cheever could not. Georgiana knew, with a heady sense of awareness, that she should not be alone with him. Her mother would be horrified!

And yet that very same menace might be of use to her, for Ashdowne appeared to be eminently capable of anything. He certainly would be able to handle a pair such as Whalsey and Cheever with ease, Georgiana decided. "Perhaps you can be of help to me," she whispered as she stared out into the night.

"Yes?" The word was little more than an exhalation,

yet it managed to harry her senses in ways she had never thought possible.

Annoyed, Georgiana forced herself to concentrate. "You see, I know the identity of the thieves, but I fear they will escape Bath unless something is done to stop them."

"Ah. And what do you suggest?" Ashdowne said. No laughter. No taunts. There wasn't even a hint of contempt in his manner, and Georgiana knew a swift sense of relief. Perhaps this assistant business was all to the good, for just sharing her thoughts with another seemed to put her more at ease.

"Well, I'm not entirely certain," Georgiana admitted. "You see, I don't really have enough evidence to tender to the magistrate, who probably would not deign to listen anyway." She paused to consider the injustice of it all before mentioning her only other option. "I'm afraid there is nothing for it but to confront one of the culprits."

"Miss Bellewether," Ashdowne said. His intense tone demanded her attention, so Georgiana glanced upward, only to shiver at the way his eyes glittered in the moonlight. "You will *not* confront a criminal."

Frowning at what sounded an awful lot like an order, Georgiana nonetheless chose not to argue, for she fully intended to use his objection as a means to her end. "Well, that's where you could…step in, as it were," she said.

"You want *me* to confront the fellow?" Ashdowne lifted one dark brow in speculation.

"Well, that, uh, would be a good job for an assistant, don't you think?" she asked, smiling tentatively. "And I would be there to do all the talking. I have little doubt that I can wrangle a confession from them, or one of them, at least, because when I spoke to him in the Pump Room, he became quite agitated in a most telling fashion.''

Ashdowne's lovely lips thinned. ''Are you telling me that some brute knocked you down this morning?''

''Well, in a manner of speaking—''

He muttered something she could not quite discern. ''You are lucky the fellow did not do more! You cannot go around accosting lawbreakers. You have no idea what that sort of man is capable of, but I've seen some in London who would slit your throat for a shilling!''

''Oh, I realize what you are saying, and I heartily agree,'' Georgiana replied. ''You see, I make it my business to follow the London newspapers quite thoroughly, especially the criminal exploits and the heroic actions of the Bow Street Runners. However, I must assure you that this fellow is not a common cutpurse.''

Ashdowne did not appear mollified. Rather, he seemed to be in quite a taking, his handsome face hard and his mouth grim. To Georgiana's surprise, he reached for her, and she sucked in a strangled breath as his gloved hands closed over her bare arms. The heat that they generated was alarming, as was the abrupt metamorphosis of her companion. Right before her eyes the Marquis of Ashdowne had changed from smooth and charming to threateningly feral, and Georgiana blinked in amazement.

Held by his hands and his glittering gaze, Georgiana felt caught between dread and titillation, between the heat of his touch and the cold of the shiver that ran up her spine. ''Miss Bellewether, you will *not* confront anyone, no matter how harmless you believe them to be,'' he said.

''Well, I—'' Georgiana opened her mouth to protest. She had not even formally agreed to take him on as her assistant, yet the arrogant man was trying to tell her what to do. This was not at all what she had imagined, but then

Ashdowne was always doing the unexpected. And this moment proved no different, for as Georgiana watched with widening eyes, his head dipped, his features blurred and he kissed her.

Georgiana had been kissed before, of course, but those country lads and military gallants had never aroused in her any enthusiasm for the intimacy. She had always thought it rather distasteful to have someone place his mouth on her own. Until now.

Quite simply, Ashdowne put those other lads to shame. He played upon her lips like a master, his first touch a mere brush, a featherlight caress that left her aching for more. And instead of giving it to her, he grazed the line of her jaw, her cheek, her eyelids and her forehead, where a curl had fallen. Then he pressed against the errant lock, with a deliberate caress that hinted of delights untold.

"You are quite a sumptuous feast, are you not?" Ashdowne whispered against her hair, and then, to her infinite relief, his lips returned to hers, enticing and molding them until Georgiana heard a low moan that shocked her as her own. She lifted her hands to Ashdowne's embroidered silk waistcoat, drawing in a giddy breath at the heat that emanated from his muscular form. He was so warm and solid and sleek that Georgiana couldn't help running her palms around to his back, beneath his coat.

As if her explorations encouraged him, Ashdowne touched her with his tongue, and she gasped in surprise only to feel him enter her mouth in a smooth invasion that seemed to affect her entire body in the most peculiar ways. Curious…that something so odd could be so delicious, Georgiana thought, for Ashdowne tasted better than anything. Although a devotee of desserts, Georgiana could liken him to none she had ever had before, his flavor a dark, rich embodiment of…passion?

The thought made its way through her dazed senses, and she realized she should not be clutching the marquis's person in such a manner. She should not let one of his elegant hands clasp the back of her neck while her head fell back, her mouth opening under his. She should not push so close to him that her breasts were smashed against his elegant waistcoat. And, most of all, she should not be moaning wantonly at the extraordinary bliss to be found in his arms.

Vaguely Georgiana heard the sound of footsteps, followed by the frustrating vacation of Ashdowne's lips. "Whom do you suspect?" he whispered against her ear, and it took her fogged brain a full minute to comprehend his question. During that time, he stepped away, and Georgiana's arms fell to her sides, empty and anchorless.

"Suspect?" she asked, her voice a breathless squeak. "Oh, uh, Lord Whalsey and Mr. Cheever."

"Ah," he said softly, already moving into the shadows. "I'll have Whalsey's house watched."

Georgiana blinked, seized by a disappointment so acute that she was tempted to call him back or throw herself against his wonderful, tall body, and beg for more, but he was backing away silently.

"Miss Bellewether!" The sound of a voice made Georgiana whirl guiltily, and she flinched at the sight of Mr. Hawkins, the displaced vicar, approaching. "I can see it is a good thing that I came outside, for you should not be here alone," he said, his eyes traveling to her bosom, and Georgiana was grateful for the darkness. She was certain that every inch of her skin was flushed right down to her toes.

"Oh. I was, uh, just going in," she managed to reply.

Mr. Hawkins looked disgruntled but offered to escort her, and she took his arm, though it was a poor replacement for Ashdowne's. Trying to marshal her muddled thoughts, Georgiana blinked as they stepped into the reception room, automatically scanning the assemblage. Immediately she noted the presence of Lady Culpepper, who was deep in conversation with a black-haired gentleman.

"I see that she has recovered from her grief," Mr. Hawkins said, with a frown in Lady Culpepper's direction.

It was an odd comment for a vicar, and Georgiana felt her wits return with the realization. "Perhaps the gentleman is extending comfort to her," she said.

Mr. Hawkins's only response was an unchurchmanlike snort.

"Who is he?" Georgiana asked, eyeing the fellow with interest now. He was tall and handsome and dressed in an elegant but understated way.

"Only one of the richest and most arrogant men in the country," Mr. Hawkins said in a derisive voice. "He's related to half the peerage, but has more money than nearly all of them."

"Oh, perhaps he's a relative of Lady Culpepper, then?"

"So they say. Supposedly he's brought someone from London just to try to recover her necklace, as if he could care! Pocket change for him, no doubt. Odd business, if you ask me."

Georgiana's head turned so swiftly toward her companion that a curl landed smack in her eye. Impatiently she blew it away while her heart took up a furious rhythm. "And just whom has he brought from London?" she asked.

"A Bow Street Runner," Mr. Hawkins said. "Though I imagine the fellow will soon be sorry he came when he has to deal with the likes of those two," he added in his most pompous tone.

But Georgiana was no longer paying attention. All she could think about was the Bow Street Runner and the expectation that, after years of following their exploits, she would finally meet one of the elite criminal investigators in the flesh! She glanced around for Ashdowne, but he was nowhere to be seen, and she spared a moment's annoyance at the man's frequent disappearances.

Perhaps he was off to Lord Whalsey's, she thought, and not a moment too soon. She would like to have spoken with the Bow Street Runner tonight, but knowing Ashdowne was keeping watch on her prime suspect gave her ease. And first thing tomorrow, she would set off to find the investigator. If all went well, she could lay her case before him and hand over the culprits by noon. Hopefully, the jewels were still in Whalsey's possession, and, if so, she might be able to personally return them to Lady Culpepper.

Then, the rather ungracious noblewoman would have to change her opinion of Miss Georgiana Bellewether. Indeed, everyone would have to take her seriously, Georgiana thought with giddy anticipation. And her long-awaited career as a renowned mystery solver could, at last, begin!

Chapter Four

Georgiana stood across the street from Lady Culpepper's residence, trying to appear inconspicuous. It was a bit difficult, because she'd been at her post since sneaking out of her own house early this morning, and she was already receiving odd looks from those who staffed the luxurious homes around her, as well as the occasional peddler. However, she refused to budge other than to pace up and down a short way, for she was a woman with a mission.

Sooner or later the Bow Street Runner who had arrived last night would have to visit the scene of the crime, Georgiana reasoned, and she intended to have a word with him when he did. But Lady Culpepper's late sleeping habits seemed to be making the inevitable interview later rather than sooner. So far the only traffic into the house had been servants and a rather rumpled middle-aged man who had gone by the tradesmen's entrance.

When the same fellow left the building a good half hour later, Georgiana thought nothing of it—until he crossed the street and came directly toward her. She frowned, unwilling to waste her time chatting with a man who probably wanted to sell her something. She had to keep her eyes and her wits upon Lady Culpepper's, or miss her chance entirely.

"Excuse me, miss," the man said politely, and Georgiana nodded. He had stopped in front of her, forcing her to crane her neck in order to see the doors to the Culpepper house. "You seem to be interested in that building over there. Would you mind telling me why?"

Surprised by his blunt manner, Georgiana studied the stranger anew. Although his clothes were of a poor cut, they were decent, and most everyone rubbed elbows in Bath. Stifling a groan of impatience, she tried to be gracious. "Haven't you heard? A Bow Street Runner has been summoned to look into the infamous theft of Lady Culpepper's emeralds," Georgiana explained.

The fellow appeared taken aback, his thick brown brows furrowing. He had a world-weary countenance, with more lines perhaps than could be accounted for by his age. Normally Georgiana would have been interested in meeting someone outside her usual realm of acquaintances, but not today; she was too busy. Nor did she have the time to relate the details of the robbery to him, should he be new to Bath and unfamiliar with the tale.

"Pardon me for asking, miss, but what does that have to do with you?" he asked, looking genuinely curious.

"I am waiting for him!" Georgiana said loftily, hoping that the man would take her tone as a dismissal.

He did not. To Georgiana's annoyance, the stranger continued to obstruct her view with his rather stocky, compact form. He showed no signs of discouragement, but bent his head in the sketch of a bow. "Wilson Jeffries, at your service, miss." *Oh, would he not go away?* There was some activity across the way, and Georgiana fidgeted to see over his shoulder.

"Miss? Just what did you want to see me about?"

"You?" Georgiana blinked in surprise.

The man nodded, his mouth curving into the ghost of a smile. "Yes, miss. I'm from Bow Street."

Georgiana took in a deep breath as her attention was drawn from Lady Culpepper's house to the fellow in front of her. Truth to tell, she had to admit to a slight disappointment, for Wilson Jeffries was hardly what she had conjured in her mind as one of London's expert thief takers. Quite naturally, Georgiana had pictured a young virile specimen, bulging with the muscles necessary to subdue his prey and with a sort of seedy cast to him—from his association with all those criminals.

She found herself eyeing a man of medium height and build, with rounded shoulders that made him appear slumped and rather tired, a weariness that was echoed in his brown eyes. With his wrinkled clothes and unthreatening demeanor, he looked more like a simple shopkeeper than a trained investigator.

Wilson Jeffries seemed neither tough nor particularly clever, and Georgiana decided right then and there that it was a good thing she had stumbled upon him. Undoubtedly, this particular Bow Street Runner was in sad need of her aid. Pleased with the thought, Georgiana smiled at him and leaned close.

"Why, Mr. Jeffries, it is not what you can do for me, but what I can do for you," she said.

When he eyed her quizzically, Georgiana explained herself with some measure of confidence. "You see, I am accounted a bit of an investigator myself, and I have studied this case most thoroughly. I was there when it happened, you know."

"And you have some information about the theft?" He had a rather skeptical air about him, but Georgiana was not deterred. It was the nature of men to be dubious of her abilities, yet this one could not afford to maintain that attitude for long, and that knowledge lent fresh enthusiasm to Georgiana's efforts.

She leaned close, lowering her voice to a whisper. "Indeed, I at once narrowed the field of suspects down to three," she said in a confidential tone.

The fellow eyed her assessingly. "Did you now?" he asked.

"Yes! And I will be happy to impart to you my deductions, including the identity of the robber himself!"

"Would you?" Jeffries said. He was certainly a man of few words, and Georgiana wondered if he used that to his advantage during the course of his questioning or if it might not be a hindrance to him. Perhaps she could not only assist him with this case, but give him a few suggestions on how to improve his technique in the future.

"I own I would dearly love to pursue a career such as yours, but, sadly, I am a victim of my gender," Georgiana admitted. "However, that does not prevent me from solving whatever mysteries I can, small ones for the most part, but this business at Lady Culpepper's is a true crime! And I am only too happy to lend my expertise to you for its speedy resolution."

"I see," Jeffries said, although he did not look at all as if he did. Perhaps he was slow but thorough, Georgiana thought, giving him the benefit of the doubt.

"Shall we walk?" Georgiana asked, for even though the Bow Street Runner seemed oblivious to his surroundings, she was keeping a wary eye out for curious passersby.

Jeffries appeared nonplussed, but when she tugged on his sleeve, he fell into step beside her. "Did you question the servants?" she asked.

"Miss, I..."

"No matter," Georgiana said with an airy wave. "I am certain of the identity of the thief."

"And just how did you decide, miss?" Jeffries asked.

"Well, as I said, I narrowed it down to three likely candidates," Georgiana explained, pleased to have the opportunity to expound upon her theories. "At first, I considered Ashdowne—"

"*Lord* Ashdowne? The *Marquis* of Ashdowne?" Jeffries stopped to gape at her until Georgiana was forced to nudge him forward once more.

When they were walking again, she continued. "I admit that he seems less likely now, but I cannot shake the feeling that he is up to something, for he is hardly the sort to frequent Bath. I ask you, why would a healthy man such as he claim to be in need of the waters?" Georgiana said. Immediately, she regretted her words as a blush climbed her cheeks. All too well, she recalled just how healthy— and hard and muscular—was Ashdowne.

Jeffries, apparently mollified, smiled slightly. "It's been my experience, miss, that it's nigh impossible to figure out the ton and their doings."

Georgiana nodded, although she thought his admission a sad commentary on his skills, for it was his job to discover motivations and such. Still, a man so aware of his own shortcomings might be more amenable to assistance than someone more arrogant, Georgiana mused, and she stepped alongside him with increasing assurance.

"Be that as it may, I have dismissed him as a suspect, for he became most interested in the investigation. He offered to assist me and is watching the culprit's house even as we speak," Georgiana said. *Or so she hoped.*

"Did he now?"

Georgiana thought she caught a sly grin on the taciturn man's face, but she ignored it, not wishing to enter into any further discussion of the marquis. She had lain awake long enough last night thinking about Ashdowne and his kisses, and she had concluded that it was a good thing the Bow Street Runner had arrived to close the investigation.

Her association with her one and only assistant would soon be at an end, effectively eliminating the need for any further contact with the incredibly handsome nobleman. Although Georgiana had to admit to a certain amount of pleasure in his company, he was just too much of a threat to her senses. Why, she could hardly think when he was near, and that would not do at all for someone who delighted in mental exercise.

No. Ashdowne was too much of a distraction even now, Georgiana mused as she forced her errant thoughts back to the matter at hand. She held up three fingers and immediately ticked off one, then another. "I also had my suspicions about a certain Mr. Hawkins, late of Yorkshire," she confided.

"Did you now?" Jeffries asked, and Georgiana was pleased to note the Bow Street Runner's increased interest.

"Yes. He is in town looking for a new living, and—"

Jeffries cut her off with a startled sound. "You're accusing a vicar?"

"Well, yes," Georgiana admitted. "For the most part, I'm certain that those who choose a religious life are above reproach, but, alas, I am equally sure that some commit the same sins as lesser men. And Mr. Hawkins is no ordinary vicar," Georgiana explained. "I have talked to him twice now, and his speech on both occasions struck me as most peculiar."

Georgiana leaned closer to her companion to impart her information more confidentially. "He harbors a grudge against the rich that cannot be put down to mere envy.

And since he is looking for a new post, I would imagine he is in need of funds.''

"You're saying a man of the cloth sneaked into Lady Culpepper's bedroom, stole the necklace and climbed out the window?'' Jeffries asked, his expression dubious.

"Why not?" Georgiana returned, straightening to her full diminutive height. "I tell you, he has something against the wealthy in general, if not Lady Culpepper in particular.''

To her immense gratification, Jeffries turned thoughtful. "I see. But you have since changed your mind about him?''

"Not really. It is simply that I have found a far more likely culprit,'' Georgiana declared. Nodding to a passing couple, she inched closer to Jeffries and spoke in a low tone as she pressed upon her third outstretched digit. "On the night of the theft, I overheard two men plotting most suspiciously. One of them I recognized immediately as Lord Whalsey, and the other I have identified as a Mr. Cheever.''

"*Lord* Whalsey?'' Jeffries echoed with a groan. "Pardon me, miss, but must all your suspects be noblemen or churchmen? Don't tell me! Let me guess. This fellow's a bloody duke, isn't he?''

Georgiana was disturbed, not by Jeffries's language, which was undoubtedly the cant of the streets, but by his accusation. She lifted her chin. "I assure you that I did not choose these men for their titles,'' she said. "And besides, Whalsey is only a viscount with pockets to let, driving him to engineer the commission of a crime.''

Jeffries shook his head, an unhappy look on his plain features. "First you accuse a marquis, then a vicar, and now a viscount. Miss, I do believe you have a most lively imagination.''

Georgiana blinked in dismay, for she sensed she was losing him. "Are you suggesting that such persons never venture onto the wrong side of the law?" she asked.

"No, miss," he replied.

"Then you must hear me out! I tell you, I did not search for Whalsey and his cohort. Quite by accident I fell upon them hatching their scheme." And as precisely as she could recall, Georgiana related her experience behind the large potted plant, leaving out the calamitous entanglement with Ashdowne, of course.

She was a bit disappointed that Jeffries did not take notes and resolved to suggest that course to him later, but in the meantime she was determined to convince him of the truth of her conclusions. And so she told him about her confrontation with the viscount in the Pump Room.

They had nearly reached that center of Bath by the time she had finished, and she had the distinct pleasure of watching him lift a hand to rub his chin in contemplation. "It sounds bad, miss, but I can hardly march up to his lordship without more evidence."

"But surely you can question him at least!" Georgiana protested. The interrogative talents of the Bow Street men were legendary. "I am certain that he would confess in a thrice!"

"I don't know, miss," Jeffries said, shaking his head again, and Georgiana was seized by a fit of temper. All her life she had been faced with skeptics and scoffers, but she had never expected this professional to doubt her. He was one of the best! He was one of her *heroes!* How could he not take her seriously?

Georgiana turned on him, prepared to demand that he at least speak with Whalsey before it was too late. She swung her reticule back and forth, tempted to use it to knock some sense into his wooden head, but she was uncertain as to the penalty for striking an official of the law. Fortunately, she was saved from that desperate choice by the sound of her name.

"Ah, Miss Bellewether. I see that you are busy already this morning."

Ashdowne! Never had Georgiana thought she would welcome the presence of the marquis, for she had accepted his assistance of necessity, but now...now she felt like throwing herself into his strong arms. Her happiness must have shown on her face, for he hesitated a moment as if startled by her enthusiasm, before smiling smoothly.

"Ashdowne! I am so glad you are here!"

"So I gathered," he said, bending over her hand with a wry expression. "To what may I attribute this sudden delight in my company?"

Ignoring the way he set her pulse pounding, Georgiana tugged her fingers free and gestured toward Jeffries. "My lord, this is Wilson Jeffries, a Bow Street Runner who is investigating the theft of Lady Culpepper's necklace."

"Jeffries." Ashdowne acknowledged the man with a nod. "But what is there to investigate? Surely you have given him the benefit of your expertise?" he asked Georgiana, lifting one dark brow.

Georgiana was uncertain for a moment whether he was teasing her, but he appeared expectant. "Well, yes, I have, and he doesn't believe me! Can you imagine?"

Ashdowne looked properly affronted, and Georgiana was immediately mollified. "Really?" he said, turning to Jeffries, and Georgiana had the pleasure of watching the Bow Street Runner squirm under the nobleman's gaze. Although he had refused to heed *her,* a marquis was quite a different story, and Georgiana found herself smiling smugly at Jeffries's discomfort. She congratulated herself on her choice of assistants, for Ashdowne really was proving himself most helpful.

After a moment of fidgeting under the marquis's unyielding stare, Jeffries cleared his throat. "Well, I suppose that I could have a little chat with Lord Whalsey, if you think it would be advisable," he said.

"Absolutely," Ashdowne replied in his dry manner so different from her own rampant enthusiasm. Georgiana wondered what, if anything, excited the marquis, and then blushed at the conjectures that followed.

"In fact, I insist upon it," Ashdowne said. "Let us all make a visit to the house he is letting, for I have a man watching the place, and he has not gone out as yet." As he spoke, Ashdowne turned in that direction, motioning for Georgiana to join him, and in reluctant surrender, Jeffries fell into step alongside them.

Unable to contain her bliss, Georgiana glanced up at Ashdowne with an expression of gratitude. Perhaps it was too much for the contained marquis, for he looked decidedly uncomfortable before flashing her a smooth grin. Too smooth, Georgiana thought, but she was so thrilled she did not want to contend with her recurring suspicions about Ashdowne. Returning his smile, she eagerly anticipated the interview ahead, planning her strategy should poor Mr. Jeffries require her help in obtaining a confession from Whalsey.

As it happened, their suspect was having a late breakfast when they arrived, but Ashdowne's name gained them entrée and they were shown to a small salon, where they waited for only a few minutes until Whalsey's arrival. Apparently he was all too eager to greet a marquis, for he hurried forward to give Ashdowne a deferential bow. But when he bent toward Georgiana, he straightened abruptly, a look of ill-disguised loathing upon his pale features.

"You!" he muttered, taking a step back, and Georgiana, far from taking umbrage, was well pleased with his reaction. Already wary of her, the man ought to confess his guilt in no time at all!

"I assume you've met Miss Bellewether," Ashdowne said, ignoring Whalsey's slight. "And this gentleman is Wilson Jeffries, a Bow Street Runner."

"Wh-what?" Whalsey blanched as he whirled toward Jeffries.

The Bow Street Runner nodded respectfully. "Good morning, Lord Whalsey. I would like to ask you a few questions, if I may."

"You most certainly may not! Wh-what is the meaning of this?" Whalsey asked, puffing with indignation.

"Nothing to get yourself agitated about, my lord. I'm here in Bath doing some investigating, and I—" Jeffries began, only to be silenced by Whalsey's loud huff.

"You've been listening to *her,* haven't you?" Whalsey accused, pointing a finger at Georgiana. Warmed by the recognition, she smiled, which only seemed to enrage the viscount further. "Surely, you cannot mean to believe the absurd prattle of this…this hoyden?" he asked, his voice rising shrilly. "Why, the woman's a lunatic! She needs a keeper!"

"Ah. That would be me," Ashdowne said softly.

Surprised, and somehow warmed, by the marquis's show of support, Georgiana glanced at him gratefully, but any words she might have formed were lost as the doors to the room were flung open by a manservant. "Mr. Cheever, my lord!" the servant announced, as the man in question hurried into the room.

To Georgiana's delight, Whalsey made a strangled

sound and turned toward the new arrival with a look of horror that made Cheever stop in his tracks. Georgiana suspected that the fellow would have turned tail and run if Jeffries had not chosen that moment to act. He rose to his feet. "Mr. Cheever, please join us, as I'd like to put a few questions to you."

Cheever remained arrested, a wary expression on his lean features, while Whalsey moved between Jeffries and the new arrival, as if to prevent their conversation. "This man is a Bow Street Runner," Whalsey explained to Cheever with a significance that no one could miss. Georgiana smiled triumphantly at Ashdowne.

"Please sit down," Jeffries said to Cheever. His voice, although cordial, held an underlying insistence that Georgiana admired. She had to restrain herself from clapping and urging him on.

Whalsey, however, did not join in her enthusiasm. He puffed his chest and his cheeks out once more, reminding Georgiana of a bellows. "This is an outrage!" he declared, most emphatically. "Y-you barge into my home, accost me, and now you are attacking my guests. Well, I—I won't have it! You, sir, may leave the premises at once!"

When Cheever inched toward the door, Whalsey shot him an exasperated glance. "Not you! You!" he clarified, pointing a finger at Jeffries. "Harassing your betters! Why, I'll have you stripped of your position!"

To his credit, Jeffries did not waver, and Cheever eventually sat on the edge of a faded damask-covered chair, where he proceeded to dart anxious glances toward a small gilt table. The only item on the worn surface was a simple wooden box that was hardly in keeping with the rather shabby elegance of the salon, and Georgiana drew in a sharp breath at the realization.

While Whalsey continued to object to the presence of the visitors in no uncertain terms, Georgiana rose and walked casually toward the table that held so much fascination for Cheever. She was immediately rewarded with a squeak of horror from the man, which alerted his partner. Whalsey whirled toward her and gaped, his face growing red and mottled.

"You! Get away from there, you wretched female!" he said.

Excitement surged through Georgiana as she ignored the warning and stepped closer. Triumph, which had so often teased her, suddenly appeared to be within her grasp at last, for the significance of the box could mean only one thing. The overly confident thieves had hidden the necklace in plain sight, disguising its value in the rough container that normally would not have drawn a second glance.

Moving behind the small piece of furniture, Georgiana gestured toward the box with a flourish. "Mr. Jeffries, I believe that you will find the stolen item in here!" she said, trying to contain the exhilaration that rushed through her. Surely, this was her finest hour! she thought, beaming at her audience.

And then pandemonium erupted.

Cheever shot to his feet, his hands fisted at his sides, but Ashdowne swiftly rose, too, a formidable figure among the shorter men. Whalsey, his blustering at an end, pulled out a handkerchief and began fanning himself as he fell onto a nearby chaise, moaning in distress, while Jeffries stepped toward her.

"I'll just have a look, my lord," Jeffries said. No one made a move to stop him as he took up a stance at Georgiana's side and reached for the lid. It stuck momentarily, but then Jeffries lifted it away to reveal the contents, and

Georgiana held her breath only to release it in a hiss of disappointment.

With dismay, she saw at once that no gold necklace lay inside, for instead of the glitter of emeralds, her gaze met the dull sheen of glass. Although she leaned forward, it was soon obvious that the box was empty except for a dark bottle. She blinked, but just as she opened her mouth to admit her shock, Whalsey spoke from his position across the room.

"You cannot hold me accountable!" he said. "I've done nothing! Whatever is in there is Cheever's, for he left that box here yesterday!"

Startled, Georgiana swung her attention toward Cheever, who was gripping the arms of his chair in a rather fierce fashion, as if he could not decide whether to push to his feet or remain where he was. He glanced wildly at Whalsey and then back to the Bow Street Runner, his face pinched into a most desperate expression that puzzled Georgiana.

"I left it here all right, but only because he paid me for it, the vain old bugger! I took the stuff, and the formula, too, but on his orders. It was all for him! What would I need with hair restorative?"

Georgiana finally found her voice. "Hair restorative?" she asked as Jeffries gingerly lifted the bottle from its berth.

"Aye, miss," Cheever said. "It's a secret formula, created by a certain Dr. Withipoll here in Bath, and nothing would do but that his lordship must get hold of some. And when the doctor wouldn't sell, that's when he called me in. It was all his doing! He forced me to steal it!" Cheever whined, eyeing the Bow Street Runner with canny intent.

"There are nigh on eighty physicians practicing in

Bath. Surely one of them could have been induced to help you with your...ah...problem, without resorting to robbery,'' Ashdowne said dryly to a sputtering Whalsey.

Having no interest in male baldness or how to cure it, Georgiana broke in upon the conversation. "But what of the jewels?'' she asked. Both Whalsey and Cheever looked at her blankly. "Lady Culpepper's necklace?'' she prompted.

Cheever's small eyes grew wide, and whatever gentlemanly ways he had put on fell away like a mask. "Now, you hold on a minute there, miss. I don't know a thing about that! I'm strictly small-time, I swear it! I ain't no jewel robber!''

"Nor am I!'' Whalsey cried from across the room. "I may be a bit short of funds at the moment, but everyone knows I get my money by marrying it, not stealing it. It's my hair I'm worried about! How will I find a rich widow, if it goes? A man can't wear a wig all the time! I simply must keep my hair!'' he declared with passionate ferocity.

Jeffries held up the bottle, and Georgiana could see that it was filled with some sort of dark liquid. "And you think this here's going to do the job?'' the Bow Street Runner asked.

"Oh, most certainly! It will grow hair on a billiard ball!'' Whalsey claimed.

"The professor swears by it!'' Cheever put in. "And you should see the head of hair he has on him!''

"A mane that he was no doubt born with,'' Georgiana muttered as disappointment swamped her. After all her careful investigation, she had not recovered the missing gems! And the nefarious scheme she had overheard had come to this: two men fighting over a stolen batch of hair restorative.

It was decidedly lowering.

Jeffries cleared his throat. "I'm afraid that whether or not this concoction works is irrelevant, for either way, it's been stolen, and I'll be returning it to the rightful owner," he said firmly. "I'll have the formula, too, if you please."

With another loud huff, Whalsey pulled a paper from his coat pocket and thrust it angrily at the Bow Street Runner.

"Is this the only copy?" Jeffries asked.

"Yes!" Whalsey snapped.

"Very good, then. I'll be in touch with you two regarding any charges that the professor might want to make against you."

"It was all his doing!" Cheever accused, scowling at Whalsey.

"I did nothing. You're the one who approached me, you housebreaker!" Whalsey retorted.

The two were still arguing when Georgiana, Ashdowne and Jeffries left the house, and it was not until they stepped outside that silence reigned once more. Georgiana, for one, was too distressed to speak, and the three walked quietly down the steps that fronted the building. So mired in her own dejection was she that at first Georgiana didn't hear the sound of a low chuckle. But by the time they reached the street, it was clearly audible. Did Ashdowne mock her?

Whirling on him, Georgiana prepared to give him a good set-down, but the look on his face stopped her. The marquis, who always seemed so elegant and assured, was grinning helplessly. "Hair restorative!" he murmured. And then he threw back his head and burst out laughing.

Watching his handsome face relax so fully, Georgiana felt her own tension ease. After all, Ashdowne was not finding humor in her miscalculations, but in the situation in which they had found themselves, which she had to admit was the silliest she had ever encountered.

Before she knew it, Georgiana was laughing, too, and then, to her surprise, Jeffries joined in with a rough growl of amusement, until all three of them were nearly making a spectacle of themselves on the streets of Bath. Her eyes watering in a most unladylike fashion, Georgiana swayed on her feet, but Ashdowne was there to lean on, and she decided that it was a most pleasant experience to share her mirth with a man.

It was only later, after sobering once more and parting with her companions, that Georgiana realized the awful truth. If Whalsey and Cheever were innocent, she was left with only two suspects.

And Ashdowne was one of them.

Chapter Five

Ashdowne stretched out upon the uncomfortable Grecian squab couch in his bedroom and propped his feet on the top of a carved stool. He had let the house, including the ghastly furniture, for the season, though he had only intended to stay a short while. Now he found himself hating the fashionable address in Camden Place. Of course, it wouldn't be the first time he had disliked his surroundings, but the pretentious trappings bothered him more than usual. *Everything* seemed to bother him more than usual, Ashdowne thought sourly.

"I need a drink," he muttered as his majordomo appeared. A canny Irishman, Finn was not the typical nobleman's servant, but he was the only member of the staff allowed close access to Ashdowne. The two had been together a long time, their association based on mutual trust rather than employment, for as Ashdowne well knew, the loyalty of a man such as Finn could not be bought.

"A difficult morning, milord?" Finn asked. He moved to a sideboard, where he poured a liberal portion of port that he soon presented to Ashdowne. Then he returned to fetch himself a good measure before perching on the ugly chinoiserie chair opposite. Camden Place had probably never seen the like of their tête-à-tête, Ashdowne thought with some amusement.

"Not so much difficult as deuced," he admitted as he swirled the wine, enjoying its rich bouquet. Although he disdained the ornate town house, some luxuries such as fine port were well worth the cost. He'd always known that, Ashdowne thought wryly as he took a sip.

Finn snorted into his drink. "How could your day be anything but odd when that Bellewether chit's involved?" he asked in his gravelly voice, the Irish lilt still evident.

"Yes, she is definitely unusual," Ashdowne mused, but missing from his tone was the acerbity that had formerly graced any discussion of Georgiana. It had been conspicuously absent ever since last night on the terrace when he had kissed her.

The kiss had been a game, really, a way to gain her confidence and as such, a seduction of necessity. Why, then, was he struck so forcefully by the memory of it? Why, whenever he saw her, was he seized by the urge for a repeat performance? Ashdowne shifted on the couch, a move that did not go unnoticed by his observant major-domo. Finn's dark eyes narrowed speculatively.

"So? What happened today? Did the runner arrest poor Whalsey?"

Ashdowne smiled. "No. I'm afraid not. The most incriminating evidence was a pilfered potion of hair restorative."

"No!" Finn brayed a low laugh.

"Yes," Ashdowne replied, chuckling at the recollection. When was the last time he had been so thoroughly, delightfully entertained? He could not recall such a catharsis as the laughter that had ensued outside Whalsey's house—or the pleasurable feeling it engendered in him. The memory, while a fond one, also was strangely disquieting. Why, after all this time, was he stimulated by none other than the Bellewether chit?

"Hair restorative? Ha! No wonder his lordship's always wearing a hat!" Finn said, slapping his knee in hilarity. "But where'd he get the stuff?"

"Apparently he and his cohort, a Mr. Cheever, cooked up a scheme to steal it from the professor who concocted it, which means our Miss Bellewether isn't quite as daft as we thought," Ashdowne said, his grin fading. "Although they knew nothing of the necklace, Whalsey and his friend technically qualify as thieves."

"If you say so," Finn said, between rumbles of laughter. "But I doubt if the Bow Streeter will see it that way."

"Perhaps. Perhaps not," Ashdowne replied. Jeffries appeared to be a decent, solid sort, not like some of his kind, who were known to be as dishonest as their prey.

"Give over, milord!" Finn said. "Even the stupidest thief taker wouldn't put stock in the girl's jabbering now."

"No. Probably not," Ashdowne agreed, shifting uncomfortably once more. And it wasn't just the hard length of couch that bothered him, but something remarkably akin to guilt, though why he should be plagued by such an alien sensation, he didn't know. He'd done nothing other than fall in with the chit's scheme. In fact, she had been inordinately pleased when he had used his influence on Jeffries.

Too pleased. Perhaps that was the problem, for Ashdowne could not help remembering the smile Georgiana gave him when he induced the Bow Street Runner to accompany them to Lord Whalsey's residence. No one in his less than exceptional existence had ever looked at him like that, as if he had pulled down the moon and stars and presented them to her! Although Ashdowne had to admit

that past lovers had often gazed at him with dazed gratitude after one of his more inventive nights, it was not the
same.

Georgiana's expression held no hint of lust for his
body—or anything else. It was more like sheer, unadul-
terated adoration. Ashdowne took a large swallow of port
as he amended his thought. *Undeserved adulation.* He had
been no more interested than anyone else in her absurd
investigation, except to make sure that it didn't impact
upon him in any way.

Ashdowne was rather ashamed of that, for his percep-
tion of the indefatigable Miss Bellewether was undergoing
a change. She had shown such pluck today that he
couldn't help feeling a certain reluctant admiration for her.
Her ideas might be skewed, but she acted on them. She
pursued her own course, without regard to anyone else's
opinion, blithely searching out mysteries in a world that
sorely lacked them.

Perhaps that's what made him so uncomfortable, for
Ashdowne well recognized her reaction. He too had once
sought excitement to feed a need within himself that few
others could begin to comprehend. But such quests were
often hazardous, and when Georgiana had baldly talked
of confronting possible criminals, Ashdowne had reacted
instinctively. The single-minded Miss Bellewether was liable to get herself into all sorts of trouble—trouble of a
far more dangerous sort than that he had already wit-
nessed.

Although Ashdowne told himself that she was no concern of his, he knew a niggling sense of worry just the
same. Of course, it was only natural to want to protect a
lovely young woman from harm, especially after the look
she had given him, but Ashdowne still decried the sensation. The chit was unnerving him in a way that nothing

had since his brother's death, and he did not care for it in the least.

"Don't tell me that the little baggage is affecting you, milord?" The sound of Finn's amusement brought Ashdowne from his dark thoughts, and he frowned in response to the all too accurate allegation.

"Of course not," he answered smoothly, but Finn knew him too well to accept the lie.

"Right!" the servant snorted. "But you have to admit that she's a beauty, with a body made for pleasing a man."

"Yes," Ashdowne agreed, though even the best of female forms had never stirred him the way Georgiana did. It wasn't the way she *looked,* but the way she *looked at him.* However, he had no intention of telling his manservant that the Bellewether chit eyed him as though he were a bloody god. Finn might hurt himself laughing.

"And I suppose it's a refreshing change not to have the lady panting after your title," the majordomo said, scratching his chin thoughtfully.

"Yes," Ashdowne agreed. One could hardly accuse Georgiana of such aspirations, for she had always seemed more leery of him than not, and unlike every other unmarried miss he had ever met, she was more interested in mysteries than matrimony. Ashdowne smiled at the thought.

"So that's her appeal?" Finn asked.

Eyebrow inching upward, Ashdowne glanced at his manservant with a wry expression. "Her *appeal?* I wasn't aware that she had any." Just because he found her stimulating did not mean he was attracted to the chit! The kiss had been a seduction of necessity, nothing more. In fact, most of the time he didn't know whether to laugh at her antics or strangle her.

Finn made a disbelieving sound as he rose to his feet. "Well, if you're not interested in her, does that mean we have to rush back to the old place?" he asked.

No doubt Ashdowne's ancestors would cringe at the family seat being referred to in such a manner, but he only smiled. Ashdowne Manor *was* old. With a pang, he realized that he ought to start thinking about making improvements, on top of everything else required of him, but his mind rebelled. He found himself longing to stay in Bath, if only for a while. For necessity or pleasure? Did it matter? Ashdowne knew it did, but he told himself that an extended visit would be in his own best interests.

"I think it might be wise to remain a little longer, just to tie up all loose ends here," he said slowly.

"Well, that suits me," Finn said, returning his glass to the sideboard. "I, for one, ain't ashamed to admit that I've a notion to see what the chit comes up with next."

Ashdowne glanced up to see Finn's back as he considered the Irishman's words. His lips curved slightly, for he, too, couldn't deny a certain sense of anticipation where Georgiana was concerned. "Yes. The whole business is becoming far more entertaining than I ever imagined," he replied.

After all, with Whalsey and Cheever exonerated, at least in the matter of the necklace, Georgiana was bound to set her sights on a new suspect. And Ashdowne, who hadn't been interested in much of anything for the past year, suddenly found himself eager to see what wild scheme she would hatch.

Finn turned to fix him with a deliberate look. "You just make sure you don't let that dizzy chit get under your skin. Many's the time a pretty face has been the ruin of a man, and I might remind you of all that you have to lose."

This time it was Ashdowne who snorted. "There's no danger of that, I assure you. I am hardly about to succumb to the young lady's extremely dubious charms." Pushing aside the memory of the feel of her in his arms, all soft and warm and willing, Ashdowne instead concentrated on her outlandish behavior. But after the discovery of the pilfered hair restorative, Georgiana's methods didn't seem nearly as silly as before.

Ashdowne frowned at the thought. "There is one thing that worries me, though," he said.

"What's that, milord?" Finn asked.

Ashdowne tilted his head, struck by an alarming feeling. "She's beginning to make a strange sort of sense to me," he said with a mixture of wonder and horror.

Finn, taking his words as a joke, burst into laughter once more, and Ashdowne tried to join in. But he couldn't quite ignore an insidious voice that kept whispering of his doom.

Georgiana sat in the drawing room, one elbow propped on the rosewood writing desk and her chin resting in her hand. She was not so somber or self-important as to lack all manner of levity, and once over her initial shock, she had been quick to see the humor in Lord Whalsey's situation. And she had found it both pleasant and novel to share laughter with a man, specifically a man such as Ashdowne.

However, the intimacy of that experience, like so much that occurred within a close vicinity to the marquis, had a peculiar effect upon her. In what was becoming a familiar sensation, Georgiana began feeling more with her heart and other parts of her anatomy, than her brain, and she had been forced to quit his company in order to think clearly once more.

Sadly, she had also required some time alone in which to swallow her disappointment. It had all been going so well—her investigation, the assistance from Ashdowne, the Bow Street Runner's attentiveness—until that dreaded box had been opened to reveal not the emeralds, but a bottle of hair restorative.

With a disgruntled sigh, Georgiana blew away a curl that had fallen over her forehead. When she thought of the precious time she had wasted on Whalsey, she let out a groan. And now Mr. Jeffries would be even harder to convince of her theories than before—although at least Whalsey and Cheever had been involved in a crime of some sort. Dear Ashdowne had made much of that once they had all recovered from the giggles outside of Whalsey's house.

Dear Ashdowne? Georgiana flung down her arm and lifted her chin in dismay. It would not do at all to begin thinking of her sometime associate in such a manner. No, she would be wise not to consider him at all. But logic told her that she needed him, or at least his influence with Mr. Jeffries, in order to unmask the culprit. Unfortunately, the wobbly thrill that went through her at the expectation of working alongside the marquis had very little to do with logic.

Reining in her wayward impulses with some effort, Georgiana straightened. She had far more faith in her abilities than in those of Mr. Jeffries, no matter what his credentials. She suspected that the poor man would never uncover the thief without her help, so she must put aside her prejudices and work with Ashdowne. She simply would have to avoid getting too close to him, and she vowed that there must certainly be no more kisses!

Firmly ignoring the sense of loss that accompanied her pledge, Georgiana tried, instead, to focus on the notes she had spread out before her. With a frown, she stared long and hard at her short list of suspects before taking up her pen and putting a line through Cheever and Whalsey. Unfortunately, she was left with only Mr. Hawkins and Ashdowne.

It had to be the vicar.

The thought of the elegant marquis climbing the side of a building for a few baubles seemed ludicrous, and Georgiana had to admit that she might have been a little precipitous in considering the wealthy nobleman as a possible robber. Even setting aside her own rapidly warming feelings toward the marquis, Georgiana had to wonder at a motive. The man seemed to have everything, so what would he want with Lady Culpepper's necklace? Although she still wasn't sure why Ashdowne was in Bath, blaming him for the theft appeared to be as preposterous as Jeffries had claimed.

Lifting the pen, Georgiana prepared to blot out Ashdowne's name, only to hesitate, her fingers suspended over the foolscap. Again, something tugged at her memory, just out of reach. But what? She laid down the pen and concentrated. There was something about the robbery that she wasn't seeing, something important...yet long moments of searching her mind dredged up nothing more than she already knew.

It must be the vicar, Georgiana thought, tossing her curls in exasperation. Unmasking him might prove difficult, for she had no evidence beyond motive and opportunity, but Georgiana never failed to rise to a challenge, and this one could provide her the rewards she had been seeking for what seemed like a lifetime. Here was her chance, and she was not going to miss it because of a balding lord's vanity.

However, she just might need some help.

* * *

Once he had decided to remain in Bath a bit longer, Ashdowne looked forward to the days ahead. There were dispatches from the family seat to be dealt with, of course, but somehow even the business of being marquis wasn't quite so stultifying here in the quaint, hill-enclosed city. He was at work in the study, a tray of sandwiches that Finn had left beside him still untouched when the Irishman interrupted his work.

"Uh, milord, there's a lady here to see you," Finn said.

Ashdowne looked up in surprise. Even in the more egalitarian Bath, women did not call on gentlemen unless they were related, and he had no family left except his late brother's wife. "Don't tell me Anne is here!" he said, staring past Finn as if to find his sister-in-law hiding behind his majordomo.

Finn snorted. "You don't really think she could gather together enough courage to make such a journey on her own, do you?"

"No," Ashdowne replied. Anne was the kind of female who was afraid to say boo to a goose—or anything else, for that matter. She was sweet and quiet and utterly boring, just the type to give Ashdowne a case of the hives, so he was greatly relieved not to welcome her to Bath. "Who, then?" he asked, annoyed with Finn, who, by now, was grinning from ear to ear.

"Perhaps I shouldn't have said *a lady,* but *the lady,* for there surely can't be another one like her."

Ashdowne opened his mouth to tell Finn just what he thought of the manservant's irritating hints when suddenly he had an uneasy feeling about the identity of his guest. But surely even she would not so totally disregard propriety, would she? "Tell me you didn't leave her on the doorstep," Ashdowne said, giving Finn a hard look as he rose to his feet.

Finn scoffed. "Of course not! I showed her into the parlor right proper."

Ashdowne was hardly appeased. Somehow the thought of Georgiana in his parlor was not much of an improvement upon Georgiana storming the gate.

He fixed Finn with a quelling stare. "Tell me she isn't alone." If she had come by herself to a bachelor's residence, he was going to strangle her! He would strangle her anyway, even if she had the entire membership of the Bath Ladies Coffee House Society with her, for decent females simply did not visit gentlemen, no matter what the provocation or company. Without waiting for Finn's reply, he stalked out of the room.

"Hold on, milord. She ain't alone! Brought her brother with her."

"Her brother? What the devil?" Ashdowne muttered, but he did not halt his steps as both annoyance and an unwelcome surge of excitement drove him forward. Pausing on the threshold in order to draw a sustaining breath, he donned a cool expression that belied his irritation. Well accustomed to keeping his thoughts to himself, Ashdowne stepped into the room, evincing nothing except the most polite interest in his guests.

Georgiana, of course, immediately pricked a hole in his hard-won reserve by rushing forward and gushing "Oh, Ashdowne!" in a breathless voice that made him seem the answer to her prayers, and drew him up short.

"Miss Bellewether," he said, nodding as best he could in the face of her obvious enthusiasm for his arrival.

"Better apologize for barging in here, Georgie." The words startled Ashdowne, for he had been too occupied with his visitor to note the other presence in the room. Cursing his unusual inattention, he swung round to face an average enough young man who didn't resemble Georgiana in the slightest. This was her brother? Ashdowne composed a greeting, but before he could get it past his lips, Georgiana launched into one of her rambling, incoherent speeches.

"Well, I suppose I must, though really I can see no harm done. You're here, and I'm happy to find you at home. I was going to send a note round, but I didn't know how long it would take to reach you, especially if you should be out. And I cannot help but feel the press of time, for each hour, indeed, each moment, might find the stolen item leaving the city and the culprit escaping prosecution!"

Ashdowne knew a reoccurrence of his previous dismay, for he followed her dialogue with alarming ease. *The chit's making sense to me!* He felt like calling Finn in to see if the phenomenon was contagious in the manner of some passing illness. Instead, he forced his features into an expression of bland agreement.

"You are speaking of Lady Culpepper's robbery, I assume?" he asked, just to assure himself that he understood her correctly. He also stifled an unexpected and unruly sense of disappointment that her enthusiasm was not for him, per se, but for his services as her investigative assistant.

Georgiana nodded, though appearing to rebuke him, as if he were being deliberately obtuse. "Desperation drove me, you see," she explained. "So when Mother asked me to take Araminta and Eustacia shopping, I instead sought out Bertrand and begged him to accompany me to find you, as I knew Mother would not be pleased if I came alone."

"Bertrand," Ashdowne said with a nod toward the young man who was now lounging against the pale silk that covered the walls of the parlor. Although any brother worth his salt would have talked his sister out of such a scheme, Ashdowne suspected it was nigh impossible for anyone to change Georgiana's mind, once it veered in a certain direction, so he simply tendered his gratitude. "My thanks for your escort."

Bertrand smiled readily. "Well, I'm just glad you didn't toss us out on our ears, which is what I told Georgie would happen should we arrive unannounced at a marquis's house in Camden Place!" The boy paused, and Ashdowne could see they were not cut from the same cloth at all.

"Please be assured that I won't toss you out," he said before turning back to Georgiana. "Now, Miss Bellewether, how can I serve you?"

Bertrand let out a choking sound that Ashdowne could only assume to be evidence of his scorn. "Don't tell me you're taken in by her nonsense, the ferreting out of suspects and all?" he asked, gawking stupidly.

The question put Ashdowne in the extremely dubious position of having to defend Georgiana, but, to his surprise, he found that the answer came readily enough. He fixed the lounging brother with an arrogant stare designed to put him in his place. "I assure you that I take your sister most seriously."

Bertrand gaped, his attention swerving back and forth between the two principles as if he could not quite figure out their relationship. His reaction made Ashdowne wonder what manner of suitors Georgiana had known, if his interest in her was so surprising. Probably callow youths like her brother, he thought, who could not see beyond that luscious body.

Dismissing Bertrand with a glance, Ashdowne turned back to Georgiana only to fall victim to The Look. She was gazing up at him as though overcome by his defense, as if no one had more nobly or more eloquently spoken up for her throughout her short life. Ashdowne checked himself, stunned for a moment as he eyed her, emotion rioting through him in a most unnerving manner. Guilt, desire and a certain misplaced pride struggled with something new and unnamed until he found it hard to control his expression.

Georgiana blinked. "Don't mind Bertrand," she said, as if his momentary lapse were due to the boy. "Give him something to eat, and he'll have no thought for anything else."

Ashdowne blinked himself, startled by the rather primitive declaration, before recovering. "Pardon my negligence. I'll send for some luncheon," he said, though it was well past the usual hour for that repast. He called for Finn, who seemed suspiciously close at hand, to bring a tray, and soon the manservant returned with sandwiches and tea and biscuits. True to Georgiana's prediction, her brother plopped down in the chair nearest the food and proceeded to happily devour it without paying them the slightest heed.

Ashdowne stared at the boy in amazement until Georgiana tugged on his sleeve, drawing him aside. "I have had a few hours to think, and now I am convinced we must act, and soon, if we are to solve the case!"

Her earnestness was nearly his undoing, but Ashdowne marshaled his resources and lifted a brow slightly. "What of Mr. Jeffries? Surely, now that he is here, he will swiftly discover the identity of the thief. After all, that is his job."

To his astonishment, Georgiana made a face and tossed her blond curls in disgust. "Mr. Jeffries! A pleasant enough fellow, I admit, but, I tell you, your manservant looks more like a Bow Street Runner than he! The man shall never come to the right conclusions without our assistance, and Lady Culpepper will never see her necklace again!''

"And what a tragedy that would be," Ashdowne said dryly. "I'm flattered by your vote of confidence, but what do you suggest we do? Surely, you don't still believe that Whalsey and Cheever are responsible?''

"No, of course not!'' Georgiana again donned her *stop being obtuse* expression, and Ashdowne tried to appear more attentive. "They were not my sole suspects! Now I have set my sights upon another, but I need more evidence.'' She frowned at the thought, and Ashdowne knew a nearly overwhelming urge to kiss her delightfully pouting mouth.

He restrained himself nobly. "What do you suggest, another confrontation?'' he asked.

"Oh, no,'' Georgiana said, grimacing so at his words that Ashdowne determined he was not acting the part of a good assistant. He immediately vowed to reform.

"As I just told you,'' she continued. "I haven't any hard evidence to back up my theory. But the man had both motive and opportunity, and what's more, he appears fit enough to have climbed up the building.''

"Ah. A feat that definitely limits the prospective robbers,'' Ashdowne said.

"Just so!'' Georgiana said, rewarding him with a smile for his quick grasp of her methods.

A good assistant definitely reaped what he sowed, Ashdowne thought, enjoying the spectacle. "But how are we to obtain the necessary evidence?'' he asked, truly curious. Oddly enough, he felt a twinge of anticipation, just to see what the devil the chit would do next. She really was the most entertaining creature.

"We shall break into his house!''

"What?'' Although Ashdowne had thought himself

prepared for anything her whimsy might concoct, Georgiana's declaration made him start. Unused to such bold speech, he glanced over his shoulder, but Bertrand was still happily devouring the sandwiches and tea, totally oblivious to their conversation. Ashdowne shook his head, wondering if he had lost the power to understand her so soon, for surely she didn't mean…

"I have given it a great deal of thought, and I do not see any other alternative," she asserted.

Ashdowne was speechless, for once, as he eyed the petite blonde who so blithely contemplated housebreaking. Never, in all of his life, had he encountered anyone quite like Georgiana Bellewether. It was unnerving, unsettling, *un*-everything, and yet strangely intoxicating, like an overdose of spirits that one was sure to regret.

"You realize, of course, that you are suggesting breaking the law," Ashdowne finally managed to say. As both a nobleman and the only one in the room with any sense, he felt it his duty to discourage what could at best be described as a foolhardy plan.

Georgiana had to consider his words for a moment, and Ashdowne could almost see the wheels turning inside that pretty head of hers. For all her foibles, Georgiana was no fool. She just needed a bit of direction, which Ashdowne had no intention of providing, he noted with an unpleasant stirring of guilt. It was enough that he stop her from coming to grief with this new scheme, he told himself firmly.

"Yes, I believe that, technically, our search could be construed as not quite legal, but since it is for the good of the case, I cannot see how anyone could object," Georgiana explained.

Ashdowne restrained his laugh manfully. "Well, the fellow whose place we're searching might see fit to find fault with us, as could Mr. Jeffries. I doubt that our illustrious Bow Street Runner views housebreaking in a good light.''

''Botheration!'' Georgiana muttered, and Ashdowne had the audacity to hope that he had finally gotten through to her. Housebreaking! He could not even begin to imagine the results if the disaster-prone Georgiana went through with her scheme. It was doomed! Surely even she—

''You're not going to help me, are you?''

For a moment, Ashdowne couldn't believe his ears, or his eyes, as the delicate creature before him gazed at him with thinly disguised disappointment. And his was a most precipitous fall from grace—from veritable god to uncooperative cur in one afternoon. It was a displacement that did not sit well upon Ashdowne's shoulders. Not only had he failed to discourage her in the slightest, but she was disgusted by his efforts! Worse yet, with or without him, the fool chit actually intended to enter someone's home without an invitation.

''It's all right,'' she said, obviously misinterpreting his horrified expression. ''I understand. A man in your position, a marquis, should not be involved in anything with the slightest hint of impropriety.''

Ashdowne might have been able to regain his composure if she had not reached out to pat his arm in a sympathetic gesture. The touch of her small, gloved hand, as well as the piteous look in her blue eyes, was his undoing. When he thought of the black deeds for which men of the aristocracy were notorious—seduction, gambling, dueling and more—as well as his own checkered past, he couldn't help it.

He burst out laughing, and he laughed so long and so hard that Bertrand glanced up from his repast and Finn, undoubtedly listening outside the door, stepped inside to see what had possessed him. But, true to form, Georgiana was unconcerned with his behavior, except as it applied to her deuced case.

"Does that mean you'll help?" she asked hopefully.

Between gasps, Ashdowne nodded, even though any sane man would take no part in Georgiana's intrigues, let alone this one, which was, no doubt, destined for the usual calamitous results. *I'm doomed,* he thought, but the knowledge served him not, for, like a moth to a flame, he embraced his own downfall.

Chapter Six

They parted with Bertrand in the Pump Room, despite Ashdowne's mild protest, for Georgiana had no intention of taking him along on their investigation. Oh, she loved her brother, but he was not someone with whom she could exercise her keen mind. Bertrand always did just what he had to in order to get by and considered anything more unworthy of effort. When he bestirred himself, he took a mild interest in the family farm, and it looked to everyone as though he would eventually succeed his father as squire and sheriff.

Most of the time, however, Georgiana considered him quite useless, so when Ashdowne voiced some surprise at their parting, she refused to call her brother back. "He would only be a nuisance," she said, shaking her head. "Besides, we hardly need him to chaperon a simple walk."

The housebreaking, of course, was another matter, which she declined to discuss in so public a place. Ashdowne, too, kept silent, although the movement of one dark brow conveyed his doubts about the propriety of them going off alone together. Georgiana dismissed such concerns with a toss of her head, for she had no intention of quibbling about appearances when the investigation lay ahead.

Truth to tell, Ashdowne was proving to be sadly pedestrian. For a while Georgiana did not believe he would accompany her at all, and she had been hard-pressed to hide her disappointment. Although she understood his position, still she had expected him to show a little more enthusiasm for her plan.

And even after he had agreed to join her in this most important endeavor, they had argued over when it was to take place. Georgiana was naturally in favor of conducting their business under the cover of night, but Ashdowne refused in a most infuriating manner. It was only after he asked her how they were to find anything in the dark that she had at last acquiesced to his scheme of entering Hawkins's lodgings in broad daylight.

When he observed that most people would be out enjoying the sunny afternoon, leaving few, if any, to mark their intrusion, Georgiana had been forced to admit that he might well be right. Perhaps she had misjudged the man, for it seemed that Ashdowne was giving serious thought to the task ahead.

Her enthusiasm renewed, Georgiana found Mr. Hawkins's direction in the book that all visitors signed upon their arrival in Bath and tugged upon Ashdowne's sleeve, ready to depart. With a long-suffering look, he attended her, and the two of them headed toward the doors only to be stopped midway through the crowd.

"Georgie!" At the sound of Araminta's voice, Georgiana winced, but there was no escaping now. Her sister was upon them in an instant, followed swiftly by Eustacia.

"There you are! Where have you been? Mother specifically told you to escort us to the…" Her words trailed off, for even the voluble Eustacia could not continue her prattling in the face of Ashdowne's elegant presence, and Georgiana knew a warm sensation of possessive pride that she had no right to feel. The handsome marquis was simply her assistant, nothing more, she told herself as she reluctantly made the introductions.

"My lord, may I present my sisters, Araminta and Eustacia?"

"Misses Bellewether. A pleasure to meet you," he said, bowing toward them in a courteous way that somehow set them to giggling. But then, *everything* set them to giggling. Georgiana was always at a loss to discover the source of their amusement and so had long ago given up trying to share their mirth.

"My lord," Eustacia said, hiding behind her ever-present fan.

"My lord," Araminta said, ducking her head close to her sister and twirling one thick curl. Much to their dismay, the younger girls had inherited the squire's brown hair, which they were always trying to lighten with some dreadful concoction. After the torment that they had put their locks through, Georgiana was surprised that they were not as balding as their father!

"We've been looking all over for you, Georgie," Eustacia said, eyeing Ashdowne coyly.

"Yes! Wherever have you been?" Araminta scolded, but without her usual acerbity.

"Ashdowne and I have been out walking and stopped in just for a moment. I'm afraid we must be on our way now," Georgiana said, inching toward the marquis.

"But Georgie!"

"Mother said—"

Georgiana cut off their growing protests with a warning look, but her sisters, as usual, did not take her seriously.

"Where are you going?" Araminta demanded.

"We're off for a carriage ride, above the city," Georgiana said, thinking quickly. And it was a good thing, too, because Ashdowne would soon become disenchanted with her siblings. And how could she blame him? Their incessant chatter rarely failed to give her a headache.

"Oh, that sounds wonderful! We shall come, too!" Eustacia cried.

"Mother would want us to join you!" Araminta said. "She said that you—"

"Sorry, but we're meeting another couple. No room!" Georgiana said, tugging on Ashdowne's sleeve. Without waiting for further protests, she pushed her way through the crowd, not looking back until they had exited the Pump Room's massive doors. Ashdowne, whose long strides had easily kept up with her, gave her an amused glance.

"Georgie?"

"A family nickname," Georgiana said with a shudder. She had been trying to put a stop to it for years. How could anyone with such a moniker ever be taken seriously?

"Which you despise," Ashdowne noted dryly. "Interesting family. I can't wait to meet your parents."

Georgiana smiled. "Although I love them dearly, you will find them much as my siblings. My father, being rather loud, would be certain to offend your aristocratic sensibilities, while my mother, though a very devoted parent, is the one who chooses my gowns."

Ashdowne gave her a long, considering look that would have set any other young woman to blushing, at the very least, before lifting his gaze to hers in a manner that made her feel all wobbly inside. "Are you certain you weren't adopted?"

Startled, Georgiana laughed aloud. Despite her best intentions, she felt an affection for the marquis that warmed her right down to her toes. Never had she felt so at ease or enjoyed someone's company as well. Unlike any other man she knew, Ashdowne treated her with respect. He listened to her, and—dare she think it?—he seemed to *understand* her. Georgiana's heart tripped as he walked alongside her, and she put some distance between them on the way to Mr. Hawkins's lodgings.

As delightful as she found him, it wouldn't do for her to become too enamored of the marquis's charms. Instead, she must focus on her quarry and how to run him to ground. Then, Georgiana vowed, Ashdowne wouldn't be the only person to take her seriously. With renewed determination, she marched forward, turning the conversation away from her family and back to the case, where it belonged.

They located their destination easily enough in a rather shabby but still genteel part of the city, and when Ashdowne paid a young boy to knock upon the door, no one answered. Georgiana had hoped as much, but she could hardly contain her excitement as they made their way to the rear entrance of the narrow apartment. Heretofore, the exercise of her abilities had been more on the mental plane, but now she found the prospect of investigating in a more physical manner most stimulating. And, she had to admit, the presence of the marquis only added to the thrill.

"It appears to encompass two floors," Ashdowne said, looking up, and Georgiana nodded in agreement, trying to focus her attention on the business at hand and not the height of the man next to her. Although she would never have thought Ashdowne inconspicuous, he managed to appear so, staying in the shadows of the small enclosed space that had once housed a garden but was now sadly neglected. She tried to follow his example and hunched against the building.

When they stepped to the entrance, Georgiana tried the latch only to find it would not turn. Stunned, she stared down at the stubborn portal in dismay. Who in Bath locked their doors? Obviously, Mr. Hawkins, and his behavior simply confirmed her suspicions about his character. No doubt, the purloined necklace was somewhere inside, for why else would the man see fit to bar his home?

However, his habits presented her with a difficult situation. How on earth were they to conduct their scarch? Georgiana glanced up at a high window, which did not appear at all accessible and then to Ashdowne, who was looking down at her with a rather smug expression, one eyebrow lifted. Did he think she would give up so easily? She scowled at him, then gasped as he pulled something from his pocket and inserted it into the lock. A nearly soundless click ensued and the door swung inward.

"Oh!" Georgiana said in breathless admiration. "Ashdowne, I take back every doubt I've had about you! You are surely the most clever of assistants!"

"Have you ever had one before?" he asked, leaning close as she slipped inside the building.

"One what?" she asked, dizzy as always when she felt him so near. The heat from his form seemed to reach out to her, although he did not touch her.

"An assistant," he said as he closed the door behind them.

"No," Georgiana said rather breathlessly.

"Ah. Then I shall disregard the compliment." He moved in front of her and then turned, his eyes gleaming in the dim interior. "What doubts?"

But Georgiana only smiled, laughter bubbling up again. With a shake of his head, the marquis began moving around the room like a cat stalking new territory, his blue eyes watchful, his body lithe and somehow always in the shadows. For a moment, Georgiana could only stare in wonder.

"What are we looking for?" He turned his head to gaze at her, and Georgiana blinked. Had she forgotten their purpose so quickly in his presence?

"The necklace, of course," she muttered, a bit flustered.

"And where might it be?" he asked, amusement heavy in his tone.

"I do not know!" Georgiana answered sharply. "Just look!"

Presumably rebuked, Ashdowne turned away and began stalking again, lifting a lid here and peeking into a cupboard there. Georgiana tried to think clearly, but it was always difficult when he was around. What would Hawkins do with his prize? she wondered. Turning this way and that, she realized that in all likelihood, the thief would not leave the jewels downstairs, but hidden as far away from prying eyes as possible. She hurried toward the steps.

Upstairs Georgiana quickly surveyed the clean but shabby furnishings, and the neat and spartan quality of the room, which hardly had the look of depravity one might expect of a thief's den. But, then again, a criminal of the caliber to execute this particular robbery was not one of the norm, Georgiana thought.

And so she set to work, spying under the mattress and in corners and through the man's linen, distasteful though it might be. She was just finishing with that chore when Ashdowne appeared, that infernal brow of his cocked slightly as if he were speculating upon her motives. "Having fun?" he asked.

"I am but seeking out all the possibilities!" Georgiana retorted, taking back some of her earlier enthusiasm for her assistant, who did not seem at all interested in the search. He wandered about rather aimlessly as she continued, determined to ignore him and find the gems on her own.

She had just completed a circuit of the small bedroom when she noticed a stack of blankets tucked into the corner under the eaves. They covered a trunk and, with increasing eagerness, Georgiana tugged it from its place. Pushing aside the covering, she jiggled the clasp, thrilled when she was able to lift the lid.

"I've found something!" she crowed as she peeked into the dark interior. Reaching inside, she came up with several lengths of dark velvet cord. Oddly enough, they looked like the kind to hold back draperies, but Georgiana could easily imagine a far more nefarious use, such as tying up victims!

"What is it?"

Georgiana nearly squeaked at the whisper, for she had not realized Ashdowne was at her elbow, bent down on one knee. She had forgotten how silently he moved.

To cover her confusion, Georgiana gestured to the cord. "Look! Rope!" She pulled another item from the trunk and held it aloft triumphantly. "And a black mask!" It was the type one would wear at a masquerades, but might just as well be used by a criminal to conceal his identity, Georgiana reasoned.

She leaned over, rooting further, and emerged with a small, tasseled whip. "And a weapon!" Of course, a gun would have been more incriminating, and indeed, this whip was among the most unusual she had ever seen....

Her thoughts were cut off by Ashdowne, who cleared

his throat softly. "Ah, Georgiana. I hardly think those are burglary tools."

"Oh, I don't know. They look very suspicious to me!" she answered, digging deeper.

"Suspicious, yes," he said, his tone one of ripe amusement. "But not in the manner you mean."

Refusing to be deterred, Georgiana stuck her head into the trunk only to feel something tickling her nose. A feather? She raised her face, but was halted in her effort to back away when she was seized by a rather ferocious sneeze. The force of it jolted her into the lid, and with a muffled shriek, she fell forward, headfirst, into the trunk, her bottom up in the air as her feet frantically sought purchase.

Although she was in no real danger of suffocating, the position was rather awkward, her skirts upended and all, and her hands smashing what might be vital evidence. Hurriedly Georgiana struggled to free herself, but she heard an ominous noise that made her panic. What was happening behind her? Where was Ashdowne?

Her face buried among a decidedly odd collection of musty items, Georgiana wondered if the vicar or his servant had returned and were even now threatening the marquis. Only when she managed to get one slipper back upon the floor did Georgiana realize that the low rumble she heard was the sound of Ashdowne's laughter.

Indignant, she threw open the lid that had fallen across her shoulders and pulled herself from the confines of the trunk. Her would-be assistant, instead of rescuing her, was seated on the floor, leaning against the wall, positively roaring with amusement. As if that wasn't bad enough, he was actually clutching his flat stomach as if he were taxed by his own hilarity. Georgiana sincerely hoped that he was in terrible pain.

"Well!" she said, tossing her curls.

She seemed to have gained Ashdowne's attention, for he stopped laughing long enough to look at her, only to burst forth once more, throwing his head back. Suspiciously, Georgiana lifted her hand to her hair and patted her curls gingerly. Her fingers lighted upon the feather, which appeared to be lodged in a particularly thick lock and stuck straight upward. Blowing out a breath of exasperation, Georgiana yanked it forcibly from her head and thrust it back into the trunk.

"There! Is that better?" she asked Ashdowne in angry accents. His raucous noise dwindled to a chuckle as he stared up at her, and Georgiana noticed his eyes were watering from the force of his mirth. It should have annoyed her more, but somehow the sight of him, so handsome, so relaxed, so very human and approachable, made her heart melt. And she had to admit that she would rather have Ashdowne laughing at her than some other man staring at her bosom.

His laughter wasn't cruel, but joyous, and Georgiana couldn't help smiling at the warmth in his expression, a far cry from the cool man she had initially met. Turning to hide her softening mood, she tucked the blanket over the trunk once more and pushed it under the eaves. She moved back to survey her handiwork, wondering if the container was in the exact same position. After a moment's study, she began backing away to get a better view, only to trip over Ashdowne's outstretched legs.

She flailed wildly for an instant before strong arms caught her, drawing her down onto his lap, where Georgiana landed with a gasp. As she blinked at Ashdowne, he reached up and swiped at his eyes with the back of one gloved hand and then shook his head. "You, Miss Bellewether, are utterly delightful."

"Well, I'm happy to provide you with whatever amusement I can," Georgiana said, wiggling as she tried to right herself.

But Ashdowne held her firm, and she glanced at his handsome face in surprise. "Ah, but I need laughter," he said. "I'd forgotten how much...I...need..." His words trailed off as his head dipped, and Georgiana's lips opened in surprise just in time to meet his own.

They were warm and gentle and as heady as she remembered. Georgiana had the fleeting notion that she ought not to let him kiss her, especially on the floor of Mr. Hawkins's chambers, but she could never hold a thought when he was this close, and her mind easily surrendered to her body.

As if it had too long been subjugated to the whims of her brain, the rest of Georgiana welcomed Ashdowne's attentions. She lifted her hands to his wide shoulders, her fingers flexing into the hardness there with pleasure. He bent her back over one of his arms, his kiss becoming deeper as his tongue leisurely explored her mouth.

Oh, it was surely the most glorious sensation! Georgiana could only cling to his shoulders as his lips moved along her cheek to her ear, where he did something amazing with her earlobe. How curious! And then he drifted lower, leaving a trail of moist, hot kisses along her throat that made Georgiana squirm and elicited the oddest sound from her.

Ashdowne murmured something encouraging against her flushed skin, and then one of his hands, which had been resting at her waist, moved upward to graze the underside of her bosom. Georgiana caught her breath in astonishment. The figure that she had always cursed now seemed to take on a life of its own, tingling and yearning in the most peculiar fashion. As his palm continued upward, Georgiana held her breath. She wanted, she wanted...

She released a low sigh as his fingers closed over one breast. Oh, the bliss! It coursed through her as he gently stroked her, his gloved fingers gliding along the bare skin above her gown, his thumb brushing the nipple that suddenly grew hard and taut.

"Oh, Ashdowne!" Georgiana murmured as sensations whirled through her. She wiggled on his lap, searching for some kind of surcease, and felt something stir and stiffen against her bottom. "Oh!" she gasped as it seemed to move beneath her.

"Yes. *Oh.* Georgiana..."

Whatever Ashdowne meant to say was lost in the click of a lock. It sounded so loud in the stillness that they both paused, the cadence of their shallow breathing the only sound that followed, and then they heard the ominous creak of a door below.

Before Georgiana could even gather her wits, Ashdowne was up and pulling her to the window. He had it open in a thrice and was himself outside in seemingly one fluid movement. Then he lifted her through, too, sliding the window shut behind them in the space of a heartbeat. Stunned, Georgiana turned to find that they were on a roof, and Ashdowne, without the slightest hesitation, led her around chimneys and dormer windows, hopping from one building to another until they reached a tall, spindly-looking oak.

Although it was not a long way down, Georgiana still balked at the precarious climb, blinking at the ground that seemed so threatening from where she perched. But Ashdowne moved with ease, his hands always ready to grasp her own or take her weight as he helped her down. Finally she slid to her feet, grazing his hard body in way that nearly robbed her of what few wits she had left.

There they remained, his hands resting upon her waist, and Georgiana braced herself for a scold. Ashdowne had surely ruined some part of his elegant clothing, besides risking his neck and his freedom, should they have been caught in the act of housebreaking. Suddenly her plan seemed more foolish than inspired, and Georgiana felt a deep remorse for having talked him into it.

She glanced up at him with some trepidation, but to her surprise, the expression on his face could only be described as exultant. He threw back his head and laughed as they stood safely hidden in the shade, leaves gently swaying above their heads. Georgiana wondered if he had gone mad as she watched him. The man did have a marked propensity for hilarity at the most peculiar moments. But, just then, he sobered, his lashes drifting lower, and Georgiana eyed him cautiously as he leaned closer.

"Thank you," he whispered, his bright eyes glittering in a way that made it difficult for her to concentrate.

"For what?" Georgiana asked.

"For the adventure," Ashdowne explained. Before she could digest that declaration, he leaned close to whisper in her ear. "I had forgotten, and owe you well for the reminder."

"Forgotten what?" Georgiana felt more confused than ever as he flashed her a white smile and bent near again.

"Life is an adventure," he declared, and right there, in the shadow of the oak, Ashdowne brushed her lips in a brief, hard kiss. Dazed, Georgiana simply stood there, until he took her hand and pulled her along behind him.

Adventure? Apparently the man thrived upon it, and as he led her through cramped back gardens to the streets of

Bath, Georgiana began to feel as though *she* were the assistant, being swept along by a force greater than any mystery.

Afternoon was fading into evening by the time they neared the Bellewether residence, but Georgiana was no closer to solving the case than she had been upon meeting the Bow Street Runner this morning. She felt as though the once-simple solution was slipping further from her fingers with each passing moment. And her assistant, while valuable when it came to housebreaking, was turning out to be part of the problem.

Ashdowne, she was forced to admit, had the most disturbing effect on her of anyone she had ever met. His very presence acted upon her like a potent drug, dulling her mind while sharpening all of her other senses to an astounding degree. When Georgiana remembered the feel of his hand upon her breast, she was struck with both an overwhelming yearning and horrendous embarrassment.

Had she really responded to his touch with such abandon? Having wished herself a man more often than not, Georgiana had disdained the feminine trappings that so enamored her sisters. She had always considered herself far above such nonsense, too logical and intelligent and clever to fall victim to the charms of any man. Ashdowne, however, seemed able to reduce her to a mindless, incoherent puddle in a manner of moments.

It was decidedly lowering.

Worse yet, this curious phenomenon couldn't have been more ill-timed, coming as it did just when she needed her wits most, when she was finally on the verge of carving out a career for herself. Georgiana blew out a breath of exasperation. Although she tried to curb her feelings for her assistant, she simply was unable to concentrate. Ashdowne was much too distracting!

Obviously, drastic measures were called for in this instance. As much as she liked the marquis and appreciated his help in her investigation, she was going to have to sever their association. The decision was a painful one, made more so by the sight of him as she halted to face him in front of the Bellewether residence. He was so tall and handsome, his eyes still glittering with the pleasure he had taken in their little escapade, his mouth curving into an easy smile that bespoke a certain relaxation that she had not seen in him before.

Georgiana's stomach dipped as she considered that she might actually be good for the man, but she refused to let herself follow that train of thought any further. Nor would she allow herself to look too long upon the features that had become dear to her so quickly. Instead, she stared doggedly at his neck cloth and prepared to dismiss her one and only assistant.

"Ashdowne, I—"

"Georgie! There you are!" Georgiana was dismayed at the sound of her father's hail. Not only was she interrupted at a most unfortunate moment, but now she would be forced to introduce Ashdowne when she wanted nothing further to do with him.

"The girls said that you were out driving with..." Her father's words trailed off as he stopped to stare at the marquis. "Ah, but who is that with you, surely not Lord Ashdowne?" he asked in a voice that told her he was well aware of the identity of her companion and inordinately pleased with the knowledge.

Trying not to grimace, Georgiana turned toward her sire, who was grinning happily. "My lord, may I present my father, Squire Bellewether."

As usual, her father barely gave Ashdowne a chance to nod his head before launching into gregarious speech.

"My lord! Why, this is a pleasure! My little Georgie out and about with one of the most famous visitors to Bath!" He glanced approvingly at his daughter, as if forming an acquaintance with a marquis was some kind of accomplishment, and Georgiana stiffened.

Despite her heightened awareness of the man beside her, she was not one of those giddy females who spent their time chasing after a husband. Why, she didn't even want the marquis as an assistant anymore! "Yes, but he was just leaving," Georgiana said, ignoring the slight lift of one of Ashdowne's dark brows.

"Oh, no! You can't leave now, my lord," her father boomed. "Not when you haven't met the family! Come, come," he said, gesturing toward the house. "You simply must see Mrs. Bellewether, and I'm sure she won't let you go until you have taken supper with us."

Georgiana stared at her father in alarm. Even before she had decided to discharge her assistant, she would never have put him through the rigors of a meal with her flighty family. And now that she was prepared to end their relationship, Georgiana wanted as little contact with the man as possible. Inviting him inside hardly seemed the way to withdraw from his company.

"Oh, I'm sure that his lordship has other engagements this evening," Georgiana said, giving Ashdowne a polite excuse to refuse the invitation. Of course, it never occurred to her that the man who had once looked down his nose at her would actually *want* to stay for supper, so when she heard his low rumble of denial, Georgiana glanced at him in surprise.

"Actually, I have nothing pressing planned for tonight," he said, his lips curling upward in a devilish manner that led her to suspect he was deliberately being obtuse. But why? Perhaps he thought she wanted to continue their discussion of the case, Georgiana decided. Giving him the benefit of the doubt, she made sure her father wasn't watching and then shook her head in what she hoped was a subtle yet forceful manner.

The movement only caused Ashdowne's brow to lift higher and his mouth to curve into a smile. "In fact, Squire, I would be delighted to accept your kind invitation," he said. Although he inclined his head toward her father, Ashdowne kept his gaze upon her, as if daring her to deny him.

Outraged, Georgiana glared at him, but she could not make her objections known more loudly, for her father was already herding them toward the house, while proclaiming his gratification in a loud voice. Ashdowne, too, appeared inordinately pleased, and Georgiana scowled at his good mood, for it surely would not last once he was introduced to the rest of her family.

Despite her misgivings, the situation could work to her advantage, Georgiana told herself, for she might well be spared what would surely be a difficult parting from her assistant. She might not have to dismiss Ashdowne at all, she mused.

One meal with the Bellewethers ought to accomplish that feat far more easily than she ever could.

Chapter Seven

As if to confirm Georgiana's suspicions, she and Ashdowne had barely followed her father into the house when they were greeted by the sound of shouting. Ahead in the front parlor, Araminta and Eustacia were plainly in view, engaged in a loud argument.

"It's my ribbon!" Araminta screeched, tugging fiercely on a pale pink confection she held between her fingers.

Unfortunately, Eustacia kept a firm grip on the other end, so that the two girls resembled nothing so much as dogs fighting over a bone. "It is not! Mother gave it to *me!*"

"She did *not!*" Araminta replied. She punctuated her words with an especially violent yank, sending Eustacia sprawling upon the floor in a very unladylike pose.

"Girls! Girls!" her father scolded, while Georgiana turned to Ashdowne with a look that dared him to complain. But instead of the horror she expected to see upon his face, the marquis wore an expression of faint amusement as he leaned close to whisper to her.

"I see you're not the only hoyden in the family," he said, for her ears only.

Georgiana blinked at him, outraged, as he straightened,

and gave her a guileless smile that further annoyed her. She a *hoyden?* Certainly not! She was not at all like either of her sisters. Georgiana formed a blistering retort, but had no chance to launch it at his smug profile, for Araminta and Eustacia had finally caught sight of him. They hurried forward, fans and handkerchiefs at the ready, while the disputed ribbon lay forgotten on the floor.

To Georgiana's dismay, they immediately began their incessant giggling. "My lord!" they gushed, surrounding Ashdowne and flirting with him in the silliest fashion. It was positively sickening, and Georgiana had to bite her tongue to stay the rebuke that swiftly formed. Her father was no help at all, booming out introductions without a thought for the misbehavior of his youngest daughters.

When Araminta nudged aside her sister to take a place next to the marquis, Georgiana had to fight an alarming urge to jerk one of her sibling's fat curls or knock her to the floor. Luckily she recognized the sensation as the same strange possessiveness in regard to Ashdowne that had come over her earlier, and so she curbed her violence. Such feelings were only natural, she reasoned, since he was her assistant.

But no longer. With displeasure, Georgiana let Araminta usurp her position, for she could not, in all good conscience, cling to it. Ignoring the pang that kept nagging her at the thought of their parting, she stepped away, only to be halted by Ashdowne's gentle yet firm touch at her elbow.

How he had done it she had no idea, but he had out-maneuvered her sisters to regain his stance beside her in a rather proprietary fashion. Although Georgiana told herself that he was simply taking his duties as assistant seriously, she could not help the warm swell of happiness that rose within her at his actions.

Despite the marquis's earlier acquiescence, Georgiana never really thought he would stay for supper, but when the time came, he very handsomely agreed. And as the evening progressed, he continued to be both gracious and agreeable, two traits that Georgiana would not usually have assigned to him.

He managed to juggle her sisters' avid attention and her father's jovial conversation, while somehow easing her mother's subtle reservations about a nobleman arriving on her doorstep. Luckily Bertrand did not appear, or her unconventional visit to Ashdowne's house might have come to light, thereby upsetting the congenial atmosphere. But Bertrand remained out, presumably dining with friends, and Ashdowne worked his charms effortlessly upon the rest of the family.

It was both admirable and irritating, for Georgiana did not need another reason to like the marquis, especially when he already was so distracting. She had not wanted to dine with him in the first place, and she found his continued presence a deterrent to her concentration. She really needed to consider the case, but she could hardly do so when he was seated next to her, his tall form exuding a warmth that affected her all too easily.

And why was he being so nice when he normally wouldn't give her family a second glance? Georgiana had thought that a few hours spent in their company would drive him from her home, but Ashdowne appeared perfectly at ease even among the most trying members of the household. Being of a suspicious nature, Georgiana immediately began to wonder about his motives. If he thought his duties as her assistant required him to handle her relatives, he was mistaken, for the man had no duties at all. He just didn't know it yet, she thought, more determined than ever to sever their relationship.

However, no matter how hard Georgiana tried to engage him in private conversation in order to do just that, she found her efforts thwarted by the rest of the assemblage. She became increasingly frustrated as the evening wore on, especially after they were forced to listen to her sisters sing and play. Although the girls were passable musicians, Georgiana was in no mood to take pleasure in their performance.

"And what of you, Georgiana?" Ashdowne said, leaning close. "Will you not join in?"

Georgiana made a sound of disgust. "Not unless you wish to suffer a screeching that might well unsettle your supper."

His rich laughter drew immediate attention—a frown from her mother, a grin from her father and two pouts from her sisters. Of course, any chance of important dialogue between the two of them was lost, and Georgiana blew out a breath of exasperation. Impatiently she began tapping her toe upon the floor until the edge of Ashdowne's booted foot nudged her into silence. Her ensuring glare only drew another burst of laughter from the impossible man.

How could he sit there calmly pretending to enjoy the mediocre musical abilities of her sisters when she was fairly squirming to get away? Georgiana fumed. She never knew what sort of behavior to expect from the man. At first she had thought him a haughty boor, but he had soon revealed himself to be her intellectual equal. Yet when she came to accept his contribution to her case, purely on a ral level, of course, he suddenly turned humorous or charming or…sensual.

His mercurial nature, while annoying, also seemed to stimulate some heretofore untapped part of her that craved such stimulation. Perhaps it was because her life was rather ordinary, her family and acquaintances utterly predictable, that she found Ashdowne so appealing.

But no longer, Georgiana told herself, as she envisioned their dissociation with a growing sense of purpose. Once rid of the erratic marquis, she would return to her stable existence of logic and reasoning, her only stimulation the mental kind. And if the rest of her female form shuddered in disappointment, Georgiana had no intention of indulging it.

She was drawn from her thoughts by Ashdowne, who stood and clapped politely. Apparently, another interminable entertainment was over.

"Thank you for the music," he said, thereby putting an end to it, much to Georgiana's relief. "And now, Miss Bellewether, I believe you promised to show me the garden."

For a moment, Georgiana only stared at him blankly. Then, realizing that he was, at last, responding to her efforts at private speech, she rose hurriedly. "Oh, yes," she said, seizing upon the suggestion.

"The garden?" Her mother's tone evinced dismay, but her father paid no heed and boomed out his approval.

"You go on and show his lordship, but don't be too long now," he said, giving them a wink that made Georgiana cringe in embarrassment. Surely the squire did not think they sought to be alone for...for the purpose of flirtation? Georgiana's cheeks flamed, but Ashdowne remained impassive, gesturing for her to join him with his usual grace. They headed toward the tall doors as the protests of her sisters rose and faded behind them.

The garden was small, as were most in Bath, in shadow. It had rained during supper, leaving a mist that Georgiana found irritating. She peered through it with a gloomy sense of frustration, for the vicar might be doing anything on a night like this. Was he even now getting rid of the evidence?

Then Ashdowne moved near her, and all thoughts of the case fled, along with most of her wits. The mist that had seemed so stultifying now swirled about her in a rather romantic fashion, enclosing the two of them in a world all their own. Georgiana registered the thought and then shuddered at the absurd whimsy.

Obviously she was not herself. As if to prove her suspicions, heat surrounded her, and the scent of Ashdowne filled her senses, doing strange things to errant parts of her anatomy. She stepped back, blindly seeking an anchor where there was none. Knowing that she must speak now before her wits deserted her entirely, Georgiana cleared her throat, her attention firmly focused on Ashdowne's boots.

"My lord—"

"Really, Georgiana, I don't see the need for such formalities between us," he replied in a tone that made her stomach dip and her body ripen like fresh fruit. She closed her eyes on a memory of his hands upon her, steeling herself against the slow sweep of lethargy that came with it.

"Ashdowne," she amended. Lifting her lids once more, Georgiana blurted out her message before it was too late. "I'm afraid I'm going to have to dismiss you. I don't want your help any longer."

The silence that met her announcement was deafening, and Georgiana dared a glance at her former assistant's face. Rarely did Ashdowne reveal himself, so it was with some surprise that she watched raw astonishment grace the elegant marquis's handsome features. While Georgiana realized she had never seen him so unguarded, the always eloquent nobleman actually started sputtering, as if struck speechless by her declaration.

Georgiana might have been amused if she had not felt so guilty for causing his distress. "I'm sorry, Ashdowne, but you're just too much of a distraction to me," she explained. "I cannot concentrate on the case."

At her words, he stopped sputtering and stared at her for a long moment. Then he threw back his head and burst into laughter, making Georgiana wonder if insanity ran in his family, for the man seemed too often amused. Perhaps, like her sisters, he found humor where she saw none. Georgiana frowned as Ashdowne recovered himself.

"I beg your pardon, but you're just so deuced... unpredictable," he finally said.

It hardly seemed a compliment, so Georgiana tossed her curls in pique. Hadn't she just been thinking that of him? "I could say the same of you!" she said.

"Really?" he asked, his grin warming her insides so that she could not hold on to her annoyance. "How delightful," he murmured, and Georgiana again felt the familiar sensation of surrender as he stepped toward her.

"No!" she said, holding up a hand to fend him off. "This is exactly what I mean. I haven't been able to think at all during supper. You are simply too unnerving."

This time Ashdowne's smile was so slow and provocative that Georgiana thought her knees might give way. "Unnerving, am I?" he said, taking another step forward. Georgiana moved away, only to come up against the wall of the house at her back.

"I like being unnerving," he said, one hand reaching out to rest against the building, thereby trapping her. His other hand brushed against her hair, and he stared, his attention caught, as if he had never seen it before. Touching a fat curl, he rubbed it between his fingers, as though fascinated by the texture, and Georgiana had to admit to a certain fascination herself. She made a low sound, and Ashdowne slowly turned his face back to hers.

"But I'll try to be less unnerving, so that you can concentrate on the case," he murmured, his expression sincere if unrepentant. "What do you plan to do next?"

Wrenching her thoughts back to her neglected investigation, Georgiana realized that she had few choices, so she blurted out the first idea that came to mind. "I suppose I'll just have to follow the vicar and see if he reveals himself."

"But I'm afraid I can't allow that," Ashdowne whispered, so close that Georgiana could feel the gentle caress of his breath.

"W-what do you mean?" she stammered. Despite the warmth that weighted her limbs, she felt a spark of outrage, for the man had no right to dictate to her.

"I'm your keeper, remember?"

Georgiana could only nod stupidly, her momentary rebellion melting away as his nearness swamped her senses.

"I'll have to come along to keep you out of trouble, so you will forget this wild notion to dismiss me, won't you?" Ashdowne asked. Georgiana fully intended to shake her head in objection, but instead she found herself nodding in yet another example of the defection of her body from her brain.

"Thank you," Ashdowne purred, and she stared at his lips, transfixed by their subtle curves and the lovely little indentation above them. "Promise me that you won't do anything foolish tonight, and I shall be at your disposal tomorrow," he added.

At her disposal? The very thought made Georgiana giddy. She wanted to taste those marvelous lips, to feel him kiss her in that deep, lush way of his, and she held her breath, awaiting his touch. But just when she expected him to put his mouth to hers, he stepped back, confounding her once more.

"I don't want you leaving your house tonight. It's not a fit night for anyone to be about, and your investigation will wait until tomorrow."

"Investigation," Georgiana repeated numbly. *Oh, yes, the case!* She pushed herself from the wall and ducked away from Ashdowne, taking in a deep draught of air to dispel his allure. "I fear that it is getting away from us. We must act, and soon," she said with as much force as she could muster. Her mind clearer, she began walking through the grass, heedless of the soaking her hem would receive. "Who knows what the vicar is doing. Do you think he's gotten rid of the necklace already?"

"No," Ashdowne answered.

"Good. Then we still have a chance to recover it!" Georgiana said. "We simply must catch him at something suspicious! Perhaps he has not even hidden the jewels at his lodgings, but somewhere else. That is why we must keep an eye on him."

"So we shall," Ashdowne said. "But I want you to promise me that you will not try to follow him—or anyone—alone."

Flustered, Georgiana turned to argue, but the marquis wore a most implacable expression that stopped her short. "Oh, very well," she muttered.

"Promise?" he asked, moving nearer.

"I promise," she said with a grimace.

"Good girl," he said.

Georgiana was going to deny the endearment, but he was looming over her again, tall and elegant and handsome, a figure of shadow and yet so much more. She felt a wash of dizziness, along with a stirring of longing, which she firmly quelled.

"But you must agree not to be so...distracting," she said, stepping back to escape his potent charm. "If we are going to work together as you demand, then we must keep our minds firmly on the investigation and avoid unseemly behavior...such as that which occurred this afternoon at the vicar's."

Georgiana's face flamed, and she was glad for the darkness, but to her dismay, Ashdowne actually chuckled. He was not taking her seriously! "Nothing at all can be accomplished by such a...flirtation," she repeated more firmly. "Logically, one must—"

Ashdowne cut her off by moving in front of her. "You are a complete fraud, Georgiana Bellewether," he said, the gentle timbre of his voice taking the sting from his words.

"Whatever do you mean?" Georgiana asked, tempted to take umbrage but unable to rouse her indignation. Ashdowne was wearing an expression she had never seen before, an odd mixture of tenderness and something else....

"No matter how much you pretend otherwise, you lead with your heart, not your head," Ashdowne said softly. While Georgiana tried to form a protest, he took her face in his hands and rubbed her cheeks with his thumbs, effectively stealing her wits.

"Just because you are intelligent and clever and resourceful, you think that makes you pragmatic, when, in fact, you are the most romantic woman I've ever met," he said, tilting her chin upward.

"That is not true at all," Georgiana replied in a breathless whisper, but it died away as his mouth at last came down on hers. He brushed against her lips, lightly nipping as if he were but tasting and not quenching his thirst.

Then, just when Georgiana would have leaned into his hard body, he drew back, leaving her with a vague dissatisfaction.

Giving her a gentle smile that she would have never expected from him, Ashdowne moved toward the door, where her mother's voice drifted out to them. "An incurable romantic," he said.

For once, Georgiana, left speechless by a nearly overpowering sense of longing, was not about to argue.

Ashdowne didn't trust her in the slightest.

According to his calculations, he had just enough time to return to Camden Place, but little beyond that. No matter what Georgiana might promise him when she was dazed with passion, eventually she would change back into a creature of logic. And then, her vow to him might be conveniently forgotten in the excitement of pursuit, or whatever she cared to call her wild-goose chases.

In the meantime, she would have to answer some questions from her family, no doubt, concerning her sudden association with a marquis. If Ashdowne had judged them correctly, the mother would issue a few judicious warnings, while the father, an optimistic but not as sensible a sort, would be less wary of a nobleman's attentions to his daughter.

Hopefully, the interrogation and the ensuing goodnights would keep Georgiana busy, for a while at least. Unfortunately, Ashdowne suspected that keeping the indefatigable Miss Bellewether occupied could be a full-time task, requiring a man with steady nerves, quite a bit of daring and a variety of talents. He realized, with a chagrin, that he was uniquely qualified for the position. Unfortunately, the realization was not nearly as alarming as it once would have been.

At first Ashdowne had disdained Georgiana's exuberance and irrational behavior, but now he was finding himself strangely enchanted. What other woman had so many facets? Where else could both reason and imagination thrive in one delectable package, along with a delightful ability to laugh at herself?

Ashdowne had long disciplined himself to anticipate all possibilities, but Georgiana left him baffled. No matter how well he thought he knew her unusual mind, she continued to surprise him. With a certain fondness, he remembered her expression when he had picked the lock on the vicar's door. Instead f appearing shocked, Georgiana had been impressed, rewarding him with a look of admiration that had oddly affected him, for where, outside of London's East End, would he find another female who would appreciate such a skill?

Ashdowne had never met a woman who downplayed her beauty, yet Georgiana treated hers as if it were naught but a nuisance. Of course, those gowns her mother chose for her were hideous, as well as practically indecent. He would choose for her more modest attire, simple fabrics devoid of ruffles and bows that let her innate loveliness shine, without drawing too much interest from other men.

But no matter what her costume, Georgiana would remain true to herself. Whether in sackcloth or silk, she would ignore her attributes in favor of her more cerebral interests and defy convention with her foibles. Oftentimes she made such dreadful faces that Ashdowne didn't know whether to laugh or to kiss her. Indeed, he rarely knew just what to do with the increasingly alluring Georgiana.

Well, he had a good idea of what he would *like* to do with the voluptuous creature, Ashdowne thought, his body growing taut. And it didn't involve clothes of any kind. For one long, delicious moment, he imagined her naked, that glorious form his for the taking, before he ruthlessly banished the vision. No matter how tempting she might be, Georgiana Bellewether was a gently bred virgin and not for him.

Ashdowne recalled how he had already overstepped his bounds with the young lady. He certainly hadn't intended to touch her today, but he had never laughed so freely as when he had watched her antics in the vicar's bedroom. And his delight had led to an expression of appreciation that went far beyond his initial aim. But he had never expected such an enthusiastic return of his ardor, either.

Truly, everything about Georgiana Bellewether was an intriguing discovery, especially the innocent passion that he had so swiftly tapped. Ashdowne paused at the rear entrance to the Camden Place house, taking a moment to savor her words. *Too distracting,* was he? He had no intention of letting the luscious blonde know that the feeling was increasingly mutual.

Unfortunately, he couldn't afford such a preoccupation, especially now, and the knowledge sobered him as he slipped into the house, calling for Finn while he headed for the study. A lamp had been left burning, illuminating a massive desk and exotic furniture, but Ashdowne rejected the hard chairs to lean against the mantelpiece. He was too restless to sit, and he pushed away from the gilded wood when Finn entered, closing the door behind him.

"So, how'd you fair with the housebreaking?" the Irishman asked with a grin.

Ashdowne lifted a brow, as if the very question offended him. "Child's play," he said, much to Finn's amusement. He tugged at his elaborately tied neck cloth, pulling the spotless material from around his neck in one elegant motion.

"And the vicar? Has he been stealing hair tonic, too?"

Ashdowne gave his servant a dry smile. "I think the only thing the good vicar is guilty of is a rather perverse taste in sexual playthings."

"Give over, milord!" Finn said with a snort. "And what did the little miss think of that?"

Ashdowne grimaced, knowing he couldn't hide a lot from Finn yet unwilling to admit too much—even to himself. He had no intention of letting the Irishman in on what he had shared with Georgiana in the vicar's bedroom. "She's far too innocent to understand, thankfully," he said, ignoring the guilt that nagged him for sampling some of that innocence.

"And a bit too dizzy besides," Finn said with a grunt, as he reached up to divest Ashdowne of his coat.

Upon hearing the barb, Ashdowne realized that some part of him rebelled against giving Georgiana so unflattering a label. "She is not quite as stupid as she appears," he muttered. "After all, she did catch Whalsey and Cheever in some sort of robbery, if not the correct one." Yes, behind that often foolish facade was a quick mind. All too quick, Ashdowne mused. Luckily it worked hand in hand with a fanciful imagination.

Perhaps that was the key to whatever allure she possessed. Whether real or imagined, Georgiana was always busy with *something*. Even a mundane rout was made interesting by her silly attempts at spying, of inventing intrigues where there were none, while uncovering one or two actual plots besides.

And all the calamities that occurred during the process...well, as long as one wasn't injured by them, Ashdowne had to admit they were usually amusing. More entertaining than a night at the theater, her foibles drew one in as though one were participating in a play. Ashdowne grinned. And no matter what happened, the young lady never lost her aplomb. Whether crashing into the orchestra or falsely accusing Whalsey, Georgiana thoroughly enjoyed herself.

"Maybe she's too smart for her own good," Finn scoffed.

"Perhaps," Ashdowne mused, his thoughts drawn back to his errand. Her family, kind though they might be, could not be trusted to keep Georgiana safe. They had no understanding of her at all, and no idea what situations she was capable of getting herself into, but he did, and that was why he had called for Finn.

"I've a job for you, if you will," Ashdowne said, glancing at his majordomo.

Finn folded the coat over an arm and nodded his head curtly. "You know it. Shall I see what the vicar's up to, if you'll pardon the pun?" he asked with a grin.

Ashdowne smiled but shook his head. "No, not the vicar. He's no threat. It's Miss Bellewether I want you to watch. She's liable to get into mischief the moment I turn my back."

"You think she might actually be on to something?" Finn asked, giving his employer a sharp look. Ashdowne could only shake his head again, feeling awkward as he contemplated his odd surge of protectiveness toward Georgiana. He had never considered himself honorable, but he could not stand by and let her boldly charge into trouble.

In the ensuing silence, Finn's mouth twisted slyly, and he regarded his employer with a far too perceptive gaze. "Developed a bit of a yen for the gel, have you?"

Ashdowne lifted a dark brow. His feelings for Georgiana could hardly be described in such terms, but he had no intention of examining them too closely, let alone expounding upon them to his manservant. He schooled his features to reveal nothing except a bland directness as he fixed his friend with a sober stare.

"Just watch her, Finn. I don't trust anyone else to do so."

Finn nodded. "All right, if you'll admit that you find her interesting," he demanded, his eyes twinkling.

Ashdowne gave a harsh laugh. "Oh, she's interesting, all right." Georgiana was so many things, it was difficult to put into words all her intriguing facets, but he sensed that Finn would not drop the subject without further explanation. Pausing to consider her for a moment, Ashdowne smiled wryly. "How long has it been since you've met a female who has fun?" he asked.

Grinning, the servant mentioned a certain lady of the ton who was notorious for her wild and wicked affairs.

Ashdowne chuckled. "No, not that kind of fun. I mean innocent joie de vivre. No matter what happens, Georgiana's having a good time, an adventure of her own making. It may be all in her mind, but she takes such pleasure in it that those around her can't help being entertained, as well."

"An adventure, you say?" Finn asked. "Seems to me I used to know a man who had a few himself."

Ashdowne disliked the reminder. "That was a long time ago, Finn," he said.

"Not so long!" the servant scoffed.

"It was another life, Finn."

"Ha! A man makes his own life," Finn muttered, turning toward the door. Ashdowne knew he would get no sympathy from the Irishman, nor did he want any. Although he counted Finn as his closest friend, the street thief turned servant could not begin to understand the responsibilities of a marquis, or how they weighed him down.

"Well, if the dizzy chit can keep you from turning into your brother, then I'm all for her," Finn said, over his shoulder.

Ashdowne quelled the sharp bite of annoyance before he spoke. "I am not my brother," he said, as coolly as possible.

"Glad to hear it, milord," Finn said. Then he slipped soundlessly from the room, leaving Ashdowne to glare at the closed door.

He wasn't turning into his brother, Ashdowne assured himself, for his brother had never really laughed, not as he had done today. The memory drew a smile from him, along with a rather alarming desire to see Miss Georgiana Bellewether again.

Here. Now. And always.

Chapter Eight

Ashdowne had never been an early riser. Like so many of his peers, he kept late hours and slept till noon. Although the assumption of his brother's duties had altered his habits somewhat, he could not remember the last time he had been up at dawn. Yet, here he was, startling the maids as he called for a quick breakfast, for he suspected that Georgiana would not lie abed for long.

Pushing aside the image of rumpled sheets and a warm, lush body that followed the thought, Ashdowne hurried through a cup of coffee and some toast. He told himself that he needed to spell Finn, who had been up all night without warning, yet he couldn't deny a certain anticipation that rose within him. It was the kind of simmering expectation that he had once known well but that had been sadly lacking in his life of late.

What would she do next?

The question drove his steps quickly into the quiet neighborhood where Georgiana's family had taken up residence. There, hidden in the shadows of a tall shrub, Ashdowne was relieved to find Finn alert and out of sight, though he was not as pleased by the manservant's knowing grin.

"You do have it bad, don't you, milord?" Finn chor-
tled. "It's been years since you've been up and about at
this hour. Why, the last time, I think it was when that
French filly turned out to have a jealous lover and—"

Cutting him off with a silent glare, Ashdowne tilted his
head toward where the Bellewether household was stirring. "No trouble?"

"Not a whit, milord," Finn answered, still grinning.
"The gel's been quiet as a mouse."

"Never left the house?"

"No. Good as gold, she was," Finn said.

Ashdowne felt a moment's relief, as well as a small
measure of pride. Georgiana had kept her promise to him
after all. Perhaps her word held true, even when her will
wasn't softened by the desire that flowed so easily between them. His own prevarications caused him a twinge
of guilt, which Ashdowne promptly dismissed.

"What now?" Finn asked.

"You go back to Camden Place and get some rest,"
Ashdowne said. "I'll take it from here."

"I bet you will, milord," Finn said with a wink. "I
have full confidence in your ability to handle one lone
female, even Miss Bellewether."

"Thank you," Ashdowne said dryly, but as he watched
the Irishman swagger off, he wondered if his friend's faith
was a bit misplaced. Could anyone really keep up with
Georgiana? Ashdowne smiled slightly at the realization
that he was looking forward to discovering the answer.
With a skill long honed, he slipped silently into a position
beneath a leafy oak not far from the house.

He did not have long to wait.

Ashdowne suspected that the rest of her family had yet
to come down to breakfast when Georgiana peeked out
the door of the kitchen, looking for all the world as if she

expected someone to be watching for her. Of course, someone was, Ashdowne thought, grinning, and he stepped from his place to approach her. Although she glanced about her carefully, she was no match for his stealth, and so was unaware of his presence until he stopped behind her.

"Looking for me, Georgiana?" he asked, leaning over her shoulder. She gasped and whirled around, but Ashdowne was prepared and caught her deadly reticule in one hand.

"Ashdowne! Oh, you frightened me! Quit sneaking up on me like that!" she scolded as she tugged her offending baggage from his grasp. She wore a delightfully disgruntled expression that made him want to kiss her, the sensation at once both alarming and pleasurable. Unable to resist the urge to touch her, Ashdowne tapped the tip of her nose and grinned at her perplexed look.

"What are you doing here?" she asked. Her thick lashes drifted low over her soft blue eyes, her lips parting invitingly, and Ashdowne knew a desire to do more than touch her. He drew in a fortifying breath and stepped back.

"Waiting for you, of course," he said. "Although I knew that you would not go off without me after giving me your solemn promise."

The blush that suffused her face at his words made Ashdowne bite his cheek to hold in his laughter. Since he often found her unexpected behavior frustrating, her transparency today was even more delightful. But he did not take her broken vow lightly, and he had better let her know it now, before…before what, he was not quite sure, and it made him frown.

"I was, uh, just coming to get you," she said, her eyes downcast.

She was not a very good liar, he thought. Certainly she was not as adept at it as himself, Ashdowne thought, feeling again the twinge of guilt that had plagued him lately. When he was in the company of the luscious Miss Bellewether, it was all too easy to forget the differences that lay between them, but they were there, vast and sobering.

"Don't come to my home alone, Georgiana," he said, more gruffly than he intended. "And don't make promises you won't keep."

"I was going to keep my promise!" she protested, blue eyes so wide and earnest that he found himself softening once more. If he didn't watch out, Georgiana would have him wrapped around her tiny fingers in no time. "I just wanted to get a head start, that's all, for I hardly knew when a gentleman of your rank would see fit to begin the day."

Her last words were muttered with a disdainful expression that made them rather insulting, but Ashdowne could hardly fault her for his habits. He chuckled, though he felt himself sinking deeper into her thrall, his good sense protesting loudly all the while.

"I told you I would be at your disposal," Ashdowne said, without elaborating upon the far-reaching truth of that statement. He watched the slow flush tinge her pale skin again, and an answering heat swept through him as he imagined her cheeks pink with something other than embarrassment, with the warmth of his attentions.

Although expert at hiding his thoughts, Ashdowne must have evidenced some hint of his desires, for Georgiana swayed forward only to straighten her shoulders and step back in a physical withdrawal he had seen before.

"I might remind you, Ashdowne," she said in a prim voice totally at odds with the rest of her, "that ours is strictly a business relationship. And I cannot have you distracting me from my purpose.''

She scowled delightfully at him, and Ashdowne nodded, keeping a tight rein on both his lust and his mirth. ''Of course,'' he answered as meekly as he could manage. Although Georgiana eyed him skeptically, she turned toward the street, and he fell into step beside her, content to let the day play out as it would.

Life, after all, was an adventure.

By late afternoon, Georgiana had to admit that her interest in the pursuit was flagging. Ashdowne was still with her, but he kept pestering her to stop for luncheon or an early dinner or sustenance of some sort. She supposed that a man who possessed the muscular form of the marquis had to take in sufficient nourishment to preserve that rather fascinating body, but she was loath to take her eyes from Mr. Hawkins for a moment.

Unfortunately, it was not as though the vicar had really done anything of note. He hadn't emerged from his lodgings until nearly noon, then had made an obligatory stop at the Pump Room, where he had spoken to several older women, possible benefactors perhaps. None looked to be in league with him in any nefarious activities, much to Georgiana's disappointment.

From there he had walked one of them to her residence before prowling the stores on Milson Street. For a man without a means of living, he had done an awful lot of shopping, Georgiana reflected. Well, not shopping, but looking, because he carried no parcels, for all his wanderings.

''Do you think he knows we're following him?'' Georgiana asked, suddenly stricken by the possibility.

Ashdowne gave her an arch look, as if she had insulted

him somehow. "The good vicar hasn't a clue," he said. Then he paused to gaze at her with a thoughtful expression. "Unless he can hear my stomach growling."

"Really, Ashdowne!" Georgiana said, taken aback by his bold speech, but she had little time to dwell upon it, for their quarry was moving again. Grabbing his sleeve, she tugged on it until he stepped forward, strolling down the street to stop in front of a milliner's bow window. Taking his cue, Georgiana lifted a hand to point out a set of gloves as she watched the glassy reflection of the opposite side of the avenue. It appeared that Mr. Hawkins was entering another establishment.

Turning slightly, Georgiana glanced over her shoulder only to groan, for the man had gone inside a pastry shop. At the sight, Ashdowne threatened to mutiny, and having a weakness for desserts, Georgiana felt her own determination waver, but she bolstered it bravely. Mr. Hawkins was her last chance for vindication, for a famous case to launch her career, and she had no intention of letting him slip by her for the sake of a sugared biscuit or raspberry tart.

"You may do as you wish, but I intend to keep at it," she told the marquis firmly. Although she fully expected him to leave her, Ashdowne remained where he was with a sigh and a shrug. Georgiana felt a warm surge of pleasure at his continued presence. He really was the most helpful of assistants, she thought, for although they had kept the vicar well within their view all day, she knew that it would have been a boring business without company.

At his insistence, she had long given up calling him "my lord." Her mother might not approve, but once they handed the vicar over to the Bow Street Runner, the case—and her association with the marquis—would be at an end. Unfortunately, instead of comforting her, that knowledge made her feel all empty inside, like a cake that had fallen in upon itself.

Ever logical, Georgiana put the odd sensation down to hunger pangs and soldiered on only to groan anew as Mr. Hawkins appeared, eating something sticky that he had obviously just purchased. Much to her dismay, he continued to feast, and in a most thorough manner. He even licked his fingers and smacked his lips, which disgusted Georgia.

"Quiet, you," Ashdowne told his stomach, and Georgiana glanced at her companion. Although she had heard nothing, she found herself staring at where his hand rested on his flat abdomen, thoughts of food fleeing abruptly. All too easily, she remembered sitting on his lap, being cradled by those hard thighs as he touched her breast, and she felt dizzy. Her skin seemed to tighten while, conversely, her insides, including her brain, seemed to grow all soft and liquid.

"Have you a craving, too?" Ashdowne's voice washed over her senses like warm chocolate, and Georgiana shivered before jerking her gaze back to his face. Whatever was he talking about? Her face flaming at the direction her errant thoughts had taken, Georgiana turned on her heel and rushed after the vicar.

During the ensuing hours her culprit made no unusual stops, had no clandestine meetings and talked with no unsavory characters. He did nothing noteworthy at all, but began walking again until they once more reached the Pump Room. Although Ashdowne made no complaint, Georgiana was thoroughly exasperated.

"Oh, doesn't the man ever do anything *interesting?*" she complained as she plopped down upon a low stone wall.

"I fear we all can't be as intrepid as yourself, my sweet," Ashdowne said, leaning casually against a buttress.

With a toss of her head, Georgiana bent down to tug off her slipper, banging it against the wall until a small pebble dislodged itself and fell to the pavement.

"May I assist you in any way?" Ashdowne asked, eyeing her foot in a proprietary fashion that threatened to reduce her to a dazed ninny again.

"No!" Georgiana answered, her temper running short.

"I could rub your foot," Ashdowne suggested in a tone that made her feel warm and gooey inside until she caught herself. She slapped her slipper back into place and glared at him before sinking her chin onto her hand.

"Don't try to cheer me up," she warned him, "for I am sunk in the dismals."

"Shall I seize him by the throat and demand he confess?" Ashdowne asked.

In spite of herself, Georgiana smiled. Although the plan had its merits, Mr. Hawkins was of a different caliber than Lord Whalsey and would not be so easily intimidated. "No," she muttered. "Let's just keep watching him."

"Until we starve to death," Ashdowne said.

"Yes," Georgiana agreed.

But just as she was beginning to think they would have to separate so that they might manage to eat, Mr. Hawkins went into a coffee shop and ordered supper. Discreetly following, Georgiana and Ashdowne took a tiny table in the shadows at the rear of the room and proceeded to dine quite agreeably.

Although she was forced to forgo the rich dessert she was considering when Mr. Hawkins finished his meal early, Georgiana was feeling much better by the time they followed their quarry back into the streets to one of the city's lesser baths. Not nearly so grand as the King's Bath or one of the other more well-known watering places, it was small and less fashionable, and, as Ashdowne noted, probably quite cheap.

After waiting a few moments, they went inside, hanging back by the doorway. Although some of the more famous spots were open only during limited morning hours, Georgiana caught a glimpse through an archway of several bathers nearly submerged in the dark waters. Although the building was made of the usual creamy stone for which the city was well-known, the pool was open to the sky, an advantage on sunny days but hardly a plus when it rained, Georgiana surmised.

Lingering behind the archway, she watched the vicar speak to one of the attendants and head toward the steps. To her surprise he pulled a book from his coat, taking it with him as he stepped into the medicinal waters. Although he soon sank lower and lower, Mr. Hawkins kept the volume with him and opened it, as if to read. But Georgiana caught his gaze drifting from the page, most notably when nearing a female companion.

"Odd," Ashdowne murmured beside her. "From what you've said, I would hardly think him such a devoted cleric that he studies the Bible while in the baths."

Georgiana made a low sound of disgust. "I don't think he's reading it at all! I suspect he comes here simply to ogle the women in their wet clothing." Although some of the baths provided their customers with smocks, the moisture made all garments cling, sometimes leaving little to the imagination.

Ashdowne glanced toward her, one dark brow lifted and a wry smile on his face, but Georgiana held her ground, for he was the one always insisting on plain speaking. "I have observed that Mr. Hawkins has a marked interest in ladies' chests," she insisted.

To Georgiana's dismay, Ashdowne's dark gaze traveled slowly down to her own breasts, which seemed to swell and preen in response. "Well, he had better keep his eyes off yours," the marquis said in a serious tone that threatened her sensibilities most thoroughly.

With some effort, Georgiana tore her attention away from her alluring assistant back to the suspect. She watched him walk along the perimeter, Bible in hand, but as if to prove Georgiana right, he looked rather slyly at the women, nodding in a superior manner whenever they chanced to pass him, but studying them when they were unaware.

He continued along in the same vein until Mrs. Fitzlettice, a rather ill-tempered wealthy widow, entered the water. Upon seeing her, Hawkins swiftly closed the volume and glanced around rather suspiciously. Apparently convinced that no one was watching, he tucked the book behind a loose stone in the wall.

Georgiana swung her face toward Ashdowne and saw her own astonishment reflected on his features. "Did you see that?" she asked.

"I'll be deuced," he muttered.

"I'm going in!" Georgiana said, lurching forward, but Ashdowne halted her with a firm grip about her arm.

"Wait!" he said. "Hawkins will see you." Although certainly not what she wanted to hear, the words were spoken in a knowledgeable tone that made her stop. He was right, of course. Both the vicar and the widow were standing too near the book's hiding place for either she or Ashdowne to retrieve it.

Georgiana frowned in frustration. "What if one of us were to cause a diversion, allowing the other to snatch the volume?'' She glanced up at her assistant hopefully, but his only reply was a look that told her in no uncertain terms what he thought of her suggestion.

Botheration! Just because he had seen her at her worst did not mean that every one of her endeavors ended in disaster. Georgiana opened her mouth to tell him so, but Ashdowne shook his head. ''I doubt if even your incomparable endowments are enough to divert the good vicar's attention from a possible benefactress, especially one whose pockets are so well lined.''

Although she colored at his description of her chest, Georgiana had to admit he was right. However, she was too impatient to stand back and wait with the ease that seemed to come naturally to Ashdowne. They had been following the vicar all day, and this was the first sign that he actually was the thief, the first real confirmation of her suspicions.

''He must have had the book with him all day,'' she whispered to Ashdowne. ''No wonder we could find nothing at his lodgings. No doubt, he carries it about with him everywhere, keeping it always upon his person! And what better place to secret the necklace than in a hollowed-out book?''

No one would think anything of a vicar carrying around a Bible, Georgiana reasoned with growing excitement. The only time he was liable to run into trouble was if a devout person, like Mrs. Fitzlettice, should ask to view a verse in the volume! That, of course, was why Mr. Hawkins had hidden it away before greeting her. Georgiana smiled. It was all falling into place so perfectly that she was practically squirming with eagerness.

Unfortunately, Mr. Hawkins was still deep in conversation with Mrs. Fitzlettice, and they continued to speak for what seemed an interminable length of time before beginning to move away from the concealed goods. The moment they started walking, Georgiana jerked forward again, only to be detained by her more cautious assistant. He inclined his head toward the pool, where, to her surprise, the vicar and Mrs. Fitzlettice were rising from the water. Apparently, they were departing together *and leaving the book behind!*

Startled, Georgiana let Ashdowne urge her out of the building and into the shadows of a nearby doorway. The sun was sinking low on the horizon, and she blinked at the dark figures who emerged from the baths. Mr. Hawkins and the widow were but the first among a line of patrons who exited, and Georgiana waited breathlessly then gasped in alarm at the sound of a lock clicking. The place was closing!

Angrily Georgiana whirled upon Ashdowne, for this impasse was all his fault. Far from assisting her, he had done nothing except restrain her unreasonably, and now it was too late! She opened her mouth to vent her outrage, but before she could utter a word, he took her hands in his and pulled her close.

"We will come back tomorrow, first thing," he promised.

Despite the lure of his words, Georgiana pulled her fingers free, determined not to let him lull her into complacency with his honeyed voice and overpowering presence. "No! The jewels are in that book, I am certain of it! And, if so, Hawkins will not leave them for long. I am convinced that he never intended to let them out of his hands," she said. "He certainly won't wait till morning to retrieve them."

Ashdowne groaned, but Georgiana ignored his protests. Tossing her curls, she glared up at her assistant defiantly and stated her case with firm intent. "We must come back when the place is deserted, but before it is too late!"

"And just how do you propose to get inside?" Ashdowne asked.

Georgiana flashed him a smile, for she knew well his talents in that direction. "Oh, I'm sure you'll think of a way."

Ashdowne glanced over at the now quiet building, then back down at her, his blue gaze glittering in the gathering twilight. "Very well," he said, muttering something about his doom. "We will return tonight, once it is full dark."

Ashdowne would not let her leave alone, and since Georgiana insisted that someone must watch the building, he had sent a passing boy back to his residence with a message, and soon his manservant had appeared. A wiry Irishman, Finn agreed to keep an eye on the place while Ashdowne escorted her home. Of course, it was wholly unnecessary, as Georgiana kept telling him, but the marquis could be dreadfully obstinate at times.

Once back at her parents' residence, Georgiana took to her bed with a headache, to later sneak out through the kitchen, meeting Ashdowne at the garden gate. Per his instructions, she wore a black cloak, and despite all logical protestations to the contrary, the clandestine nature of their investigation roused all her senses.

Their circuitous route through the alleys and dark streets of Bath served to increase her excitement, and by the time they reached their destination, Georgiana was certain that no matter how famous she should become, she would never forget this night, her first real case, or her one and only assistant.

Although Georgiana did not see the Irishman, Ashdowne assured her that he was there, watching in the shadows, and would alert them should the vicar, or anyone else, approach. The neighborhood was quiet, the darkness nearly complete as they stood before the doors to the baths, and Georgiana took a moment to appreciate her companion. She could have managed without him, but there was something about Ashdowne that inspired confidence above and beyond her own.

He was dressed all in black, without even the white of a neck cloth to relieve the starkness of his costume, and he moved with a lithe grace that she could only admire. He was tall and strong, and Georgiana had no doubt that he could subdue any miscreant who might be so bold as to approach them. He was, she decided, entirely competent.

But, more than that, Ashdowne emanated a power and danger that struck Georgiana in a way she had never before known. She was not frightened of him. Indeed, the look of him, with his face hidden in shadows, his gloved fingers moving silently as he bent to pick the lock, merely enhanced her excitement, until she wondered if the man himself could possibly eclipse her interest in the investigation.

It was a sobering thought and one that made Georgiana look determinedly away. She was too near him, she decided. Therein lay the problem, for whenever she was close to Ashdowne, her brain seemed to shut down, while giving sway to the rest of her body. She would do well to keep her distance, she reminded herself.

A soft click drew Georgiana's attention back to her companion, who flashed her a white grin before pushing open the door. He really was quite talented, she admitted, for had she been here alone she would have had to use a tool or something equally incriminating to gain entry.

"Can you teach me how to do that?" she whispered.

"No," Ashdowne answered, and before she could reply, he was pulling her inside and closing the door behind them. Immediately, the baths seeped into her awareness, the warm, moist air surrounding her, the unpleasant odor of the famous waters more subtle than usual because of the open roof. Georgiana tried futilely to gain her bearings in the utter blackness of the area near the entrance, but Ashdowne seemed to possess the senses of a cat, for he somehow managed to light a small, shuttered lantern.

It gave out little more illumination than a candle, but at least it would not be as susceptible to breezes and stray drops of moisture. And it guided their way toward the pool. As they approached, the stones became slippery, and Ashdowne reached out to take hold of her arm, aiding her in an unnecessary but thoughtful fashion toward the steps.

There he stopped, and Georgiana felt the eerie silence deep in her bones. Although the smallest of the city's baths, the place seemed cavernous in the darkness, with no attendants or patrons to fill it, and with its ceiling open to the sky far above them. Stars twinkled high overhead, while moonlight cast a pale sheen across the black water. Georgiana shivered.

"I'll go in," Ashdowne said as he released her. "You stay here and watch the lantern, for I don't care to be mucking about in total darkness." Georgiana turned toward him with a comment, but it died upon her lips when she saw that Ashdowne was removing his coat. *Right there in front of her.* She watched as he shrugged out of it, flexing his wide shoulders in a most disturbing manner.

Oblivious to her scrutiny, Ashdowne laid the garment carefully upon a step, then sat down and began to take off his boots. Swamped by a sudden wave of dizziness, Georgiana sank down beside him. For some reason, her legs were threatening to give out.

She was too close to Ashdowne, Georgiana realized, scooting away slightly. And although she tried not to look, his movements were so interesting that she could not help herself. His shirt must be black, for his face, shadowed and intent, was the only part of him touched by the lantern's faint glow. Even his stockings must be black, Georgiana noted as her gaze dropped lower. She told herself that there was nothing shocking about seeing them, yet the ritual bespoke an intimacy that set her insides to wobbling.

Deliberately Georgiana turned her face away, but she could hear the low thump of his other boot and then a rustle. Oh, my, was he removing his *stockings?* Georgiana glanced furtively downward and got a glimpse of a bare, arched foot. All thoughts of her purpose here fled as she was struck by the most peculiar desire to reach out and touch Ashdowne.

Georgiana made a small strangled sound, which he didn't appear to notice, thankfully, for he stood, rising tall above where she sat upon the step. "I want you to stay here," he said, and she nodded dazedly. Resting her chin in one palm, she simply stared at him as he stepped into the pool, the dark water rising to cover his ankles, his lower limbs, his thighs and higher...

Suddenly Georgiana wished for more light as she discovered a heretofore unknown fascination with Ashdowne's backside. Never before had she looked at a man's behind, but now she felt bereft when Ashdowne's disappeared into the pool. Once he began moving farther away, she felt better, staring at the image of him that nearly disappeared into the blackness. Where was he going? She stood and stepped down one slippery stair.

"I believe it is more to your left," she said, lifting her

arm to point toward where she thought the book was hidden.

"*Georgiana,*" Ashdowne muttered in a harsh manner that was entirely uncalled for, in her opinion. "I told you to stay where you are," he commanded. Although she could not really see him out there in the darkness, Georgiana took umbrage at his tone.

"I am simply trying to direct you," she returned with a frown.

"Well, *don't.* Sit down on the step and *stay there.*" This time there was no mistaking the threat in his words, and Georgiana bristled at the thought of him ordering her about.

"I must remind you, Ashdowne, that you are the assistant here, and I am the investigator," she said.

"You are also the one most prone to producing calamity. Now, hush, and don't move!"

Georgiana did not accede well to arbitrary commands, especially when issued by an arrogant male who had no right to mandate her actions, and so she stepped forward. "Now, see here, Ashdowne," she began, then faltered as her slipper struck something.

With sickening dread, Georgiana heard one of the marquis's boots roll off the step onto another. And another. Botheration! Did it have to be so dark in here? He should have brought a real lantern, not that minuscule light, and anyway, wasn't it just like a man to leave his effects scattered about in everyone's way? But before the dratted thing could tumble all the way to the pool, Georgiana hurried downward, grabbing wildly at nothing except air, until she heard the dull plop of something striking the water.

"What was that?" Ashdowne asked.

"Nothing," Georgiana murmured as she approached

the water. Would the boot sink? Blinking, she thought she could make out the once-fine leather floating near the edge of the pool. Now, if she could just inch forward and reach it…Georgiana knelt beside the bath and bent over only to see the lump bob out of reach. Scooting closer, she leaned and stretched, but the movement was too extreme.

For a long moment, she wavered off balance, knowing a rueful regret that she had not listened to Ashdowne, before she fell, headfirst, into the warm waters.

Chapter Nine

At first Georgiana was disoriented by the dark liquid and dragged down by the weight of her gown, then her toe struck bottom, and she managed to right herself, planting her feet solidly. She had just begun to rise above the water, spitting and blowing, when a pair of hands closed around her waist.

"Damn it, Georgiana! I told you to stay put!" Ashdowne's anger was unmistakable, his shadowed features intense even in the moonlight. She tried to explain, to sputter a protest, but he was too close. And he was *wet.*

Dragging in a breath, Georgiana felt her insides wobble like jelly as she took in the dark hair dripping water onto his broad shoulders. He must have swum to her in his haste, she thought dimly, as her gaze followed one drop down his throat to his chest, where his dark shirt clung to wide muscles. Her heart started thumping in a most outrageous manner, and her lips parted, seeking more air, for the moist darkness seemed suddenly close and stifling.

"Are you all right?" Ashdowne asked, and Georgiana forced her attention back to his face. She had a full minute to stare into his glittering eyes, during which his alarm turned into something else entirely. He once more looked upon her as though she were, if not a bug, at least something he was likely to devour. Georgiana had time to draw in another breath before he pulled her to him, his mouth descending on hers with a violence she had never imagined.

And then she lost herself there in the darkness, the warmth of the water palling against the heat of Ashdowne's body and his hands, steaming through her clothes where he touched her. His palms slid up and down her back and then tugged at her shoulders, and before she knew what he was about, her gown was down at her waist, her breasts pressed against the solid wall of his chest.

And then he touched them. With a low cry, Georgiana arched backward as his fingers explored each curve of her skin. Slick with moisture, they slid over her flesh, drenching her in sensation she thought was incomparable until his lips settled there, his tongue rasping against her nipples, his mouth covering her to suckle one and then the other.

Wild feelings shot through her, from her breasts to every part of her, settling most fiercely at the juncture of her thighs, and Georgiana wriggled helplessly in an effort to ease the heaviness there. Finally she felt her legs parted by the firm thrust of Ashdowne's hard thigh. It pressed right against the spot that so inflamed her, and she nearly wept with relief. Dear Ashdowne, he knew exactly what to do!

''Ashdowne,'' she whispered, clutching at his back as her equilibrium faltered. His shirt had come loose, and Georgiana slipped her hands beneath to boldly stroke his skin, smooth and firm and wet. There was something about the water that heightened her senses, Georgiana realized. It was her last coherent thought before her brain surrendered to the rest of her, giving up its dominion gladly.

"Ashdowne," she whispered again. She felt the wall at her back, heard the low lap of the water and saw the twinkle of stars overhead before he took her mouth once more. Her arms went around his neck, holding him close, as his thigh grazed her. The sensations that slight movement engendered were beyond her comprehension, but Georgiana embraced them, unable to stop, unable to do anything but moan and cry out, bereft, when he shifted.

Murmuring low words of comfort, Ashdowne lifted her higher, pushed her skirts up and stepped between her thighs, so that her most private part was bared beneath the water. But before she could utter an embarrassed protest, he pressed against her. Instead of his leg, she felt the front of his trousers, only that thin layer of material separating her nakedness from the hard, powerful bulge there.

It was beyond anything Georgiana could ever have imagined, and for once, she couldn't get too close to Ashdowne. She wiggled, seeking some kind of surcease from the feelings building inside her as his body rubbed against her in a primitive rhythm that left her gasping, wanting, *needing*...until the darkness and the water and Ashdowne enveloped her in a driving heat that peaked as she cried out, drowning in incredible pleasure.

Georgiana would have sunk down into the luxurious embrace of the pool, her legs no more substantial than the night breeze, were it not for Ashdowne's firm hold upon her. He thrust against her, harder, with a fierceness Georgiana had not known he possessed. Then his ragged groan echoed in the silence as he shuddered, his tall body shaking as if with the force of her own exultation. Had he known similar bliss?

"Oh, Ashdowne," Georgiana murmured against his

throat, too wobbly to do or say anything more complex. And in the utter stillness the only sound was of their own rapid breaths, slowly returning to normal. But would she ever be normal again after what had transpired? Georgiana wondered as she gradually returned to her senses. What miracle had Ashdowne worked upon her? What magic was this that only he could conjure?

Finally he lifted his head, and Georgiana tilted back her own to meet his gaze. He looked slumberous and satisfied, but the wry, rueful curve to his lips confused her. She opened her mouth to speak, or perhaps simply kiss him again, with a more leisurely ardor, when a noise echoed in the silence.

The door.

Georgiana stiffened as Ashdowne's hand came over her lips, and he pulled her deeper, dragging them low until only their faces lingered above the water, his body tense against her. She looked, wide-eyed, toward the steps, where the lamp she had been bidden to guard sat pointedly spreading its dim glow over the edge of the pool.

"Milord?"

Georgiana felt Ashdowne relax and let her own muscles ease their cramped vigil as she recognized Finn's voice. Although she expected the marquis to rise, he did not, but remained where he was, holding her tightly beneath the water. And it was truly not until that moment that Georgiana realized her skirts were floating high, while her upper garments were somewhere about her waist. She made a mortified sound that was muffled by Ashdowne's fingers.

"What is it?" he called to Finn.

"You've been in here a good while, milord, and I thought I heard a shriek. I was worried that something had gone amiss, but I see that I must have been mistaken.

So, you just take your time and pardon the interruption, if you will,'' he said, his voice gravelly with amusement.

''We've had trouble finding what we came for, but we won't be long now,'' Ashdowne assured his servant. Not until the door closed once more did Ashdowne release her. Pulling her gently to her feet, he tugged at her bodice and soon had everything righted in a most competent fashion while Georgiana blinked at him dazedly.

She was still standing there, looking foolish, when he turned and strode toward the fallen stone, easily retrieving the book, while Georgiana could only stare at it in surprise. Was that why they had come? For the book? In the exotic enchantment of Ashdowne's embrace, she had forgotten everything, and still her mind was so slow in functioning that he had to take her hand and urge her forward to where their lantern glowed like a tiny beacon in the darkness.

''Hmm. What's this?'' he said, and Georgiana, who could not remember blushing during their deepest intimacy, now did so as he slowly lifted his once-shiny, expensive boot from the water to drip rather dramatically. Luckily Ashdowne could not see her flush in the darkness.

''It looks like a boot,'' she said rather unnecessarily.

''Ah. And a familiar one at that,'' Ashdowne added, shooting her a wry glance that she refused to acknowledge as they rose out of the water. The soggy leather fell onto the step with a squish, and Georgiana knew she could put off her reckoning no longer.

''I, uh—'' she began, turning to face him.

''Never mind. I won't decry the loss of one boot when…'' Ashdowne's words trailed off as he reached up to stroke her cheek with a wet finger. Georgiana closed her eyes and shivered. ''It was for a good cause,'' he said in a low voice that made her legs weak and her wits wander. "But it's growing late, and I must take you home before you catch a chill."

The possibility seemed absurd when Ashdowne's very presence filled her with heat, but Georgiana nodded dazedly, and he stepped away. "Wring out your gown as best you can, and then we'll have a look at the book."

The book! Georgiana straightened abruptly, her errant thoughts returning immediately to the evidence at hand. The euphoria that Ashdowne's touch induced changed into a different sort of thrill altogether—the excitement of the case. Although she wanted to reach for the volume at once, she dutifully pulled up her skirts and twisted them until the worst of the water was out, while Ashdowne donned his boots and coat. Of course, her gown was ruined, but since it was a beribboned lavender one of her mother's choosing, she spared little thought for it.

Her thoughts were all upon the book, and her hands trembled in expectation when she finally turned toward Ashdowne. Despite his dousing, he managed to look just as handsome and elegant as ever when he presented it to her, and Georgiana was seized by a sudden feeling for him that went far beyond his appearance. He could have inspected the prize himself, but instead he let her do the honors, and the gesture made her stomach dip, as well as something else, higher up in her chest.

Drying her hands upon her cloak, Georgiana reached out to take the vicar's tome. She opened it with extreme care, but to her disappointment, no hidden compartment revealed the necklace. Instead, she looked down upon a drawing of some sort. Georgiana leaned closer and realized that it was a picture of a man and a woman, both totally devoid of clothing.

"But this is not important at all!" she protested.

"That depends upon your point of view, I would imagine," Ashdowne said dryly.

With a sound of frustration, Georgiana held up the volume by its spine and shook it, yet no jewels fell out. Then she began leafing through the pages, but they all turned freely. There was no hidden compartment, only more pictures. Unable to believe her eyes, Georgiana let the book fall open and stared at it in dismay, her gaze riveted by a drawing in which a man intimately held a woman in the air, her legs wrapped around his waist. Turning the book this way and that, Georgiana blinked.

"Is that possible?" she asked.

Ashdowne cleared his throat. "Yes. Certainly," he said softly. And suddenly she realized that what looked so astonishing was not that different from what she had been doing only moments ago. If she had but lifted her legs and…Georgiana drew in a sharp breath at the memory of that incredible pleasure.

Abruptly she turned the page only to see the same sort of intimate activity, although this time the man was positioned behind the woman. "Oh, my," Georgiana whispered. The baths once more felt close and stifling as she became increasingly aware of Ashdowne's presence at her back, looking over her shoulder. How would she feel if he stepped closer, pressing himself against her? She stifled a groan and turned the page.

Here, the woman knelt before the man, her mouth enclosed about a certain engorged part of his body, and, caught between startlement and curiosity, Georgiana nearly dropped the evidence completely. Her face flamed as she remembered that part of Ashdowne's body rubbing against hers. How would he react if she dropped to her knees and…the moist warmth of the baths pressed down on her, robbing her breath, and she shut the book with a loud thump.

In the ensuing silence, the heat inside her dissipated, replaced by a wave of disappointment. She had been right in that the book was no Bible, yet neither was it a secret hiding place for the stolen necklace. "But I don't understand," Georgiana muttered in frustration. "Why would he carry this about with him in the baths?"

"I suspect you were correct to begin with, that Mr. Hawkins is not partaking of the waters for his health, but for the titillation of seeing ladies in wet clothing. Beneath the surface, the...uh, evidence of the direction of his thoughts would not be visible."

Georgiana blinked as she realized just what sort of evidence Ashdowne was talking about, and she made a sound of distress at the thought of their suspect walking about in such a state.

"Yes. Let's hope that's all he does in there," Ashdowne muttered. "Or the idea of climbing into that odoriferous water becomes infinitely unappealing, my own, uh, lapse, notwithstanding."

Although Georgiana didn't quite understand what Ashdowne was saying, certain words resonated loudly in her mind, most especially "unappealing" and "lapse." She drew herself up to her full height and turned to face him, focusing firmly on his throat. But with the absence of his neck cloth, she was able to see the muscles in the strong column, a definite deterrent to her concentration. "I regret, uh, putting you to all that trouble in the bath," she murmured.

"I would hardly call it trouble," Ashdowne said, reaching out to take her hands and draw her closer. "You, Miss Georgiana Bellewether, are an utter delight, and being with you is always a...pleasure." His voice deepened on

PLAY "LUCKY 7" AND GET
THREE FREE GIFTS!

HOW TO PLAY:

1. With a coin, carefully scratch off the silver box at the right. Then check the claim chart to see what we have for you — **FREE BOOKS** and a gift — **ALL YOURS! ALL FREE!**

2. Send back this card and you'll receive brand-new Harlequin Historicals® novels. These books have a cover price of $4.99 each in the U.S. and $5.99 each in Canada, but they are yours to keep absolutely free.

3. There's no catch. You're under no obligation to buy anything. We charge nothing — ZERO — for your first shipment. And you don't have to make any minimum number of purchases — not even one!

4. The fact is thousands of readers enjoy receiving books by mail from the Harlequin Reader Service®. They enjoy the convenience of home delivery . . . they like getting the best new novels at discount prices, BEFORE they're available in stores . . . and they love their *Heart to Heart* newsletter featuring author news, horoscopes, recipes, book reviews and much more!

5. We hope that after receiving your free books you'll want to remain a subscriber. But the choice is yours — to continue or cancel, any time at all! So why not take us up on our invitation, with no risk of any kind. You'll be glad you did!

YOURS FREE!

PLAY LUCKY 7 FOR THIS EXCITING FREE GIFT!

THIS SURPRISE MYSTERY GIFT COULD BE YOURS FREE WHEN YOU PLAY

LUCKY 7!

**Visit us on-line at
www.romance.net**

The Harlequin Reader Service® — Here's how it works:

Accepting your 2 free books and gift places you under no obligation to buy anything. You may keep the books and gift and return the shipping statement marked "cancel." If you do not cancel, about a month later we'll send you 6 additional novels and bill you just $3.94 each in the U.S., or $4.19 each in Canada, plus 25¢ delivery per book and applicable taxes if any.* That's the complete price and — compared to cover prices of $4.99 each in the U.S. and $5.99 each in Canada — it's quite a bargain! You may cancel at any time, but if you choose to continue, every month we'll send you 6 more books, which you may either purchase at the discount price or return to us and cancel your subscription.

*Terms and prices subject to change without notice. Sales tax applicable in N.Y. Canadian residents will be charged applicable provincial taxes and GST.

If offer card is missing write to: Harlequin Reader Service, 3010 Walden Ave., P.O. Box 1867, Buffalo, NY 14240-1867

BUSINESS REPLY MAIL
FIRST-CLASS MAIL   PERMIT NO. 717   BUFFALO, NY

POSTAGE WILL BE PAID BY ADDRESSEE

HARLEQUIN READER SERVICE
3010 WALDEN AVE
PO BOX 1867
BUFFALO NY 14240-9952

NO POSTAGE
NECESSARY
IF MAILED
IN THE
UNITED STATES

the last word, and Georgiana blushed to the roots of her hair. Grateful that he could not see, she felt the slow, languid sweep of his lure engulfing her, and she deliberately looked away.

She wondered just how far her assistant might take this flirtation between them. The pictures in the book had both alarmed and excited her, and being of a curious nature, naturally she was interested in human experience in all of its forms. However, she knew that society as a whole, and her mother in particular, would not approve of that sort of fact-finding.

She pulled her hands away and stared down at her sodden slippers. "About that, uh, pleasure..." Her words trailed off, lost in the confusion of Ashdowne's nearness.

"I'm sorry, Georgiana," he said, lifting a hand to brush her cheek. And despite all her fine resolve, she turned toward his touch like a flower to the light. "I never meant for things to go that far, although my only regret this evening is that you didn't find what you were looking for, or did you?"

Georgiana was uncertain of his meaning. Sometimes the man talked in riddles, and how could she concentrate on anything when he was looming over her? She moved back, farther away from him, and tried to concentrate. "I might remind you that you were to keep your mind upon business, not that...other," she said rather stiffly.

"I beg your pardon," he said, his tone one of mild amusement.

Georgiana chose to ignore it as she strode across the stones, her thoughts once more upon the case. "Obviously, the necklace is not in the book, but Mr. Hawkins is still our chief suspect," she said, then paused to consider the vicar before continuing determinedly. "Sooner or later, he will slip up and reveal himself to us. In the meantime, we will have to keep a close watch upon him.''

''Indeed,'' Ashdowne said dryly. ''From all appearances, I shouldn't care to get too close to the good vicar.''

Georgiana slanted her assistant a reproving glance before giving in to the laughter that threatened, and it was with muffled chuckles that they made their way out of the building into the darkened streets of Bath. Once outside, she was again seized by exhilaration, the disappointments of the evening forgotten in the excitement of hurrying through the night.

Yet, as they slipped silently among the shadows, for the first time in her life, Georgiana wondered if it was the case that so compelled her—or her assistant.

Georgiana's doubts lingered into the dawn and beyond. Although she told herself that emotion must not cloud her judgment, her discovery of Mr. Hawkins's peculiarities had dampened her enthusiasm for following him about. Perhaps she could not distance herself from her suspects well enough, Georgiana mused, a discouraging thought that she put aside to ponder later.

She was hard-pressed to hold any thought at all, thanks to an extremely annoying preoccupation with her assistant. Try as she might, Georgiana could not deny a new, deeper awareness of Ashdowne that was even worse than the distraction she had suffered before. And who could blame her, after what they had shared in the baths? What exactly they had shared, Georgiana was uncertain, although she knew enough of reproduction to realize that her virtue remained intact. Still she could hardly claim to be unchanged by such a momentous event.

After sneaking back to her room, she found the evening's events had replayed themselves unceasingly in her otherwise orderly mind. When she had finally managed to fall asleep, her dreams had all been of Ashdowne, and she had awoken tangled in her bedding, feeling hot and tired and frustrated, a sensation which, to a lesser degree, had plagued her throughout the morning.

Although Georgiana told herself quite firmly that theirs was a business association, it was difficult to focus on the business part when memories of a quite different sort of relationship kept intruding. To make matters worse, Ashdowne looked even more handsome and wonderful in the light of day when they resumed their pursuit, and Georgiana found herself watching him instead of their quarry.

She couldn't help but notice the way his dark hair brushed his collar, the soft curve of his lips, the graceful movement of his gloved hands and the hard muscles of his thighs. And she *remembered*. She knew the feel of those thighs wedged between her own, the thrust of his body against hers, the slippery slide of his wet skin and the moist heat of his caresses. Shuddering, Georgiana wanted to forget what had happened, while, conversely, she yearned to repeat it all again.

Never had she been so confounded, even by the most difficult of cases. To add to her confusion, Ashdowne appeared cool and elegant, as if he hadn't a care in the world. Georgiana would have thought she imagined the intimacy between them if it were not for the occasional glimpse of something like hunger in his eyes, which made her skitter away.

Such glances made Georgiana wonder again just how far Ashdowne planned to take their…experimentation. Although the notion of delving further into such mysteries was quite tempting, Georgiana knew a genteel young woman such as herself should not even consider such a course. Nor could she dismiss outright certain concerns about the marquis himself.

Did he engage in such behavior with every woman he met? Georgiana did not care to be one of an interchangeable array of females, no matter how curious she was to learn more of the pleasures to be found in his arms. Although she would not wish Ashdowne to worship at her feet, as did her most ardent suitors, Georgiana wanted him to feel *something* for her, some small modicum of affection, along with a respect for her abilities.

Unfortunately, Georgiana could deduce little from his rather closed expression, and she did not feel comfortable broaching such a topic, especially since she was supposed to be concentrating on Mr. Hawkins. But so far, her suspect had done little to garner her interest.

Indeed, the vicar's day had progressed much like the one before. He had spent the morning in his lodgings, presumably in undeserved rest, before visiting the Pump Room. And there he remained, talking with various elderly widows, while Georgiana and her companion tried to remain unobtrusive.

Had she been alone, Georgiana was certain she would have done very well. However, Ashdowne was simply too handsome and grand to blend in well with the crowd. She had wanted him to wear a disguise, but the marquis, as was his wont, laughed uproariously at the suggestion and tapped her nose. In an effort to avoid any further touching, Georgiana had dropped the subject.

Now she could see the foolishness of her capitulation, for although they were partially hidden by a screen near the orchestra, Georgiana could see a matronly woman bearing down upon them with a daughter of marriageable age in tow, leaving her with no doubt that her companion had been spotted. Stifling a groan, Georgiana turned to flee, and felt Ashdowne's gloved hand close around her arm.

"I'm following the vicar," she whispered, attempting to escape, but Ashdowne held her fast, drawing her near.

"No, you aren't," he said mildly. He looked down at her with a bland expression that suggested he was engaging in some pleasantries when he was, in actuality, keeping her prisoner. Georgiana opened her mouth to argue, but she never had a chance to speak.

"My lord! What a pleasure it is to see you gracing our beloved Pump Room! Truly, we did not expect such a treat this afternoon, did we, my dear?" the woman asked, turning toward her daughter. The girl, a tall slender blonde, obediently shook her pale curls and smiled in a coquettish fashion at the marquis.

Georgiana wanted to roll her eyes or heave up her breakfast, but she settled upon a polite smile instead. Her effort was wasted, however, for all the attention that was paid it. "You remember my daughter, Forsythia, do you not, my lord?" the matron asked, pushing the girl forward.

Ashdowne muttered some civility that set the mother to extolling Forsythia's talents, which were exceeded only by her beauty, in her mother's eyes at least. Georgiana had a more critical opinion, especially concerning the lack of manners in both women.

Georgiana might well have been a stain upon Ashdowne's sleeve for all that the ladies had noticed her—which was just as well, of course. Georgiana certainly did not want to draw attention to herself. Yet she couldn't help feeling a bit proprietary about the marquis. After all, he was *her* assistant, and she did not care for the way Forsythia was batting her eyelashes at him.

In fact, she had a sudden desire to pluck those eyelashes

out, one by one. It was a most unwelcome notion for someone who prided herself on objectivity and a logical, ordered mind. Georgiana had always considered herself far superior to the rest of the feminine population with their petty jealousies, but now she appeared to be prey to the same sort of nonsense. Lately it seemed that she did not even know herself. And who was to blame? Ashdowne!

Frowning at the companion who was deep in conversation with his admirers, Georgiana realized she had forgotten all about Mr. Hawkins, who might well be escaping while she was trapped here at Ashdowne's side. Gritting her teeth resolutely, she inched away from her assistant and was drawn back easily by one strong arm.

"Pardon me, but have you met Miss Bellewether?" Ashdowne asked in a casual tone that belied his grip upon her. "Miss Bellewether, may I present Forsythia and her mother..." Ashdowne paused to gaze blandly at the matron before him. "I fear I do not recall your name, madam."

"Mrs. Gilcrest," the woman said, her toadying smile momentarily faltering. "But tell me, my lord—"

"Ah, you must excuse us," Ashdowne said, glancing over the lady's shoulder as if something there had engaged his attention. And before she could respond, the marquis was moving away, dragging Georgiana with him, until they found a new corner behind two portly gentlemen who appeared to be asleep in their seats.

"It simply will not wash!" Georgiana muttered as he finally released her, her pique over sharing him with his devotees still lingering. "Now that you've been spotted, we'll be fair game for all the eligible females and their mothers!"

"Shh," Ashdowne said, inclining his head toward the entrance.

Georgiana was in no mood to be shushed, but her curiosity was stronger than her annoyance, and she looked in the direction he indicated and spied the vicar deep in conversation with Lady Culpepper herself. Georgiana found the sight most intriguing, especially in light of Mr. Hawkins's vocal contempt for the woman. "See, he's lording it over her," Georgiana whispered.

"Lording what?" Ashdowne asked.

"The theft! After years of study, I know the criminal mind," Georgiana replied. "I suspect our thief gains a perverse pleasure out of playing the supplicant, while knowing that he is in possession of the very thing that means the most to her."

"You're right about the perverse part," Ashdowne said dryly. "But I think it far more likely that he is currying her favor, perhaps in an effort to gain the living her family endows at their seat in Sussex."

Georgiana dismissed that supposition with a wave of her hand, too intent upon their quarry to argue. Finally the vicar was doing something interesting, so she kept her attention upon him, despite her assistant's disturbing nearness.

"And, Georgiana, love, someday you must enlighten me as to your knowledge of the, uh, criminal mind, as you call it," Ashdowne said in a seductive voice, his whisper brushing against her ear with startling familiarity.

Georgiana felt a dizzying awareness, which she firmly quelled as she watched Lady Culpepper sweep from the room. The vicar was left with an unpleasant expression upon his face, his feelings quite obvious, though swiftly masked when he recovered himself. "See?" Georgiana asked Ashdowne in a triumphant tone.

"What? I admit that he dislikes the woman, but so do most of those who know her," the marquis answered. And then their conversation was, by necessity, cut short, as their quarry moved forward. Not wanting to draw attention, they remained in their position behind the sleeping gentlemen, while keeping the vicar well within their sights.

The Pump Room was not very crowded, so Georgiana had no difficulty keeping an eye upon Mr. Hawkins. It was interruptions and distractions along the lines of Mrs. Gilcrest that concerned her. So far, they had been able to avoid members of her family and her limited number of acquaintances, but Ashdowne was far too well-known to avoid discovery, and soon they were marked once again.

This time, it was Ashdowne who gave a low sound of warning, and Georgiana flinched, fully expecting to see another determined mother bearing down upon them, but it was a man who appeared before them. He was as tall as Ashdowne, with black hair and eyes of a dark, rich green that nonetheless seemed curiously impassive. With some surprise Georgiana recognized him as Mr. Savonierre, the man who had brought the Bow Street Runner to Bath.

Having seen him only from a distance before, she had noticed little about him, but now she realized that he was quite a striking figure. Being of a similar height and coloring, at first glance he reminded her of Ashdowne. However, Savonierre's features were harder, and he emanated a coldness that was far chillier than the marquis when most aloof. Georgiana felt a shiver snake up her back.

"Ashdowne." Savonierre inclined his head, but his expression was not one of cordial greeting, and his eyes were shuttered, as if a world of secrets existed behind them. Although Georgiana could not name it, she sensed something about him that was distinctly disturbing.

Ashdowne, too, must have felt it, for he answered with a distinct lack of enthusiasm. Outwardly he was serene and polite, but Georgiana could feel the wariness in him and she wondered at it. Who was this man?

"Taking the waters, are you?" Savonierre asked, and the marquis responded with a shrug. "How unusual to find a man of your particular talents here in Bath, or perhaps, in light of events, it is not that unusual, after all," Savonierre murmured, as if intimating something that was lost upon Georgiana.

"No more unusual than your own visit," Ashdowne said. "I would think Brighton more to your liking."

"Ah. But I am here for a reason, a familial duty, as it were," Savonierre said. "Surely, you know that I count Lady Culpepper among my connections?" he asked, the question oddly taunting. When Ashdowne only nodded, as though bored, Savonierre smiled slightly, like some sort of predator. He moved forward, as if to menace them, and Georgiana stepped back, though the marquis held his ground.

"I came straight away when I heard about the stolen emeralds," Savonierre explained. He glanced toward the crowd and then back to Ashdowne. "I admit to being a bit disappointed with the Bow Street Runner I hired. It has been four days, and he has not yet unveiled the thief."

Georgiana, too, was a bit disenchanted with Jeffries, but she had to admit that his plodding pace was to her advantage. "I have my own suspicions," she said, seizing upon the subject most dear to her heart.

But before she could speak further, Ashdowne broke in. "Have you met Miss Bellewether? She is an amateur investigator and has been following the case quite closely.''

"Indeed?'' Savonierre's attention swung toward her, and Georgiana noted the intensity of his gaze. Although she usually embraced an opportunity to expound upon her theories, she felt uncomfortable under such intent scrutiny. Her tongue seemed to cleave to the roof of her mouth, as if he had stricken her mute with that piercing stare, and so, for once, she did not elaborate.

"Perhaps I shall succeed where Mr. Jeffries cannot,'' she stated simply, when she finally managed to speak.

Instead of scoffing like other men, Savonierre glanced from her to Ashdowne and then back again, an odd smile twisting his mouth. He inclined his head toward her, his green eyes glinting. "Perhaps you will, Miss Bellewether. I shall look forward to it.''

Savonierre's tone held a dark edge of promise that made Georgiana draw in a sharp breath, and she held it as he bowed and left, expelling a low sigh of relief at his departure. "Who is he?'' she whispered to Ashdowne. "And why does he hate you so?''

For a moment, Ashdowne said nothing, but stood staring after Savonierre with such a dangerous expression that Georgiana feared he might go after the man with violent intent. Anxious, she tugged on his sleeve until he turned toward her, his face rigid.

"He has certainly taken a dislike to me, but I have no idea why. He is, however, a very powerful man and one not to be trifled with.'' Casting a last look in the direction that Savonierre had taken, Ashdowne seemed to recover his usual aplomb. He took her arm, giving it a gentle squeeze that Georgiana presumed was one of friendly encouragement until she realized that he was urging her forward into the crowd.

Mr. Hawkins, drat him, had disappeared.

Chapter Ten

To Georgiana's immense relief, they soon spied the vicar exiting the Pump Room and fell into their positions behind him. Although she expected a further repetition of yesterday's schedule, this time Mr. Hawkins turned away from the shops toward a more residential area.

Keeping a good distance away, they nonetheless managed to follow their quarry through winding streets to a rather shabby neighborhood. It was less genteel than the one in which he lived, but not so inelegant as to cause Georgiana alarm. She felt eminently safe with Ashdowne, and although he kept wanting to turn back, she would have none of it.

"This is exactly the sort of place where he is most likely to reveal himself," Georgiana argued. "Why, he might be on his way to a dealer in stolen goods. We might very well catch him in the act!"

"That is what I'm afraid of," Ashdowne muttered, but he grudgingly stayed beside her. Georgiana dismissed his concerns with an airy wave, for she was firmly focused on the case again and eagerly anticipating its resolution. Although Ashdowne seemed to view her resurgent enthusiasm with some reluctance, he voiced no more complaints, and Georgiana was able to give her full attention to the vicar.

And Mr. Hawkins definitely was up to something. When he turned into an alley and stopped before a door there, Georgiana nearly clapped her hands in glee, for it certainly looked as though he was making his move. As if to confirm her suspicions, the vicar looked about him furtively before knocking, but he did not note Ashdowne or Georgiana, hidden behind the corner of a building across the way, peeping out intermittently.

Hawkins wasted no time slipping inside when the worn door opened to admit him, and Georgiana hurried across the street, anxious to inspect the place. Unfortunately, there was nothing to be learned in the alley, so she made her way into the building's back garden, a sadly ill kempt area littered with refuse. There, another door was flanked by two tall windows, and Georgiana motioned for Ashdowne to hurry as she climbed upon some broken stone to peep through the glass. A tiny, dark kitchen met her gaze, and she groaned in frustration.

Unwilling to give up, she dropped back down to the ground and, heedless of her skirts, clambered over the dirt and trash until she reached the other window. But it was too high for her to see in, and she glanced about, ready to direct her assistant to move some of the fallen stones, when she was arrested by sounds from inside the very room she was trying to view.

Extremely *odd* sounds. Puzzled, Georgiana moved closer to the building and listened. At first, all she could hear was a low moaning of sorts, punctuated by a sharp cracking noise. As she stood still, the latter became more pronounced, the moans more like groans of pain, and Georgiana glanced toward Ashdowne in alarm.

"He's murdering someone in there!" she whispered in

horror. Then something about the shouting struck her as familiar, and with dawning dread, she recognized Mr. Hawkins's voice. "No," she amended. "Someone's murdering him!" With a low cry, Georgiana rushed toward the rear entrance, intent upon stopping the carnage. No matter that he was a thief and a contemptible creature, she could not stand by while Mr. Hawkins met his end.

"No! Wait!" Ashdowne called to her softly, but Georgiana was in no mood for caution. The door swung open easily, and she entered the dim kitchen, where the stale odors of food mixed with a rather overwhelming reek of perfume. She paused for but a moment to catch her breath when Hawkins's harsh shout rent the air. Hurrying toward the sound, Georgiana halted at the threshold of a small, rather tawdry room and stared in astonishment.

The good vicar, so stoic and superior during their brief conversations, was bent over a red velvet chair, his naked behind sticking up in the air. Standing over him was a woman, dressed in a bizarre costume and wielding a whip. It was such an incredible scene that Georgiana made no further move to aid him, and she wondered why he continued to remain prone, for he was not bound in any way.

In fact, he appeared to be welcoming the woman's punishment, which Georgiana could see now was no ordinary whip, but one made of soft material that did not seem to be causing any damage to the vicar's stiff rear. He wiggled his posterior, as if eager for the treatment, even as he howled and begged for mercy.

For her part, the woman, dressed in high, tassled boots, some sort of tight military coat and little else, appeared to be wholly bored by the exercise. She had a real whip that she cracked loudly against the floor, while, in between yawns, she used the paltry substitute upon Hawkins.

The whole situation was so shocking yet absurd that Georgiana was caught between a gasp and a laugh and, struck speechless, she simply stood frozen in her place until she felt the heat of a hand against the small of her back. It was Ashdowne, of course, but Georgiana's nerves were strained to the limit, and she jumped in startlement, drawing the attention of the scantily clad woman.

She turned toward them, her expression one of irritation rather than horror at being caught in such circumstances. "Here now, only one customer at a time," she said. Angrily she turned back toward the vicar's bum. "If this is your idea, you can forget it right now. I work alone! I'm an artist and won't have none of your bloomin' orgies!"

"What?" Hawkins's head lifted, and he choked in outrage, yanking up his trousers as he struggled to gain his footing. "What are you doing here?" he cried, gaping at Georgiana and Ashdowne. He turned upon his companion. "If you think you can blackmail me, I've news for you, wench. You'll not get a farthing from me!"

"Hold now, gent! I don't know nothing about these two!" she said, throwing up hands that still gripped the whips.

"I apologize for the intrusion," Georgiana said, sensing that her intervention was necessary. "But I am investigating a certain theft, and I have reason to believe that *you* know something about it."

"Me?" the woman squealed. "I don't know nothing about any thievery, miss. I just do what they pay me to, and if they happen to lose a bit of change when their trousers are down, well, then, I can hardly be blamed for it, can I?"

"Be at ease, madam, for it is not you we wish to speak with, but your client," Ashdowne said, stepping forward. Leaning close, he said something to the woman, and

Georgiana suspected he slipped her some money, too, for when he moved back, she was all smiles.

"Well, then, I'll just leave you to do your, uh, business, shall I?" she said, exiting the room with no further protestations.

Hawkins, however, was livid. "See here, what do you think you're doing?" he charged, though it was hard for him to maintain a dignified stance while gripping his trousers.

In any event, Ashdowne was wholly unaffected by his blustering. "Is this how you lost your last position?" he asked in a deceptively soft voice. He strolled forward to finger the small whip that the woman had left behind, then pinned Hawkins with a contemptuous stare. "By getting a little too close to your female parishioners?"

"I did not! It was all Lord Fallow's fault! I was just comforting and attending his wife, especially during his long absences, when he suddenly took affront and tossed me out for no good reason," Hawkins replied. As if remembering himself, he drew himself up straighter, though one hand still held the fall of his trousers. "And what I do in private is no one's business except my own!"

"As long as you're not entertaining someone else's wife," Ashdowne said dryly.

"Be that as it may," Georgiana interrupted, "our concern here is with Lady Culpepper's necklace. If you return it at once, we shall try to persuade her not to press charges in the case."

Hawkins gaped at her in a dumbfounded way that sent a sense of foreboding skittering up her spine, for either the man was a consummate actor or he knew nothing of the theft. Unwilling to accept the latter conclusion, Georgiana lifted her chin. "It is quite obvious that you harbor a dislike for Lady Culpepper—"

Hawkins cut her off with a fierce snort. "It's the entire class I hate, a bunch of lying hypocrites, lording their wealth over the rest of us," he said, with a discreet glare in Ashdowne's direction. "But I did not take her necklace! How could I? I was there at the ball the whole time, not climbing up the side of the building! If you ask me, the blessed thing was never even taken. The old witch is probably collecting the insurance money for it, while selling off the pieces."

Georgiana realized this was not the first time she had heard Hawkins tender such a theory. And, as an impartial investigator, she had to consider the possibility that his accusation might be true.

Thankfully, while she was lost in thought, her assistant stepped in. "Perhaps you would care to tell us exactly where you were at the time of the theft," Ashdowne suggested.

Hawkins eyed the marquis with undisguised loathing. "Why me, my lord? There were plenty of other people there. Any one of them could just as well have committed the crime. Yet, you choose to accost me. Why? Is this some sort of retribution for my views upon the aristocracy, or is it another one of Lord Fallow's rebukes?" Rigid with fury, the vicar finally managed to button his trousers. "Well, he can't blame me for this! I was with a certain lady in the linen closet."

One dark brow inched upward on Ashdowne's face. "Indeed?"

"Indeed!" Hawkins replied. "And lest you think I am lying, just ask the woman herself. It was Mrs. Howard!"

Georgiana started in surprise at his admission, for she knew the lady, as well as Mr. Howard, her husband, but Hawkins showed no evidence of embarrassment over his behavior. The fellow certainly deserved to be whipped, she thought, though since he enjoyed it, the punishment was hardly fitting.

"And now, if you will excuse me," he said. "I will thank you to leave me alone!" Drawing together the shreds of his dignity, the vicar turned and strode through the doorway with a stiff stride, unaware that his shirt hung loose down his backside, flapping as he walked.

Georgiana stared after him, and the manner of his gait, coupled with the dingy shirttail, was too much for her. A giggle welled up in her chest at the sight and at all that had gone before. Who could have imagined the staid, pompous vicar paying a fancy woman to *spank* him? It was really too absurd, Georgiana thought with a bit of hysteria.

Although she tried to restrain herself, when she turned to look at Ashdowne, Georgiana knew it was hopeless, for he too appeared to be barely containing his amusement. And as soon as the door shut behind the vicar, the two of them sagged against each other as they gave in to boisterous laughter.

Once her amusement died away, Georgiana visibly began to droop, like a hothouse flower that had been exposed too long to the vagaries of an English climate. Her shoulders slumped, her smile faded, and, oddly enough, Ashdowne felt as if the sun had gone down with it. He would have taken her in his arms, convincing her to forget all about Hawkins and the stolen necklace, but even he realized that the pleasure parlor of the mistress of punishment was hardly the place for such distractions.

Of course, a gentleman would never have let her wander into this neighborhood, and especially not an establishment such as this one, but Ashdowne had never accounted himself a gentlemen. He didn't feel the slightest shame over what they had seen, which had really been little enough. Rather, he thought it had all been highly humorous, as had Georgiana.

She was not the type of woman he had to shield from the world, as was his fragile sister-in-law. Anne would have fainted dead away at the sight of a man's bare buttocks, let alone the mistress whipping her client. Indeed, most well-bred young ladies, boring creatures all, would have reacted with shock and horror, but Georgiana was nothing if not adventurous. She embraced life in all of its infinite variety, hungry for experience, thirsting for knowledge and lusting for mystery.

Ashdowne shifted slightly as he redirected his thoughts from that last observation. And if, during the course of her exploits, Georgiana caused a few calamities, well then, that was why he was along—to protect her from herself. And this instance, Ashdowne realized, qualified as one of those times. Although she was in no physical danger, Georgiana was spent emotionally. And no matter how hard he might once have laughed at the notion, now he found himself oddly affected by her mood—and determined to elevate it.

So he gathered her close and took her to a coffeehouse, where he plied her with the rich desserts she had forgone the day before. Leaving his own syllabub untouched, Ashdowne tried to bolster her spirits as she fiddled with her silver.

"It wasn't your fault," he told her. "Your reasoning was sound." That was true enough, for the vicar had made his hatred for the upper class quite apparent. If, in Ashdowne's opinion, he was woefully incapable of managing the stunning theft, then Georgiana could hardly be blamed. Perhaps she didn't realize the skill, precision and coordination necessary to perform such a feat.

"And how were you to know that he was in the linen closet? Obviously, he was most secretive about it," Ashdowne murmured.

"Yes," Georgiana answered glumly as she stuck her spoon into the rich confection. Then she paused to slant him a glance. "Do you think he was lying? Will Mrs. Howard verify his story?"

Although the woman in question might be reluctant to admit to her liaison, Ashdowne thought it highly unlikely that Hawkins was spinning a Banbury tale. "I do not believe that the vicar would have concocted such a story had it not been true," he hedged, unwilling to disappoint Georgiana further. Clearly discouraged, she sighed, blowing a fat curl from her forehead, and Ashdowne watched the play of her lips with fascination.

Drawing in a deep breath to clear his head, he tried to remember what he was going to say. Ah, yes. "I will speak to Mr. Jeffries about it, but I suspect that Hawkins is simply a bad vicar, not a thief," he said.

At least, like Whalsey, the man had been guilty of *something,* Ashdowne mused, but he did not think Georgiana would be heartened to hear it. So he kept silent, watching her as she finally placed the tip of the spoon in her mouth, taking great pleasure in the creamy taste. She took such pleasure in it that Ashdowne hardened at the sight of her fluttering lashes and beatific expression.

He wanted her to look like that for *him,* not some dessert. Then again, the thick, whipped concoction might very well be used to good advantage, Ashdowne thought wickedly. He would like to spread it over those creamy breasts of hers and...he swallowed, his mind changing track as he watched her lick her silver. On second thought, perhaps the froth could be applied to appropriate portions of *his* body and Georgiana could do the honors with that lovely little tongue.

She appeared to be awfully good with it.

Ashdowne drew in a harsh breath. He was well aware that his fascination with Miss Bellewether exceeded various and sundry boundaries, including those he had set himself. Never had he intended to do much more than kiss such an innocent, and yet there was the small matter of the little episode in the baths, where he had brought her to release, while spilling himself into his breeches like an untried boy.

Ashdowne's lips curved at the memory of the incident, which he refused to regret. It had been a most pleasurable, humbling experience and one he longed to repeat, for every time he looked at Georgiana, he desired her. He had but barely glimpsed her breasts, had not seen the rest of her, and so he knew a fierce longing to see all of her, naked. And, as enjoyable as their little encounter had been, it seemed to have just whetted his appetite for more traditional lovemaking.

Watching while she consumed the syllabub with a delight that was palatable, Ashdowne wanted to be the object of that delight. He wanted her hands on him, her mouth on him, her soft curves surrounding him, with an intensity that was remotely alarming. Even ignoring his lingering reservations about the woman herself, this interest of his could bring trouble to them both, if only because of her station in life. And then there was the whole wretched business of the theft.

When Georgiana's pink tongue snaked out above her lips to catch an errant drop of the dessert, Ashdowne broke out in a sweat. He accounted himself an experienced man, well versed in the intricacies of seduction, but there was something about Georgiana's innocent sensuality that nearly undid him. His erection was so painful that a small sound escaped him.

"I agree totally. This was simply too much," Georgiana said, pushing her bowl away. She glanced toward him, her eyes widening. "But you haven't even touched yours! Here, just have a taste," she insisted. And to his dismay, she took his spoon, dipped it into the syllabub and held it out to him.

Although he knew it would only test his restraint further, Ashdowne could not resist. His blood pounding out a rhythm that sounded suspiciously like *doom, doom,* he caught her gaze with his own, letting her see his desire as he sucked on the proffered utensil. Her hand faltered and he captured her wrist, lifting the spoon back to his lips. Then he shamelessly licked away every drop of the dessert, while he watched her blue eyes cloud with a passion that fed his own.

For one long moment, Ashdowne, who prided himself on his ability to remain alert in all situations, felt as if the coffeehouse and its occupants faded away. Only a vague awareness of their surroundings kept him from lifting her to the table and letting his tongue taste a treat sweeter by far than the syllabub—her mouth, followed by every inch of white skin, culminating at the juncture of her thighs. His nostrils flared in a primitive reaction so far removed from his urbane existence that he jerked his hand from hers.

The spoon fell, clattering onto the table and awakening them both to an awareness of their surroundings. Ashdowne could have cursed himself for his slip. What if someone had seen them? What was he thinking to behave in so suggestive a manner when they were in a public place? He was already testing the bounds of propriety by appearing so often as Georgiana's escort.

Unfortunately, he had no answer to that because he rarely seemed to be thinking at all when Georgiana was around. Something about her made him throw caution to the wind, ignore his instincts, act on impulse and indulge his suddenly overactive appetite for her. It was maddening, yet so strangely exhilarating that he could not help himself.

"I, uh, think that's enough," she said, looking away from him in a way that was deuced annoying. Despite what every sensible bone in his body was telling him, he didn't want her withdrawal. He wanted to take her back to Camden Place, send all the servants away and make love to her on every piece of garish furniture in the house.

"Oh, what are we to do?" Georgiana whispered in a plaintive tone that made Ashdowne draw a deep breath. It was his responsibility to wrest control of this dangerous attraction between them. Determinedly he banished the images invoked by his desires and donned the sober expression of an attentive listener, of a man who could be counted upon to honor her wishes and...

"Now Mr. Jeffries will be even more disinclined to put his faith in me," Georgiana said.

With a jolt, Ashdowne realized that it was not their unsatisfied ardor that upset her, but the bloody case. He had to bite back a shout of laughter as he schooled his expression to polite interest once more.

"Being a man, you can have no notion of the obstacles placed before me," Georgiana complained. "Your very gender assures you a modicum of respect, no matter how fanciful your notions. Why, even Bertrand, who failed to apply himself to any of his educational opportunities, is taken more seriously than I!"

Although Ashdowne found it difficult to imagine anyone according much respect to her lackadaisical brother, he had to admit that she might well be right on all her other points. It was a sad commentary on the male population, but he rarely held his peers in high regard.

"One look at me, and all but the most discerning see a buffle-headed doll, a witless creature to be admired for her outward appearance, something over which I had no control whatsoever! Indeed, my so-called beauty has been no blessing, but a curse," Georgiana moaned.

Ashdowne began to feel the weight of his own part in her predicament, a resurgence of guilt that he swiftly tried to dislodge. "You are viewing your appearance in the wrong light, Georgiana," he said. "You have always worked against it, when, instead, you must learn to use it to your advantage."

"How?" she asked, her expression a study in bafflement.

Guilt pressed down upon him again, only to be ruthlessly jettisoned. "In the hands of a superior seamstress, you would be incomparable. Dress yourself as befitting your God-given gifts, and present yourself so to the world. When the world comes calling, show it that you have a mind, too. Let your beauty get you in the door, while your wit keeps you there!"

"What door? There is no one here to impress but dandified bucks and gouty old people!" Georgiana said.

"Not in backwater Bath, but in London," Ashdowne said, warming to his own suggestion. "There you could be the toast of some of the most elite salons, where discussion of events isn't limited to the latest gossip, but turns on politics and art and literature." He knew he could gain entrée to such groups with his title, if not on his own past merits, and the thought of Georgiana shaking up some of the intelligentsia made him smile.

He eyed her expectantly, and for a moment she simply

stared at him, perhaps transfixed by his sudden, unusually impassioned speech. Despite himself, Ashdowne found himself waiting for The Look. For once, he deserved it, for he could see her admitted into the most exclusive of societies. But instead of gazing at him as if he were a god, Georgiana donned an expression of exasperation.

"But, how on earth am I to get to London?" she asked. "Papa could never be induced to go. He is already complaining about Bath, for he wants his daily comforts. He is a man of routine and does not like it disturbed, even for the better."

It was Ashdowne's turn to stare stupidly back at her as he realized just how ridiculous he must have sounded. He had spoken as if he could sponsor her, when, of course, he could not, for she was not related to him in any way. At the realization, he felt deflated, as if all his wild enthusiasm had been drained away, leaving him empty.

"I beg your pardon," he muttered, feeling foolish. The situation he had described would be her ruin, should she appear in his company alone, yet, perversely, he could not picture her with anyone else. "Have you no relatives in London?" he asked.

"No," she replied.

"No one at all you could visit or who might take you with them?" *Besides me,* he thought.

She made one of her delightful faces, as if deep in concentration, and he fought against his entrancement. "Well, there is my great-uncle, Silas Morcombe," she admitted.

Ashdowne felt a surge of relief. "Perhaps your uncle could contrive to take you for a visit," he suggested.

Georgiana looked thoughtful. "Perhaps. But I doubt if Mother would agree, for she considers him sadly ramshackle and would fear that he would not observe the correct proprieties. He's a bachelor, you see, and never cares much about anything except his latest studies. I would not expect him to squire me about to any drawing rooms, even if he could spare the time.''

Resting her chin in her palm, she sighed, and the soft sound did something to Ashdowne's insides. "No. It would be better if I could become famous, then others would come to me, no matter where I am,'' she said. "If only I could solve this case, then I would, at last, gain the respect I crave. Not only would I be vindicated, but I could finally make use of my expertise.''

As Ashdowne watched, Georgiana's eyes took on a hazy glow, her lips curving into a smile that made him ache in places he didn't expect and didn't care to examine. He felt himself sink into the sweet lunacy that was Georgiana, escape at once both impossible and uninviting until she spoke again.

"It has been my greatest wish, you know, to become a sort of a consultant and to have people from all over the country present to me their mysteries,'' she murmured, and Ashdowne's fey mood vanished with startling abruptness.

He had been amused at first, then entertained and even rather enthralled by Georgiana's efforts to solve the theft of Lady Culpepper's necklace, but he had never imagined that her desire went beyond the gratification of apprehending the culprit. Now he saw her attempts for what they were: the achievement of a lifelong dream.

The guilt Ashdowne had so successfully kept at bay landed on his back in a thrice, and he frantically sought some way out of a conundrum far more complex than any Georgiana had ever studied. He told himself that the realization of her dream did not hinge upon this theft. There would be other cases, he knew, even as he admitted that none would be so infamous, especially in genteel Bath.

But what of London? Perhaps he could coax her uncle or someone else to take her there. Ashdowne knew he could force his sister-in-law to sponsor Georgiana, but he didn't have much faith in that vapid creature's judgment. And the thought of Georgiana loosed, unprotected, among the males of London was too horrible to contemplate. Nor did he care to entrust some scholarly great-uncle, who did not obey proprieties, with Georgiana's safety.

In fact, the only person he trusted to watch after Georgiana was himself, and swift on the heels of that acknowledgment came a series of wild thoughts. They churned through him, a relentless parade of mad possibilities that left him reeling though he tried to maintain some semblance of normalcy.

Obviously he failed, for Georgiana soon noticed his silence, and she blinked in surprise when she turned to look at him. "Oh, dear, you are as distressed as I am! How thoughtless of me not to take your own disappointment into consideration," she said, patting his sleeve in gentle sympathy.

And because he could not voice a coherent thought, Ashdowne only nodded, eager to go home and sort through the maelstrom in his mind. He needed to be alone, he knew that much, for he doubted his ability to think clearly when faced with a certain pair of limpid blue eyes.

Chapter Eleven

Ashdowne was still reeling when he arrived at Camden Place, after returning a glum Georgiana to her parents, for the brisk walk had done little to bring order to his unruly thoughts. He felt hot and tingly, like someone who had survived a lightning strike—or a man torn between his good sense and a lot of wild ideas, he thought grimly.

"I need a drink," he called to Finn as he strode into the study. There he fell into one of the hard armchairs, for once not noticing the discomfort of his furnishings.

"Right, milord," Finn said, hurrying after him. He closed the door and moved to the sideboard, eyeing Ashdowne over his shoulder. "But what of the miss? Have you abandoned her to her own devices?"

At his words, Ashdowne frowned. He had been so consumed with his own thoughts that he had forgotten about Georgiana's annoying habit of getting into trouble in his absence. "She's fresh out of suspects for now, at least," he muttered, more to reassure himself than his servant.

Finn said nothing as he crossed the room with a delicate crystal glass and handed it to his employer. Murmuring his thanks, Ashdowne took the port and stared into the depths of the liquid as if seeking an answer there. When none appeared, he related his afternoon encounter with the mistress of punishment, much to Finn's amusement.

Finn's robust laughter was a welcome diversion, but Ashdowne's uneasiness must have been apparent, for the Irishman's amusement faded as he studied his employer shrewdly. "You should have let the vicar take the blame for it," he said.

"What? The theft?" Ashdowne asked. At Finn's nod, he shook his head. "The vicar isn't guilty of much more than unpopular polemics. And he's right about most of the ton being a bunch of hypocrites." He paused to fix his gaze on Finn. "Do you know that he suggested Lady Culpepper's necklace was never stolen, but simply broken down in a plan to collect the insurance money?"

"Did he now?" Finn asked in a speculative tone, and the two exchanged a look fraught with meaning. "But what of the miss, milord? What will she do now? She'll be looking for another suspect before long."

"Perhaps her interest in the case will dissipate at last," Ashdowne said hopefully.

Finn scratched his chin. "I don't know, milord. She seems quite fierce about the whole thing."

"Yes, I know," Ashdowne acknowledged. If only she felt that passionate about him instead of some deuced mystery! His disgust turned to a kind of horror as he realized that he was becoming jealous of a *case*. Just how low was he sinking? He rolled his shoulders in an effort to ease the tension that had seized him ever since Georgiana had confided her dream.

"Unless you can distract her," Finn suggested slyly.

"Yes, but—" Ashdowne began, only to jerk as the Irishman slapped him on the back.

"Aye. Now, *there's* your answer, milord," he said

heartily. "And I've no doubt of your abilities in that regard."

Ashdowne smiled weakly. He was glad that Finn had such faith in him, but truth be told, he was not quite sure anyone could keep Georgiana distracted for long. A man would have to have the stamina of a...

"Shall I keep a watch on her until you can make sure she's occupied with other matters?" Finn asked.

"Yes. Thank you," Ashdowne muttered as he tried to ignore his accelerating heartbeat. He thought of himself as a worldly gentleman, with his share of love affairs, so why did the thought of distracting Georgiana excite him so? He stifled a groan as his attention returned to all the other questions that plagued him.

Vaguely he noted Finn's agreement and subsequent departure, but neither the port nor the conversation had brought him any closer to making sense out of the mad thoughts that careened through his brain. The indecision was doubly frustrating, for usually he was the most meticulous of thinkers. In the past, his very life had depended upon careful planning and foresight, yet now he felt as if one petite blonde had totally disordered his existence with a simple toss of her curls.

And, despite the clamor of his good sense to the contrary, Ashdowne knew it would never be the same again.

A night of serious contemplation had restored Ashdowne's equilibrium, if not his reason. He knew what he wanted all right, but his entire body rebelled against it. Well, not *every* portion, to be exact, just enough to make him hesitate. And even setting aside his lingering doubts, he was not one to take such a precipitous step lightly. There was a part of him that wasn't ready, no matter what the provocation. And there was another part that warily guarded all his secrets.

The irony of his situation was not lost upon him, yet Ashdowne knew an urge to let matters take their course. Although at odds with his calculating nature, it drove him to Georgiana's residence, where he coaxed the dispirited investigator out for a carriage ride, while fending off the invitations of her younger sisters.

She didn't want to join him, really, and Ashdowne felt the snub right down to his boots. Along with the prick to his pride came an overwhelming desire to prove to her just how well she liked his company. It was a rather primitive sensation, the kind that presumably fueled the Norse invaders who dragged their stolen brides back home without a twinge of guilt. He was more civilized than that, Ashdowne told himself as he rolled his shoulders in an effort to be rid of the tension that gnawed at him.

Although some sticklers for propriety might not approve of Ashdowne escorting a genteel young woman in his curricle, the two of them had thoroughly flouted conventional custom so often lately that he refused to consider a chaperon. And they could hardly speak freely in front of another about Georgiana's beloved case. Or at least that's what Ashdowne told himself in order to justify taking her off to some secluded grove above the city.

And Georgiana's father, whether from lack of good sense or an optimistic view toward a title for his daughter, was fool enough to entrust her to him. Although Mr. Bellewether's jovial good wishes fell in well enough with Ashdowne's plans, he felt a surge of annoyance at the man for not safeguarding Georgiana.

When *he* had a daughter, he would take better care of her, Ashdowne vowed. And, surprisingly, the notion of siring children was not so startling as it once might have been. He pictured cherub-faced girls with golden curls sprawling on the lawn in front of the family seat and smiled, firmly ignoring the now familiar thrum of *doom* that accompanied the vision.

Handing Georgiana into the waiting curricle, Ashdowne climbed up beside her and breathed a sigh of relief that he did not have to spend the morning lounging outside of the vicar's apartments, waiting to follow him. The pleasure of having Georgiana all to himself was an anticipation that built rather feverishly, despite Ashdowne's best efforts to quell it.

However, it wasn't long before he realized that the case still stood between them, for Georgiana sat beside him in dour silence, her lovely face drawn up into a glum expression, her pretty shoulders slumped. When she sank her chin into one gloved palm, Ashdowne decided he had never seen a female look so positively *disappointed* to be in his company. He didn't know whether to laugh or be insulted, but that was Georgiana.

No matter what, she was always interesting, he thought with a smile, although he didn't like to see her so dejected. But all his efforts to point out the buildings of Bath or make conversation did little to cheer her, and finally, Ashdowne began to wonder if he should suggest a new suspect. Only the absurdity of the notion, along with the desire to steer clear of Bedlam, kept him from doing so.

To his delight, Georgiana perked up when they reached the hills that encompassed the city, and even Ashdowne could admire the greenery and tall oaks. After tethering the horses, he tossed aside his gloves and lay his cloak upon the grass. He urged Georgiana to sit, but she seemed transfixed by the view of the city below.

"It is beautiful," he murmured, moving to stand behind her.

Georgiana made some noise of agreement, then pointed to the pale stone buildings in the distance. "Look how well you can see the houses!" she said, leaning forward and squinting as if she would focus on some particular dwelling. Turning to him suddenly, she blinked. "I wonder how closely you could view the doings with a spyglass."

Ashdowne simply stared at her a moment, then burst out laughing. Leave it to Georgiana to ignore the romance of such a spot while considering the practical applications of her visit. If she wasn't so entertaining, he would have taken insult. Any other woman alone with him here would not be thinking of what was happening in the city, but any other woman wouldn't see suspects behind every corner, either.

Georgiana's unique perspective was both alluring and frustrating, for his thoughts were such that he wanted her attention on himself, for once, and not her case. "Surely, there must be something else in Bath besides robbery that could draw your interest," he suggested wryly.

"Yes, but I am still unsettled by the theft. I keep feeling as if I'm missing something," she mused thoughtfully.

Ashdowne knew what he was missing, but he was trying to keep his rampant desires in check. Despite the casual air he had long presented to the world, he was very aware of all that went on around him. It was necessary. He had to consider every detail and plan accordingly, for the slightest miscalculation could spell disaster. Never before had he allowed himself to become diverted from the business at hand, and yet, ever since meeting the intriguing Miss Bellewether, he had felt his control slipping.

It was slipping now.

Although he felt like Achilles going in for a boot fitting or Samson asking Delilah for a trim, the ominous sense that Georgiana meant his downfall was somehow all mixed up with the wild notion that she could well be his salvation. Ashdowne could no longer judge what was best. He knew an urge to surrender entirely to the force that had seized him and let it take him where it may.

Stepping behind her, Ashdowne leaned close in order to catch the delicate scent of her curls. He felt her sway toward him, and he knew a gratifying salve to his pride. Despite her behavior to the contrary, Georgiana was drawn to him, and her standoffishness became a challenge, filling him with a rush of excitement that made his body tighten.

He moved closer, laying his hands on her shoulders, and for one moment she leaned against him, her head resting upon his chest, before she jerked away to turn and glare at him accusingly. "I thought we agreed to keep to…business," she said, her face deliciously pink.

"Actually, I had a more permanent relationship in mind," Ashdowne said, reaching for her.

Totally ignoring the import of his words, she stepped back, holding up a hand as if to ward him off, and he grinned at her rather panicked expression. No woman had ever refused his advances, let alone *fought* them, but Georgiana's seeming reluctance only incited his passion. Although he would never force her to do anything, Ashdowne knew from experience that she could be easily persuaded, and he fully intended to coax her willingly into his arms.

"No! Don't come any closer," she said, as if well aware of his intentions. "My mind gets all muddled when you are too near." Her mouth took on a prim little twist that made him want to feel it relaxing beneath his own, but he remained where he stood, and when he raised a hand toward her face, she swatted it away. "And no touching!" she said.

Ashdowne tried his best to look innocent. "What if I but take your hand?" he asked.

"Well, I—"

Before she could answer, he caught one of her hands in his own, while lifting his brows, as if to question her wariness. But Georgiana remained chary, frowning at him in a manner that told him she knew him too well. "All right, but *just* my hand," she said grudgingly.

Ashdowne laughed in pure delight, anticipation flooding his veins at her eventual surrender. He had never been a rake, prone to prey on young women, but this game with Georgiana was too enticing to relinquish. Once before he had made her moan and sigh and cling to him, had brought her to exquisite release, and he would do so again. He gazed into her dazed blue eyes and knew that she was aware of the power he wielded.

But Ashdowne had no intention of rushing anything. Making no sudden moves that might scare her away, he simply stood before her, holding her hand in what could be construed as a most innocent gesture. Then, very slowly, he began to rub his thumb over her palm, against the soft kid of her gloves, though he longed to strip the concealing fabric from her, to feel her bare skin as he had the other night in the baths.

The memory rushed over him, kicking Ashdowne's desire to a new level as he stared down at her tiny wrist, enchanted by its delicacy. Lifting her wrist to his mouth, he pressed a kiss to her pulse point, smiling when it tripped erratically beneath his lips. He glanced up at her face, already flushed, to see her staring at him in rapt fascination.

Once certain he had her attention, Ashdowne took the

edge of her glove in his teeth and tugged, watching her eyes widen and her lips part on a startled breath. Tugging gently, he slowly revealed an inch of pink palm and then another. He took his time, as if he were undressing her body for his viewing, and found that the ritual heightened his own excitement, as well as Georgiana's.

Her delicate fingers followed as he edged the glove down to the tips and tossed it aside. With a groan, he pressed his mouth to the center of her palm as he tried to rein in his burgeoning passion. The delicate scent of Georgiana filled his nostrils, and he licked the tender skin on the inside of her hand, creating little circles. Moving on, he traced her fingers with his tongue, finding each tip and each indentation between.

Finally Ashdowne looked up, catching her gaze with his own, and took one small finger into his mouth. He sucked on it, watching her blue eyes glaze over as she blinked in an endearing manner. His own groin jerked in response, but he held himself still, his only movement the suckling of her fingers, the only sounds in the quiet grove that of their shallow breathing. Slowly, tenderly, he bit at her tiny nail, and she gasped and swayed, her legs giving way.

Ashdowne moved forward to catch her and press her back against the smoothness of his cloak spread upon the grass. He felt light-headed, aroused beyond anything he had ever known, and he had done nothing but lavish attention on her hand. With a low sound of straining impatience, he rose over her, eager to ply the rest of her body.

But something stopped him.

Hovering over her, his weight on his arms, Ashdowne stared at her beautiful face and paused. Her cheeks were flushed, her lips parted, and her head was thrown back, so that he could not mistake her desire. But her eyes were closed.

"Georgiana. Look at me," he whispered.

Her lashes fluttered open to reveal a glimpse of hazy blue depths before drifting shut once more. Ashdowne remained prone just inches from her lush form, his groin throbbing painfully, every part of him screaming for release, for the pleasure to be found here, with her. He had but to lower himself and...

Instead, he rolled away and groaned, throwing an arm over his face. It would be so easy to take her, or even to satisfy them both and still leave her a virgin, but he felt a fraud, as if he had somehow robbed her of her choice in the matter. As absurd as it seemed, he wanted her to greet his lovemaking with her eyes wide-open, welcoming, *wanting him* no matter what. No matter all that stood between them.

With another groan, Ashdowne realized that he was just as mad as Georgiana! First he had begun to understand her, which was alarming enough, and now he was thinking like her, in bizarre convoluted ways that made no sense to anyone with wits! Muttering a curse, Ashdowne sat up and rose to his feet to stare unseeing at the panorama of Bath below.

"Ashdowne?" He felt her hand tugging at his sleeve, but he did not trust himself to face her. What would he see in her eyes? Dazed passion? Rebuke?

"Just the hand, remember?" he said as lightly as he could manage. "I was only to touch your hand and nothing else." He turned then, with a casual grace he had long ago perfected, his expression bland.

"Ashdowne?" Whatever she was going to say was lost to the wind, as the sound of horses reached them. They both swung toward the path, where a pair of hack horses pulling what looked like some sort of converted cart came into view.

"There you are!"

Ashdowne recognized the cries but couldn't believe his ears—or his eyes. Barreling toward them were Georgiana's sisters in a ramshackle conveyance, driven by her brother Bertrand.

Ashdowne spared a moment to send up thanks that he was not right now under his companion's skirts, deeply embedded in her gorgeous body, while he stared in amazement at the vehicle that came to a halt. Georgiana's sisters, sporting matching parasols and frothy gowns, waved and giggled and fluttered their fans in greeting.

"We've been looking all over for you!" Araminta, the rather strident one, scolded. "Luckily, Miss Simms said you headed this way."

"Mother sent us to fetch you!" Eustacia said, with a sidelong glance at Ashdowne that was intended to be beguiling but fell far short.

Bertrand, as usual, said nothing, having no doubt expended his meager supply of energy to search for them when he could be lounging in the Pump Room.

Georgiana, looking unrelated to any of them, glanced toward them and then back to Ashdowne, as if torn, until he nodded toward her family.

"You are obviously wanted," he said, noting the new blush that pinked her cheeks at his soft words. Despite his frustration, Ashdowne had to admire her mother, who obviously had more sense than her gregarious husband. She was a wise woman not to trust him with her daughter, and Georgiana was wise not to give herself to him.

"Well, I suppose I must go," she said, though she looked less than enthusiastic about joining her siblings.

When she leaned close as to impart some fond farewell to him, Ashdowne drew in a sharp breath.

"I was hoping we might find Mr. Jeffries and see if he had shed any new light upon the case," she confided.

Ashdowne stared at her, astounded that after what he considered a most momentous morning, all she could think about was the damned case. His pride flinched, along with the rest of him as he acknowledged his place in Georgiana's world. But she was eyeing him expectantly, so he arranged his expression accordingly.

"Meet me in the Pump Room after luncheon, and we'll see what we can do," he said. She nodded furtively, and he smiled. "Try not to get into any trouble without me," he added, touching her nose in a gesture of affection that was all he trusted himself to do.

She nodded again, and after several minutes of good-byes, Ashdowne waved as he watched the Bellewethers disappear down the hill. In the ensuing silence, he sighed, turning around to take in a view that had somehow lost its luster. Finally he moved to retrieve his cloak from the grass only to spot an errant piece of kid leather. He stooped to pick it up, rubbing the material between his fingers lovingly.

Georgiana's glove. Tucking it into his pocket, he climbed into the curricle. He would return it to her later this afternoon, he told himself, but he knew he would not. Although he had never been the sentimental sort, he was deuced if he was going to give back the glove. He frowned, once more unable to sort out any thoughts but one.

He was doomed.

It seemed to Ashdowne as if he had finally begun to concentrate upon the correspondence from his bailiff when Finn knocked, although the manservant had been told not to interrupt him. Knowing that the Irishman disapproved of the boring business that came with the marquis's title, Ashdowne suspected some manufactured emergency.

"This better be good," he muttered as he bid the majordomo enter.

"A woman to see you, milord," Finn said, his face impassive. "I put her in the drawing room, pending your instructions."

Ashdowne, who had spent entirely too much time thinking about Georgiana, didn't hesitate, but surged to his feet. He had warned her about coming to his residence, but she never heeded him. *Never.* The frustrations of this morning still simmering, he was beginning to think a lesson was in order. His jaw set, his face grim, he stalked toward the drawing room, pausing at the threshold to prevent her escape as he issued his threat.

"Bertrand had better be in there with you, or you're a dead woman," he said in a deliberately low voice. He never shouted, and he was not given to displays of temperament, but Georgiana could surely try a saint.

Only after the words had left his mouth did Ashdowne see the disarray in the room before him. Boxes and trunks littered the floor, a maid stood to one side, and the woman whose back was to him gasped and whirled around. To his horror, he saw immediately that it was not Georgiana, but a female with a taller, more slender form and dark hair.

Biting back an oath, Ashdowne recognized Anne, his dead brother's wife. She stood staring at him, brown eyes wide, lips trembling, looking for all the world as though she might faint dead away. Knowing Anne, such a fit of vapors was a distinct possibility and one which Ashdowne hurried forward to forestall.

"Anne! I beg your pardon," he said, but as soon as he took a step toward her, she stumbled backward, as if he were somehow frightening. Unfortunately, his brother's wife seemed to view the entire world as rather terrifying, and Ashdowne, despite some effort, had been unable to convince her otherwise.

"What are you doing here?" he asked, as the realization that she had undertaken a journey on her own struck him full force. Anne had never traveled until Ashdowne, weary of her continued presence at the family seat, had pushed her off to visit relatives in London—to disastrous results. Upon returning home, she had sworn never to leave again, yet here she was, appearing on his doorstep without notice.

And regretting it, apparently. "Oh, I knew that I should not have come," she whispered in her thin, reedy voice. And before Ashdowne could garner any explanation, she burst into tears and ran from the room, leaving her maid to glare at him while he frowned in annoyance.

Admittedly, since his assumption of the title, he had not been the carefree, reckless charmer of his youth, but he had never caused any other female to run, crying, from the room. Yet, this was not the first time Anne had fled his presence. At first, he had taken her mourning into consideration. Finally he had simply grown weary of her fragile sensibilities and packed her off to London—much to his later regret.

Now he knew better than to expect Anne to behave in anything but a fearful manner, and he heaved a sigh as her maid hurried after her. Instead of catching up on his correspondence, it looked as though he would have to spend the morning coddling his gentle but exasperating sister-in-law. It was one of the more onerous of his duties as marquis.

"Well?" Finn asked, appearing in the doorway.

Ashdowne shrugged and sent the Irishman a hard look. "You could have warned me," he said. Glancing at the clock, he hurried toward the stairs. He was to meet Georgiana in the Pump Room soon, and no matter what happened here, he wasn't about to be late. There was much still to be resolved between them, including the wretched investigation into Lady Culpepper's theft.

Chapter Twelve

Georgiana was trembling. She paced the confines of her room, trying to concentrate but failing abysmally. And although she had changed her gloves several times since returning home this morning, she kept staring at her quivering fingers as if the errant digits no longer belonged to her.

They belonged to Ashdowne.

And it didn't seem to matter that she had never believed in such romantic nonsense. Despite all her fierce denials, Georgiana felt giddy and warm and light inside, all the so-called symptoms of a woman who had succumbed to the sort of emotional upheaval to which her sex was prone. It didn't take someone of Georgiana's special abilities to deduce that her hands weren't the only part of her the handsome marquis had claimed.

He was perilously close to stealing her heart.

And that was a theft Georgiana had no interest whatsoever in investigating. She was a practical young woman, one who made it her business to examine all the pertinent facts, and the facts in this case pointed to only one thing: Ashdowne was a marquis and, as such, far above her reach. This absurd attraction between them could only lead to her ruin, and she must put a stop to it.

But knowing wasn't the same as doing, and Georgiana dithered and paced, undecided as to what step to take next. One moment she was determined not to meet him at the Pump Room, yet the thought of forgoing his company left her bleak. She really didn't want to see him, but, paradoxically, she couldn't wait to see him. She didn't need him...except to continue living and breathing. And worst of all, she *never* dithered! Ashdowne was turning her into a *woman,* complete with the most distasteful attributes of her gender: illogical, emotional and *romantic.*

To Georgiana's mind, ladies were essentially witless creatures who fluttered their fans and concerned themselves with flounces and new gowns and such unimportant fare. Always more interested in the male world of cogent thought, Georgiana didn't want to be like that. Why, the very notion of turning into her sisters made her cringe in horror.

And yet she couldn't shake this feeling of euphoria that had seized her. The truth was she loved being with Ashdowne. He listened to her. He made her laugh. He played her body like a finely tuned violin. With a maudlin frown, Georgiana sank down in a chair, plopped her chin in her hand and contemplated just how much being a woman appealed to her after all.

Now the face and form she had long decried seemed a blessing, a wonderful instrument of pleasure in the hands of the marquis. And that most female part of her, her heart, heedlessly held sway over her head. So, despite her formidable brainpower, her long moments of pacing and rumination were all for naught, and with a sigh of surrender, Georgiana let the errant organ lead her toward the

Pump Room for her meeting with the man who would steal it from her.

She didn't have to look for Ashdowne long, for word of his grand presence in the company reached her ears as soon as she entered the building. Georgiana knew a moment's irritation, for why could the man not be more circumspect? If only he would wear a disguise, as she had suggested! If only he were anyone other than a rich, handsome nobleman...but then he would not be Ashdowne, and her interest would undoubtedly not be engaged. Oh, fickle heart that was the downfall of her gender!

Dismayed at such feminine whimsy, Georgiana made her way through the crowd, but often paused to listen, as was her wont. This time, however, she was not too pleased by what she heard, for it was Ashdowne they were discussing at length: Ashdowne and his sister-in-law.

His *sister-in-law?* Ashdowne had said nothing of his relative's imminent arrival this morning when he had been toying with her fingers! Tugging at her glove, Georgiana realized that the opportunity for conversation may not have presented itself. But still, why had he made an appointment with her when he was engaged by his sister-in-law?

Georgiana's unease was not improved by the gossip that flitted around her. Over and over she heard turbaned matrons admire what a lovely couple they were: Ashdowne and his brother's widow! And much was made of how he might have comforted the grief-stricken woman at the family seat they shared.

It was all supposition and innuendo from disgruntled mamas and their daughters, Georgiana told herself, and certainly none of her business anyway. And yet, when she caught a glimpse of the two of them, her newly discovered heart thundered its dismay, for Ashdowne's sister-in-law was *beautiful*. Tall and slender, with dark and silky hair caught up in an elegant style, she moved with a delicacy and grace that made Georgiana feel like the worst sort of clod. The abrupt awareness of her own deficiencies only made her more clumsy, and she knocked into a chair, neatly toppling the occupant's wig.

Frantically she tried to upright the outraged gentleman's coiffure while not drawing Ashdowne's notice. Luckily for her, the marquis seemed focused solely on his lovely relative, and Georgiana watched him lean close to whisper something that drew a shy smile from the lady's lips. Georgiana's own mouth quivered perilously as she fought against the absurd urge to cry. *She never cried!*

But she had never felt this awful, wrenching envy before. Ever since engaging her assistant, Georgiana had known a possessiveness that made it nearly impossible for her to share his company with others. But her giggling sisters and the simpering Bath ladies who chased his title were one thing, while his elegant sister-in-law was something else entirely.

This woman obviously was not after his title, and she didn't giggle. Indeed, she exhibited such a serene, refined demeanor that Georgiana felt too loud, too busy, too dowdily costumed and too uncomfortable in her woman's body. And not only did this lady seemingly possess everything that Georgiana lacked, she was Ashdowne's relative! She had a past with him that Georgiana could not claim, a family tie that would never be severed.

Although she knew she should pity the poor widow and be glad that the two remaining family members could share their grief, Georgiana harbored a spiteful and petty dislike for the marchioness that made her despise her femaleness once more. This riot of inappropriate emotions that took control of her was worse than lowering. It was untenable.

And so, instead of moving toward the marquis and his lovely sister-in-law, Georgiana turned aside and headed from the room. She did not want to face them, to let Ashdowne see this horrid, twisted creature she had become, or to extend a cordial greeting to his brother's wife when she felt nothing but antipathy for the woman.

She straightened her shoulders and went looking for Mr. Jeffries. It was time she quit letting her heart do the leading and turned her attention back where it belonged: on the case. A good brainteaser was just what she needed to rid herself of these female weaknesses, and the Bow Street Runner might well have some new information. If they put their heads together, surely they could solve the theft, Georgiana told herself, without her assistant's help!

After all, she had begun her investigation without him, she mused, as she sent a note round to Mr. Jeffries's apartments. She had not even wanted to take him on, for he had been one of her suspects! She was reminded that, with Whalsey and the vicar out of the running, the only name left on her original list was that of the marquis.

The thought was a bit unsettling, Georgiana realized. But, of course, the notion of Ashdowne as the thief was too ludicrous now even to entertain, and so she simply must begin again, looking at the case with fresh eyes. As much as Georgiana hated to admit it, she was out of ideas, and Mr. Jeffries, for all that he seemed a bit slow, might well shed some light where she saw none.

She did not have long to wait, for the Bow Street Runner himself responded to her query, and Georgiana, waiting outside the Pump Room, felt cheered by the sight of the shabbily dressed investigator. She waved happily, and he nodded in greeting, his brown eyes curious as he approached.

"You sent for me, miss?" he asked.

"Yes," Georgiana said. Turning her steps toward the crescent, she gestured for him to join her. "I fear I have most discouraging news for you."

"Oh?" Jeffries asked with a look of surprise.

"Yes," Georgiana said, heaving a great sigh. "I have come to believe that Mr. Hawkins might well be innocent—of the theft, I mean," she amended hurriedly. The vicar, with all this strange propensities, could hardly be termed pure in any other sense.

"Well now, miss, I guess you're probably right about that," he said, rubbing his chin thoughtfully. "I sent someone to make inquiries at his last post, but I don't think they'll turn up anything worse than a bit of…indiscretion," he added, clearing his throat.

Georgiana nodded dispiritedly. "Well, he claims to have been in the linen closet with Mrs. Howard during the time in question, but you might want to see if you can verify it."

Jeffries looked at her with a mixture of surprise and grudging admiration. "I'll do that, miss. And I'll have someone keep an eye on him, though I honestly don't think he's got the necklace. He's a queer one, all right, but not the sort to plan such a daring theft."

"He's far too busy," Georgiana said. "Between toadying up to potential patrons and his other…activities, I don't see how he could find the time!"

Jeffries laughed. "Well, you've found some guilty fellows, miss, just not the right ones."

Georgiana frowned. "But if not the vicar, who?"

Jeffries shook his head. "That I can't tell you, miss. I don't mind saying that this one has me stumped. I've talked to all the servants, and not a one of them seems to know anything. All of them claim the fellow outside the bedroom door never left his post or dozed off. And although I have a list of all the guests, most of them are accounted for, too, except for some who would never be able to do the deed.''

"Unless someone came who was uninvited," Georgiana mused aloud.

Jeffries nodded. "And unnoticed." He paused to rub his chin again. "The locked room is a bit of a puzzle, isn't it? It almost reminds me of…" His words trailed off, and he shook his head. "No. It's been too long, and Bath's too far afield.''

Georgiana was about to ask him what he was mumbling about when she caught sight of Mr. Savonierre entering one of the finest homes in the Royal Crescent, the most elite address in Bath. She shivered, despite the warmth of the day, at the sight of the black-clad gentleman, for there was something about him she found unnerving. Remembering their conversation at the Pump Room yesterday, she turned to Jeffries.

"I believe Mr. Savonierre is becoming impatient," she commented. "Ashdowne says he is very powerful. He won't make you sorry you took the case, will he?" Although she had led a sheltered life, Georgiana knew that the wealthy often abused their authority with little regard for others. And she would feel terrible if the Bow Street Runner lost his position or was replaced.

Jeffries smiled grimly. "His black looks and acid tongue are making me sorry already, but I don't think he'll toss me on my ear just for trying to do my job. He's a strange one, but fair, I think.''

Georgiana glanced at the house Savonierre had entered, an elegant place she had heard he was making his own.

"If he's so devoted to Lady Culpepper, I'm surprised he doesn't stay with her," she mused.

"Oh, I think he did at first, but after the theft, he let his own place over there," he said, with a nod toward the tall stone facade.

Georgiana blinked, uncertain for a moment whether she had heard Jeffries correctly. "But just yesterday he said that he came *straight away* after hearing about the burglary. I thought he arrived afterward, bringing you with him," she said.

Jeffries shook his head. "Oh, no, miss. He was here that night. The servants said as much, for he locked the room right up after the theft and took charge."

Georgiana stared at the Bow Street Runner, her thoughts awhirl, her pulse pounding. "But I didn't see him at all! He never made an appearance at the ball, I'm certain of it. I wondered how he had learned of the theft so quickly. If he was there, why didn't he show himself? And why would he put it around town that he didn't arrive until after the robbery?"

Obviously sensing the direction of her thoughts, Jeffries gave her a wide-eyed look of alarm. "Oh, no, miss! Surely you're not going to accuse one of the richest, most powerful men in the country of common thievery!"

"And why not?" Georgiana asked, her excitement growing. "I find it very curious that Mr. Savonierre kept such a low profile before the theft."

Jeffries snorted loudly. "He *always* keeps a low profile, miss. That's Savonierre. They say he but whispers and the government jumps to do his bidding, that Prinny himself—"

Georgiana waved away his protests, for they were hardly pertinent to the case. Far more interesting to her was her observation that no matter what his relationship to Lady Culpepper, Savonierre was as out of place in Bath as was Ashdowne! With a sharp sensation of relief, Georgiana realized that he no longer was the sole suspect on her list as she gleefully added Savonierre. After all, the man was a perfect villain: dark, aloof, mysterious and not very nice.

Unfortunately, Jeffries had yet to be convinced. "What's a man like that want with the necklace? He's got more money than the prince himself! Why, he probably could buy a hundred emeralds, with the size of his purse, and be none the worse for the purchase," he said, dismissing her theory outright.

Georgiana glanced thoughtfully toward Mr. Savonierre's elegant home, unable to give voice to the strange feeling that tugged at her. Although she put no heed in feminine intuition, she knew that Savonierre had been in the right place at the right time under an extremely odd set of circumstances. And he was just the sort who would treat a criminal act as a game that he alone could win, while laughing at the pathetic efforts to identify him.

Her thoughts were interrupted by Jeffries, who snorted suddenly. "And why hire me? To catch himself?"

"The perfect camouflage," Georgiana murmured. "Perhaps it amuses him to watch us flounder for the truth while he remains out of reach, someone we would never suspect."

"But why?" Jeffries persisted.

"I don't know," Georgiana answered honestly. "But something tells me that there's more to this theft than mere money."

Jeffries, however, remained skeptical, and he warned her away from Savonierre in no uncertain terms. "No one's ever gone up against him, miss. He's dangerous," the Bow Street Runner muttered more than once.

"Indeed!" Georgiana replied, but her mind was already made up. She intended to prove to Mr. Jeffries and everyone else just how dangerous—and guilty—was Mr. Savonierre. Parting company with the Bow Street Runner, who was still shaking his head, she strode on alone as she contemplated her next step.

Although she refused to feel intimidated by her newest suspect's reputation, Georgiana realized that he was not cut from the same cloth as Whalsey or Hawkins. He was far too clever to admit to anything, and he was not a man one could easily follow without detection. A worthier opponent than the others, perhaps, Mr. Savonierre would nonetheless be far more difficult to apprehend.

Georgiana felt a sudden, sharp pang at the absence of her assistant but told herself she would do better alone, especially considering the enmity that existed between Ashdowne and Savonierre. She remembered all too clearly their last encounter, when those two had faced off like predators, trying to draw blood with taunts cloaked in civility. Sleek and elegant and deadly, they reminded her of nothing so much as a pair of jungle cats.

With a gasp of startlement, Georgiana halted in the middle of the walkway, heedless of the strollers who gave her a wide berth. "*The Cat!* Of course!" she murmured, blinking in stunned shock at the turn of her thoughts. All along, she had felt as if there was something about the case she was missing, some connection that wavered just out of reach. But now it came back to her with vivid clarity. Lady Culpepper's robbery reminded her of another, not here in Bath, but in London—and more than one.

An avid follower of the cases of the Bow Street Runners and professional thief takers, Georgiana read as much as she could about the crimes that plagued the city and the men who solved them. And one of the most notorious burglars of recent years had been The Cat.

No one knew his real identity, of course, because he had never been caught. They simply dubbed him The Cat because of his ability to get in and out of his victims' homes with ease, disappearing without a trace through locked doors, and...open windows! Lady Culpepper's seemingly impossible crime was just the sort of thing that had once been attributed to the daring criminal.

And the open jewel case! That, too, was typical of The Cat. One of the reasons for his popularity in the newspapers was his odd penchant for discriminating choices. He usually never took more than one item of jewelry, albeit a very expensive one, but oftentimes he had left a case or box, the rest of its contents within plain view, as if to taunt the authorities—or his victims.

He preyed only upon the very wealthy, whose losses would be as nothing, and he never took too much. That apparent lack of greed, along with his stealth and daring, had captured the imagination of Londoners. It was speculated that he was one of the elite, of course, for how else could he gain entrance to so many exclusive homes and balls? Indeed, he stole only the most exquisite of gems, usually during a house party or rout of some sort, disappearing without a trace, only to strike again days, weeks or months later. Even many members of the ton seemed amused by his antics, as long as he had not robbed them.

Georgiana had read the details of the various cases avidly, certain that if only she had access to such social circles, she could find the rogue. But she had been stuck in the country, her only contact the papers that her uncle saved for her, often weeks old by the time she read them. She had never been to London, had never moved among the ton, and The Cat had never been caught.

Georgiana tried to remember exactly when the news had dwindled, but certainly the last robbery had been committed more than a year ago. Months had gone by without a case that could be attributed to The Cat, and eventually the interest of the public shifted elsewhere. The newspapers speculated that he had been caught for some other crime and executed without fanfare, or that he had been killed, perhaps by some denizen of the criminal world.

Maybe, Georgiana mused, he had simply been changing his location. She knew that beyond the immediate environs of London, the country was in the dubious hands of sheriffs and local magistrates, many of whom were ill suited for their jobs. Some were dishonest, some simply unprepared and most hampered by lack of money and staff. And very little communication occurred between the various authorities.

Had The Cat spent the past year in rural environs, lifting a priceless piece of jewelry here and there from the lavish homes of the aristocracy? If so, it would remain a local matter unless someone called in Bow Street, a rare occurrence. And the city's journalists, Georgiana's best source of information, would probably not hear of it, either.

Perhaps London had become too confining or precarious a place after so much publicity and so The Cat had moved on, traveling between house parties and places like Brighton, where the fashionable liked to retire. But why Bath? Surely the pickings here weren't as good, Georgiana mused. Then again, the Culpepper emeralds were quite famous. Perhaps The Cat had a yen for them that went beyond their face value.

Sinking down upon a low wall, Georgiana contemplated the evidence. Although she suspected the untrustworthy press of exaggerating some of The Cat's misdeeds, she knew that the man she sought must be extremely agile and far more clever than even she had calculated. Mr. Cheever and the vicar, her first two suspects, were not intelligent enough to have carved such a career. Nor would they move in the kind of circles where The Cat had been known to strike.

But not so her third suspect, Savonierre.

Georgiana blinked, a hot flush of excitement staining her cheeks. He would fit into the most elegant and elite company, a man wealthy in his own right, whom none would suspect of such nefarious dealings! Why would he do it? Because he thrived on danger and secretly despised his titled connections, Georgiana decided. What better way to show his contempt without severing his ties to them?

Surging to her feet, Georgiana knew that this time she had the real culprit! Only, how was she to prove it? She realized that she must place Savonierre at the scene of not just this robbery but the other thefts, as well. And to do that, she needed to discover his movements a year ago and earlier, especially during the height of The Cat's infamy.

She could ask his servants, of course, but she was not prepared to rouse any suspicion at this point. Nor did she want the intimidating gentleman to discover her interest. No, she needed to track his movements without his knowledge, Georgiana mused, and the place to begin was in the very newspapers where she had first learned of The Cat's existence.

With a smile of triumph, Georgiana hurried toward home, for she knew just where to get them!

It took some convincing, but Georgiana finally managed to pry permission from her parents for a visit to her great-uncle. She suspected that her mother's general disapproval of Silas Morcombe was overcome by an eagerness to separate her eldest daughter from a certain marquis, which was fine with Georgiana. And so she had only to bribe Bertrand to go with her, which she managed to do by handing over her pin money. She never used it for the fripperies intended, anyway, and thought it far better spent on a case than a trip to the milliner's.

A coach was hired, and although Georgiana spent the rest of the day inside the stifling equipage, the journey passed far more quickly from Bath than from her country home, and the travelers were greeted with much enthusiasm by Silas by nightfall.

It wasn't until after a late supper, with Bertrand nodding in a comfortable chair, much in the manner of her father, that Georgiana was at last able to confide in her great-uncle the nature of her visit.

"I need to go through your newspapers," she said as he moved about the cozy room, piled high with books and papers of all sorts, searching for his glasses. "They are upon your head, Uncle," Georgiana said.

"Ah, yes, of course," he said, pushing the spectacles over his eyes and sinking into a worn but well-padded seat. "Now, where were we?"

"Your newspapers," Georgiana reminded him.

"Ah, of course, of course," he said, smiling. "Well, they are all there in the attic, years of the *Morning Post,* the *Times* and the *Gazette,* but you had better wait until morning to examine them. Looking for anything in particular?" he asked, giving her a sly glance.

"Yes," Georgiana answered. "I am working upon a new case."

"I thought as much," her uncle replied.

"It might even have been mentioned in the papers. Lady Culpepper's famous emerald necklace was stolen, and I was right there! Naturally, this is my most important investigation. I am counting upon it to assure my success."

Morcombe frowned, muttering to himself absently at her mention of the victim. "Culpepper. Culpepper. Ah, yes. I've heard of her. Not at all the thing, as your mother would say." Although he didn't move in the highest circles, Silas always knew a bit about everyone.

"Well, I admit she is rather high in the instep, but that is hardly unusual where the ton is concerned," Georgiana said.

"No, that's not it. The trouble's gambling, m'girl, and it's done in better people than Lady Culpepper," Silas said.

"Oh! You mean she's been losing her fortune at the tables?" Georgiana asked, surprised. She remembered the vicar's accusation that the emeralds had never been stolen at all, but broken up and sold by their owner. Although she had dismissed the possibility, it seemed to keep returning like a bad penny.

"I don't think there's any chance of her going to debtor's prison, but she is an inveterate gamester and there have been rumors of the worst kind surrounding her play," Silas explained.

Georgiana blinked at him aghast. "You mean, she...cheats?"

Silas chuckled at Georgiana's expression of horror. "I certainly can't vouch for the truth of it, but that's what I've heard. And it's a fact that she seems to win large sums quite frequently, especially from green young women who could not be expected to tell if she palmed a card or two."

"Oh! But that is too bad of her!" Georgiana said, and she wondered if this information could impact upon the case. Apparently Lady Culpepper was unscrupulous, at least when gambling. Would she go so far as to steal her own necklace? But what of Savonierre? What was his role? And The Cat? Having just discovered the connection between the Bath robbery and the notorious thief, Georgiana was not willing to give it up so easily.

"Perhaps one of the young ladies decided to get back some of her own by stealing the necklace," Silas suggested.

"Perhaps," Georgiana admitted reluctantly. But she really could not imagine any female of the ton accomplishing the daring theft, particularly someone who could not tell when their opponent was cheating at cards.

Resting her chin in her hand, Georgiana blew out a breath, dislodging one fat curl from its place over her eye. "The case is certainly turning out to be a lot more complicated than I originally thought," she said glumly.

Silas smiled. "All the more challenge for you, dear," he said as he reached for his pipe.

"Yes," Georgiana murmured, for Silas was right. She had long desired a test of her intellect, and at last she had found it, though she might have wished for a nemesis other than the rather frightening Savonierre. Somehow, she had felt an odd sort of kinship and admiration for the thief, which had not transferred well to any of her suspects, she realized with a frown.

It was rather disappointing, but one hardly had a choice when dealing with criminals. And Georgiana knew she had to focus on the eventual rewards that might result from her efforts. All during the long ride in the coach, she had imagined her success. If other thoughts, most notably about a certain marquis intruded, she pushed them aside, intent upon not only solving this case, but others, as well. Just imagine, if she should unmask The Cat!

Tomorrow she would look through the papers and gather more information, Georgiana resolved. And if it led to the identity of the famous burglar, all well and good. For now, however, she felt the effects of a long day, much of it spent in travel, and various bits and pieces of evidence whirled together in her mind, leaving her more confused than ever.

"It is all very curious," she murmured. "Very curious, indeed."

Chapter Thirteen

Despite her new surroundings, Georgiana found that Ashdowne was not easily dismissed from her thoughts. Even asleep she could not escape him, for she spent the night dreaming of him—heated, yearning visions, intermixed with odd nightmares in which both he and Savonierre turned into beasts—that left her cranky and out of sorts.

Finally abandoning all hope of rest, Georgiana headed toward the attic, where she spent a fruitful day going over the old stacks of newspapers. Of course, interesting items were always catching her attention, but she tried to limit herself to Savonierre's movements. They were not hard to find, for he was a favorite with the gossips.

"'Mr. Savonierre hosted an elegant and well-received rout last night,'" Georgiana read aloud. She made a note of the date, ignoring the details about the food served and the various luminaries in attendance. Then she picked up the next paper.

"A certain wealthy and renowned Mr. S—was seen squiring a very married Lady B—to the opera last night," another story reported without mentioning names outright. Indeed, most of the articles pertained not to Savonierre's alleged influence in government circles, but his penchant for attractive companions. Georgiana frowned in disapproval.

But Savonierre wasn't the only one whose dalliances made the newspapers. "The younger brother of the Marquis of A—continues to cut a swath through town. Last night alone, he was seen at no less than four entertainments," read one account. And although she told herself that she didn't care, Georgiana felt her stomach twist in response.

"Johnathon Everett Saxton, younger brother of the Marquis of Ashdowne, was seen at Lord Graham's ball, surrounded by ladies. His wit and charm are well-known to make him a favorite," Georgiana read. Although she tried to ignore the frequent mentions of Ashdowne when he was only a younger brother, his name kept cropping up in the pages, leaping before her eyes as if through no will of her own. Unfortunately, it seemed as though he and Savonierre kept much the same schedules, which was not unusual, considering that they were both members of the most elite circles.

Still, his continued appearance made her oddly apprehensive. If she didn't know better, she might have imagined *him* to be The Cat, Georgiana thought, laughing uneasily. Although she pushed her feelings for Ashdowne into some hidden place inside her where she didn't have to examine them too closely, she couldn't help making note of his movements.

Meanwhile, she made a chart of Savonierre's locations, so that she could more easily track his presence, along with a list of where and when The Cat had struck. Interestingly enough, the thief had never stolen anything from Savonierre, a small piece of information that appeared to confirm Georgiana's suspicions.

Originally she had thought only to study those newspapers from the years when The Cat's infamy was at its zenith, but once begun, Georgiana's task held her attention into a second and even a third day of scrutiny. In the more recent editions, she looked for any mention of a crime outside the city that resembled The Cat's methods, but found nothing at all. It was as if the master thief had disappeared from the face of the earth.

Unfortunately, her concentration was broken every so often by a bored Bertrand demanding that they return to Bath, but Georgiana refused to heed him. "Go away!" she called, diving back into her newspapers. As much as she hated to admit it, she found the vast lines of printed words comforting, for there were few nuances to be found among the bald statements. Facts were her forte, and far easier to deal with than people.

However, Bertrand must have finally enlisted her great-uncle against her, for the older gentleman bestirred himself to bring her a luncheon tray on the third day of her seclusion. Pushing aside a great heap of papers, he sat himself down to face her, and Georgiana was forced to put aside her work.

"Are you finding what you sought?" Silas asked, taking off his spectacles to clean the lenses with the end of his coat.

"Yes," Georgiana answered. "I have lists and charts, and it looks, from a cursory examination at least, as if my suspicions were correct. I can't tell you what a help it has been to be able to sort through your collection," she added, genuinely grateful.

"I'm glad they have been of use to someone," he said with a small smile as he returned his glasses to his face. The eyes behind them were fraught with intelligence as he examined her, and Georgiana felt oddly uncomfortable under his gaze, like an errant student who had disappointed his teacher.

Finally, as if he had seen all that he must, Silas leaned back against the wooden boards behind him and surveyed his cluttered attic. "Bertrand is growing impatient," he said.

"I know. As if I could *not* know when he comes up here banging on the door every other hour!" Georgiana complained. "Although I intended only to look at the older papers, I've been searching for some reference to the thief's whereabouts in recent months, which is taking longer, naturally," she explained.

"Is it?" her uncle asked, and Georgiana found herself flushing. "If you are researching your case, you are welcome to stay here as long as you wish, my dear. But if you are simply burying yourself in my attic, hiding away from other things that are not so easily examined—"

"What tales has Bertrand been telling you?" Georgiana demanded, blushing. If her continued presence here was more palatable than a return to Bath and all the attendant folly there, then who could blame her for lingering? Somehow the urgency that had once pressed her to finish the case no longer drove her as forcefully, and her once-clear purpose was all mixed up with thoughts of the man who had begun to overshadow the investigation itself.

"He mentioned a certain marquis," Silas said gently.

"My assistant!" Georgiana protested. "Ashdowne is my assistant, nothing more." Glancing away from her uncle's penetrating look, she picked up a paper and stared at it unseeing. Leave it to Silas to suddenly emerge from his scholar's daze to query her when she least expected— or desired—such concern!

"Very well, then. But would you take a bit of advice from an old man?"

"Of course," Georgiana said, feeling like a churl after all her great-uncle had done for her.

"Good," he said with a gentle smile. "Don't make the same mistake that I did and become so immersed in your studies and projects that you forget about people."

When Georgiana looked at him blankly, he laughed softly. "I've had a good life, and I've enjoyed it, but your grandfather made the better choice. He had Lucinda and your mother and the grandchildren..." Silas trailed off with a wistful expression that surprised Georgiana.

"But they're all so silly!" she protested.

Silas laughed again. "Ah, but family is family, no matter how silly, and a joy to an old man. If you bury your nose in books or newspapers or cases, you miss out on a lot of life," he cautioned. "You're a beautiful girl, Georgiana, and I wouldn't want you to end up like me, all alone." With that, he rose to his feet and headed toward the door. "I'll leave you to your research, for now," he said.

Georgiana stared after him, dumbfounded. She had certainly never thought Silas envious of her grandfather, especially since her grandfather had always complained about the children underfoot when they visited. She shook her head, rustling the paper in her lap. People were so difficult to understand, it was no wonder that she preferred hard facts.

That errant thought led, rather circuitously to Ashdowne, and Georgiana felt a pang of guilt for not being totally honest with her uncle. Ashdowne was more than just her assistant, but what? That was the question she had been trying to avoid, yet as if her very thoughts conjured his name, Georgiana focused on the page in front of her, where the marquis himself was mentioned.

"A certain Lady C——, well-known for her expertise in

the card room, won a shocking amount of money from the marchioness of Ashdowne at Lady Somerset's ball last evening. Her brother-in-law is presumed to stand good her vowels, while the young woman has left town the wiser.''

"Uncle! Listen to this!'' she called, reading the report aloud to him as he stood in the doorway.

"Hmm. It appears that your assistant is well acquainted with Lady Culpepper's rather dubious reputation.''

"Odd. He never said a thing about it,'' Georgiana mused. He had never mentioned his sister-in-law, either, she thought with a frown. Would Ashdowne find it galling to pay a debt he had not incurred, especially when the lady in question was rumored to cheat at cards? Yet such losses were not uncommon, and perhaps the marquis would not notice even a "shocking" sum.

Georgiana fought against an oddly unsettled feeling, as if there was much more to be resolved between Ashdowne and herself than she had ever considered, and she knew a sudden urge to hear his comments on the matter. Instead of solving the case to her satisfaction, her days of study left her with a sense of unfinished business. But it was clear to her that staying here amid the old papers would see her no closer to the completion of her investigation. And it was time to quit hiding from herself.

"Wait for me, Uncle! I'm coming,'' she called over her shoulder as she gathered up her lists and charts. She would need every bit of evidence to convince Mr. Jeffries that Savonierre was not only the thief, but The Cat himself. And she clung to her theory with a ferocity driven by desperation. It had to be Savonierre, Georgiana thought.

Anyone but Ashdowne.

Mindful of her uncle's warning, Georgiana greeted her family with new enthusiasm, even though her sisters' giggles grated upon her and she could hardly bear her father's good-natured teasing. According to him, a certain marquis had been quite put out at her sudden departure from Bath, having called upon her more than once while she was gone. At this news, Georgiana was torn between elation and disbelief, for if Ashdowne was busy with his beautiful sister-in-law, why would he notice she was missing?

But he had noted her absence, for it wasn't long after her return that he arrived to invite her to walk with him. Although outwardly as elegant and composed as always, Ashdowne was not himself, for Georgiana sensed something simmering beneath the surface of his polite expression, a tension that she had never seen in him before. Had he discovered some important clue while she was away? Or was this a final goodbye before he returned home with his sister-in-law?

Georgiana eyed him with some anxiety as they engaged in mindless conversation with her family, anticipation and dread warring within her. When at last they managed to escape her sisters, with her father's rather obvious assistance, Georgiana wasn't certain she wanted to be alone with her erstwhile assistant.

For a long while they walked in silence, making Georgiana wonder why he had called upon her. She was trying to gather her thoughts to say something—anything—when he finally spoke. "You might have told me you were leaving Bath," he said, his harsh tone making the words sound like an accusation, and Georgiana blinked in surprise.

"I wanted to do some research at my great-uncle's house," she explained.

"The one who cannot be trusted to squire you about London?" Ashdowne questioned sharply.

"Well, yes, but we didn't even leave the house. I spent the whole time going over old newspapers."

"Old newspapers?" Ashdowne's voice revealed his skepticism, and Georgiana was forced to stop and face him.

"Yes, old newspapers. What on earth has gotten into you?"

Far from showing chagrin at his behavior, Ashdowne's dark brows lowered and his gorgeous mouth thinned. "I suppose I assumed I might be notified of your movements. As I recall, we were to meet in the Pump Room three days ago, but you never appeared. Did you consider that I might be worried about you?"

Georgiana colored, remembering her cowardice upon seeing him with his lovely relative. "Well, I...I didn't really think you would notice," she mumbled.

His dark brow shot up. "You didn't think I would notice." He spoke the words in a deathly calm manner, but Georgiana had the growing suspicion that he was angry, perhaps even furious. And she had once wondered what would incite him? Apparently, her failure to appear had loosed a temper she was unaware he possessed.

"I beg your pardon. I should have told you I was leaving, but the idea came upon me quite suddenly, you see," she said, which was true. "I had the most amazing revelation about the case!"

Although she would not have thought it possible, his expression grew even more black. "The case!"

"Why, yes. It's most thrilling, and I suppose I should have notified you at once, since you are my assistant—"

"Your assistant," he echoed, his eyes glittering with a virulence Georgiana could not comprehend.

"Why, yes," she said, unprepared for the raw emotion that seemed to emanate from him. Accustomed to dealing with facts and logic, she had only just begun to recognize her own feelings and was at a loss to understand Ashdowne's sudden ferocity.

"Well, maybe I want to be more than your damned assistant. Maybe I'd like to be a man, for a change. Maybe..." Ashdowne turned away and threw up his hands. "Oh, hell. I don't even know what I want. Since meeting you, I can't think clearly!"

Georgiana blinked at his vehemence, though she shared the sentiment. But what did he mean about being a man? Wasn't he going to aid her any longer? Taking him literally, she voiced her concern in tremulous accents. "Don't you want to be my assistant?"

Ashdowne stared at her as if she had grown two heads, and then, as was his wont, he burst out laughing. "Lud, Georgiana, I don't know whether to strangle you or drag you off to bed, but I've missed you."

Georgiana's heart swelled at his words, along with other parts of her body that took special note of his threat *to drag her off to his bed?* He stepped close, and Georgiana eyed him warily, mindful that they stood in full view of passersby. "Oh, Ashdowne, you shouldn't say such things," she murmured.

"Why not?" he asked, as he took her trembling fingers and placed them on his arm, leading her forward once more.

Because they make me want things I can't have, Georgiana thought ruefully. "Because I can't think when you do," she said instead.

"And I can?" Ashdowne asked, lifting one dark brow.

"Of course, you can. I haven't done or said anything to disturb you," Georgiana protested in bewilderment.

"You don't have to," he muttered. "All you have to do is stand there and breathe."

"Well, it seems we are in a quandary," Georgiana said.

Although oddly affected by his admission, she had no idea what he intended to accomplish with it. Like herself, he did not seem entirely at ease with her influence upon him.

"I see only one solution," Ashdowne said, frowning as if considering something distasteful. "One way to assure that, in the future, you do not hare off to your uncle's without telling me."

"Now just a moment," Georgiana protested. "I did not hare off. I was studying the case." Disliking the scowl he wore and the words he used, she suddenly realized that he had not inquired at all about the investigation, and she lifted her chin. "Just in case you're wondering, I made quite a breakthrough."

"Really?" Ashdowne asked dryly, his tone reflecting frustration rather than enthusiasm.

"Yes, really. Of course, if you have no interest in the case any longer—" Georgiana began, only to be cut off by her companion, who halted his steps.

"Very well. Go ahead and impart this amazing discovery of yours before you burst," he said.

With a smile, Georgiana leaned close to impart the information she had shared with no one. "I believe our thief is none other than The Cat!" she whispered, only to draw back in surprise.

Ashdowne, who so rarely revealed himself, gave her a startled look that bordered on horror.

"You *have* heard of The Cat?" Georgiana asked, puzzled.

"Of course, I've heard of The Cat," Ashdowne said harshly. "But—"

"Then you must realize that his methods are exactly the same as those used in Lady Culpepper's robbery," Georgiana said.

"I hardly think—"

Georgiana, thrilled to be expounding her discoveries, didn't let him finish. "He was never caught, you know, and I am convinced that he was but biding his time in the country, waiting to strike in a new location. And that location is Bath!" she concluded with a flourish. Breathlessly she waited for Ashdowne to wax eloquent over her cleverness, or at least evince his approval.

Contrary to Georgiana's expectations, Ashdowne did not appear impressed. In fact, the elegant marquis scrubbed at his face with one gloved hand as if trying to awaken from a nightmare.

"Georgiana, you really don't imagine Mr. Hawkins to be The Cat?" he asked her, his exasperation apparent.

"Oh, no!" she said. "I've found an even better suspect in Mr. Savonierre!" Georgiana explained triumphantly.

Unfortunately, Ashdowne didn't share her enthusiasm. He stared at her, all expression leaving his face as it went rigid. "No." He shook his head. "No, Georgiana. This has gone far enough."

"Whatever do you mean?" she asked, disappointed that he was not excited about her deductions. After all, it was not as though Mr. Jeffries had recognized the similarities between this case and those of The Cat. She alone had made the connection, and she wouldn't mind receiving a pat on the back for her trouble. Instead, Ashdowne was glaring at her.

"It was bad enough when you were chasing after Whalsey and Cheever and that misguided vicar, but Savonierre is dangerous. You have to stop this nonsense right now," he said, his generous mouth carved into a hard line.

"Nonsense?" *Had he said "nonsense"?* Was that really how he viewed her investigation? "What do you mean?" she demanded. "You asked me to take you on as my assistant, so I thought you were different from other

men. Do not tell me that you are the same sort of condescending, overbearing male as the rest of your gender!''

"No, I'm not. I admire you, Georgiana. I do, but I think
you are too clever for your own good. You cannot accuse
the most powerful man in the country of pilfering jewelry!'' Ashdowne said with a determined look that only
outraged her further.

"And why not? I tell you that I spent days tracking his
movements in old newspapers, and he was in the right
place at the right time.''

"Georgiana, that means nothing,'' Ashdowne said.
"I'm sure there are a dozen members of the ton who
attend the very same functions.''

"Actually, no,'' Georgiana said, coming perilously
close to losing her temper. Did he think she was stupid?
"In fact, I noticed only two people who seemed to be
where The Cat appeared most of the time. One was Mr.
Savonierre, and the other was *you*.''

Ashdowne stared at her hard for a long moment before
shrugging carelessly. "It is gratifying to know that my
movements are followed with such enthusiasm by the
newspapers. However, you should not believe everything
you read,'' he said in a dismissive tone. Before her eyes,
he had seemingly transformed, turning back into the Ashdowne she had first met, aloof and forbidding.

"My dear girl, you are clever, but worldly unwise,'' he
added, his voice dripping with a contempt that belittled
all of her skills in one breath. *Dear girl?* What happened
to *Georgiana, my sweet?* she wondered, remembering
with flaming cheeks the endearments he had once whispered to her.

"I really wouldn't put too much stock in coincidental
appearances reported by unreliable gossips,'' he advised
her in an arrogant fashion that made her want to smack

his handsome face. "As for The Cat, he's gone. Probably dead and buried, murdered in the act of thieving some trinket." He paused to lift one dark brow. "Unless you know differently?"

"Of course, I can't prove that he still lives, but neither can you convince me that he's dead," Georgiana said. She suddenly had the odd notion that she would know if so worthy an opponent no longer lived, and she rejected Ashdowne's theory as easily as he had her own. Pausing to try to order her thoughts, she glanced up at him only to gape in total bafflement. "What is the matter with you?"

"I suppose I don't like being accused of being a common thief," he answered smoothly.

"The Cat is hardly a common cutpurse, and I'm not accusing you," Georgiana said. "I told you that I think Savonierre is the guilty one."

Far from appearing mollified, Ashdowne's face grew even harder. "And I told you to leave him out of this," he said, reaching out to grip her shoulder in a harsh grasp that made her gasp. "If you have to persist in this mystery solving, then find someone harmless with whom to play out your delusions. But stay away from Savonierre."

Delusions? Shaking off the touch she had once longed for, that had once left her a dim-witted foil to his attentions, Georgiana tossed her curls. "You have no right to order me about!"

"Oh, don't I?" Ashdowne demanded. Although he still wore the cool facade of the marquis, Georgiana caught a glimpse of the turmoil that lurked behind those startling blue eyes, and she could only stare at him, baffled by the changes in his demeanor. They were both so caught up in each other that neither one heard footsteps approach until it was too late.

"My, my, Ashdowne. Are you aware that you're in

public? I don't know what you're about, but it certainly appears to the casual onlooker that you're intimidating a lady. I hesitate to interfere, but my gentlemanly honor requires that I intervene. Is there anything I can do, Miss Bellewether?''

Georgiana was so overwrought that it took her a moment to realize that her prime suspect stood before her, tendering his services. "Mr. Savonierre! You're just the man I wanted to see!" she blurted out.

His lips curved slightly. "What a fortuitous coincidence. Shall we walk together, then?" he asked, holding out his arm to her.

Georgiana was so put out with her assistant that she nodded, thoroughly enjoying the expression of outrage on Ashdowne's face that was quickly masked. Let him stew! He had no business telling her what she could do and treating her so poorly. She was sadly disappointed in him, as well as hurt by his behavior.

"Actually, Miss Bellewether and I were having a private conversation," Ashdowne said, stepping forward as if to block their path.

Savonierre gave him a look of arch incredulity. Staring pointedly at the body that halted their progress, he made it clear that Ashdowne's manners appalled him. "It appears that your conversation is over. Am I right, Miss Bellewether?"

"Yes," Georgiana answered softly. She had nothing further to say to Ashdowne until he calmed down and began acting like himself. Although something flickered in his eyes at her breathless reply, she lifted her chin and turned back to Savonierre.

"Well, then, if you will excuse us, Ashdowne?" For a long moment, Georgiana thought that the marquis wasn't going to move, that he might actually come to blows with

Savonierre, and she immediately regretted her stance, but ever so slowly, with an insolence that astounded her, Ashdowne moved aside and bowed slightly, his gaze touching hers in mute accusation.

Although he was most certainly the villain in what had passed between them, Georgiana felt like crying. Instead, she tossed her curls and walked past him without a backward glance, determined to turn her thoughts back to the case and away from such messy things as the feelings that Ashdowne invoked in her.

"Actually, I can't count it a coincidence that I chanced upon you, for I was searching for you." Savonierre's silky tones made Georgiana start, and she looked up at the man she had so blithely joined. His words were vaguely alarming, and though she tried not to show it, she sensed his awareness.

"I was wondering if you've learned anything new about Lady Culpepper's robbery," he explained, his lips curling slightly, as if he were amused by her wariness.

Only that you're responsible, Georgiana thought, stifling an inappropriate giggle that rose in her throat. She shook her head, unwilling to lie outright, and tried to marshal her thoughts.

Savonierre was like Ashdowne in many ways, tall and dark and handsome, and with an innate sense of power that she supposed came with enormous wealth and noble relations. But there was a calculation in Savonierre that was not evident in Ashdowne, even at his worst. Ashdowne could be dangerous, she knew, for she felt it whenever his body tensed, as if every bit of him was alert and ready to pounce. But Savonierre oozed danger all the time, even in the most simple and innocent of situations, as if beneath that polished exterior lurked a primal animal searching for prey.

Perhaps it was the threatening posture that had made Georgiana uncomfortable in his presence long before she had laid the theft at his door. Or perhaps it was his intensity. Although Savonierre had never gaped at her bosom, Georgiana had the odd sensation that he could see beneath her clothes. His dark gaze was simply too piercing. Or perhaps it was his detachment. He was ever smooth, going through the motions of polite society when she had a notion that it meant nothing to him. Indeed, what would he care about? she wondered.

As if aware not only of her scrutiny but every thought in her head, Savonierre slowly turned toward her, a slight smile on his hard mouth. Georgiana's palms began to sweat inside her gloves and she struggled to open her fan, her heart thumping out a warning. She had always taken the burglary very seriously, but now she felt its gravity in a way that she had never known when pursuing Whalsey or Hawkins. At last she spread her fan, and although she had never learned the intricacies of flirting with it, now she was heartily glad of the breeze it sent across her flaming cheeks.

"I take it the investigation is at a standstill, then?" Savonierre asked, smoothly persistent.

Georgiana stammered a reply as she tried to concentrate. Unfortunately, her mind, ever distracted by Ashdowne, kept harking back to their row instead of staying put on the case. Angrily determined not to waste this opportunity mooning over her assistant like some lovesick fool, she at last managed to come up with an idea. If only she could think of some way to turn the tables on Savonierre...

"Unless you know something that I don't?" Georgiana asked, hoping to blame her shaky voice on the rough walkway as they turned toward the stone bridge that curved over the river.

Savonierre slanted her a questioning glance under his dark lashes, but Georgiana said no more. "Perhaps a visit to the scene might help," he suggested. "In truth, I was seeking you out to invite you to a small rout Lady Culpepper is holding this evening. I was hoping that I might escort you and then perhaps we could discuss the theft in more detail."

Savonierre acted as though the public streets did not provide enough privacy for such speech, and his attitude made her wary. But Georgiana could not deny a desire to see the house once more, especially with Savonierre giving her entrée. Perhaps she could even speak to the servants, she mused, as they strolled onto the bridge. "That would be lovely, thank you,"

"Very good. I will look forward to seeing you there, then," he said, his considerable strength tugging her toward him as they neared the center of the stone span. Uncomfortable with such closeness, Georgiana tried to put more distance between them, but Savonierre held firm. Finally she managed to pull from his grasp, only to have the sudden movement throw her off balance. Wildly she flung out her arms and tried to regain her footing, but she seemed destined to fall headfirst into the river below until a strong hand pulled her back from the railing.

"Don't get too close to the edge," Savonierre warned her in a harsh voice, and Georgiana shook her head blindly. Had the man tried to push her off the bridge, or was he simply threatening her with that possibility? Like a cornered animal, she had to fight the urge to surrender all, blurting out her theories and apologizing for them before fleeing for her life.

It was only when she managed to finally look at her

companion that Georgiana realized he was just as shaken as she was, if not more so. For once, the wealthy and powerful Savonierre appeared to have lost his poise. His face was white as a sheet, his mouth turned down as he took quick, shallow breaths, and Georgiana stared at him in amazement.

"I fear you've discovered my weakness," he said as he visibly recovered himself, his expression once more one of cool detachment. "I have no love of heights," he said curtly, replacing her hand upon his arm and leading them toward the shore.

Georgiana stumbled along beside him, her mind awhirl. The Cat afraid of heights? But that was impossible! He was known for his daring and agility! Georgiana wanted to argue with him, and her mixed feelings must have shown, for he turned his attention toward her, his dark gaze ominous.

"I trust that I can be assured of your confidence in this matter," he said in a silky yet menacing voice. "I would hate to have to take action against so lovely a young lady," he added, the threat implicit.

Georgiana nodded numbly, unsure whether to believe his confession or not. Savonierre was just clever enough to fabricate the falsehood in order to throw her off the track, but that would mean he knew she was aware of his identity. And how could he know? Fervently Georgiana wished that Ashdowne was not behaving so oddly, for she could well use his input.

The thought made her pause in horror, for if Savonierre really was afraid of heights, then she was left with but one man among her list of suspects: Ashdowne.

Chapter Fourteen

Georgiana stood in the Pump Room, fidgeting with her fan while Bertrand lounged nearby. Normally she would be listening eagerly to the elegantly dressed ladies in their evening gowns and the gentlemen who danced attendance upon them. But tonight she was fidgeting, her impending meeting with Savonierre uppermost in her mind.

She had spent the few hours since their parting trying to frame some questions for her chief suspect, but it was a most challenging task. Perhaps it would be best to begin with the subject of his arrival in Bath and his whereabouts during the theft, she mused, wondering how to query him without being too obvious. She frowned in concentration only to blink at the sight of Ashdowne ahead of her in the crowd, striding purposefully in her direction.

Georgiana glanced about helplessly for some way to avoid a confrontation with him, but the only person in the vicinity was Bertrand, who would be no help. Although she was not usually a coward, she had quite enough to think about without entering into another argument with her assistant. *If he even was her assistant.* After his behavior this afternoon when he had forbidden her to work on her own case, Georgiana certainly did not consider him worthy of the position. To say nothing of the heartache that she was steadfastly trying to ignore.

Georgiana's dismay grew when she caught sight of the grim expression he wore as he heedlessly brushed past matrons and their daughters, and she felt a frisson of unease dance up her spine. Wishing to avoid another display of his baffling wrath, she turned abruptly toward Bertrand, but she had barely opened her mouth to engage him in conversation when Ashdowne stepped between them.

"Excuse me, but I'd like to speak with your sister," Ashdowne said, in a preemptory manner that left Georgiana gaping. She had half a mind to refuse him an audience, but the look in his eye held a warning that made her reconsider.

"Yes, what is it?" she asked as he crowded her against the wall. He really could be quite intimidating, and it took all of Georgiana's will to lift her chin to meet his gaze. When she did, her first thought was that he did not look well. He looked…distracted. Harried. Unhappy. And Georgiana felt her earlier disapprobation melt away. Instead of sparring with him, she wanted to lift a hand to his face and smooth away the lines that formed there.

"I'm sorry," he said. So soft and gruffly did he speak that Georgiana hardly heard him.

"What?"

"I apologize," he said, louder this time. "I realize that I sounded rather curt earlier today, but I'm just trying to protect you, Georgiana. I'm your keeper, remember? It's my job." He sounded so sincere that she smiled. He'd always been autocratic, with a tendency to order her about; it was undoubtedly a flaw in his character. But he was still the most wonderful man she had ever met, and she felt that old, familiar weakening in his presence.

"What about the case?" she asked before her wits began their usual defection.

Ashdowne drew a deep breath, as if steadying himself. "We'll work something out," he said.

Georgiana's resultant euphoria at his gentle assurance lasted a full minute—until she saw his sister-in-law gracefully moving through the crowd. "And what of your sister-in-law?" she asked, scowling at the beautiful woman. "It's bad enough that I must stand and watch every mama with an eligible daughter foist them upon you, but I don't care to watch you dote upon her, too!"

As Ashdowne stared at her with a dumbfounded expression, Georgiana flushed. "All right. I admit it. I'm jealous, which is an entirely feminine trait that I loathe, but if I am to place myself under your protection, then I should be entitled to your full attention, and...well, they've got you practically marrying the woman!"

"Anne?" Ashdowne gave her an incredulous look and then burst out laughing. "I can't imagine a more horrifying prospect!" he said between gasps for breath. And although Georgiana could have wished for more circumspect behavior in the Pump Room, she was so thrilled by his denial and so pleased to see him laughing again that she could hardly fault his outburst.

"Anne is the most tedious creature imaginable, and though I know my duty toward her, the poor woman gives me hives. I have yet to discover how she managed to travel here, for she is the most timid of females. She appears to have some reason for her abrupt arrival, but every time I think to pry it out of her, she either bursts into tears or runs away like a frightened hare. Perhaps *you* could find out for me," Ashdowne suggested. "It is just the sort of mystery at which you excel."

At his warm words of praise, Georgiana felt something

shift inside her, something that made her want to weep, not with sorrow, but with joy, something that made her very glad to be a woman, after all. It must have shown upon her face, for Ashdowne's expression softened, and for one terrifying moment, she feared he might kiss her then and there—in full view of all those around them.

Instead, he touched the tip of her nose. "You, on the other hand, are utterly delightful and though the gossips apparently have taken no notice, I have. And I would very much like to speak to you privately about prolonging our association," he said.

Georgiana managed a wobbly smile, relief at their reconciliation overwhelming her. "You'll still be my assistant?" she asked.

Ashdowne groaned. "Certainly, but what I had in mind was a more—"

"Ah, Miss Bellewether." The silky tones of Savonierre speaking her name brought an abrupt end to Georgiana's brief idyll. So intent had she been upon the marquis that she had forgotten all about her promise to Savonierre, but here he was, claiming her attention in his imperious fashion, while Ashdowne, flinching as if he had been struck, gazed at her in question.

"You'll have to excuse us, Ashdowne, but we have an engagement," Savonierre said, smoothly taking Georgiana's arm. She flushed, uncomfortable under the marquis's regard yet unable to explain her plans for the evening with Savonierre standing right there.

For one wild moment, Georgiana considered crying off the rout, but when would she have another chance to question Savonierre, who just might be lying about his fear of heights? And she wanted so desperately to gain entrée to Lady Culpepper's house. Sending Ashdowne a pleading glance for understanding, she knew she could not forgo this opportunity to view the scene of the robbery.

As Savonierre urged her forward, Georgiana remembered her reluctant chaperon. "I, uh, brought my brother Bertrand," she managed to stammer. After that odd business on the bridge today, she was not about to go anywhere alone with Savonierre, and she held her ground as she glanced around for her brother.

"I'm coming," Bertrand said, loping up beside them, and although Savonierre gave her brother an arch look, he accepted the unexpected guest gracefully. Ashdowne, however, was so still that Georgiana felt a wrenching dread, made all the worse after what had just passed between them.

"Goodbye for now, my lord," she said to him, but he only stared at her, his eyes bright and hard as Savonierre led her away.

Georgiana blinked, swamped with melancholy despite her hopes for the investigation. Beside her, Bertrand, oblivious to all the undercurrents, was no comfort, while to her right, Savonierre was a chill and ominous presence. And for the first time in her life, Georgiana had to wonder if this case was so very important after all.

She felt terrible, her throat thick, her heart heavy, as if she had betrayed Ashdowne in some way. He was just her assistant, Georgiana told herself, yet she could no longer delude herself in that manner. Even she recognized that Ashdowne was so much more than that. Suddenly, with a piercing pang, she realized just how much more, for somehow over the past weeks, she had fallen in love with the elegant marquis—in all of his guises.

The knowledge, although gratifying in some ways, left her more dismayed than euphoric. Indeed, if this was what her great-uncle Silas thought he was missing, Georgiana

could not wholeheartedly endorse it. Love was not the
panacea that her mother and sisters professed it to be, but
an emotion fraught with pain and anxiety. Although she
wanted nothing more than to turn around and rush back
to Ashdowne, blurting out the truth, she had no idea how
he would respond to her confession. With horror? Amusement? Embarrassment? She quailed at the thought.

And right now, she had her hands full with Savonierre.
Pushing her blossoming feelings for Ashdowne back into
the general direction of her heart, Georgiana fought to turn
her attention to the man beside her and the speedy resolution of the case that seemed, now more than ever, to
stand between her and happiness.

If she missed the protective presence of her assistant,
at least she had possessed the foresight to bring her
brother along, and for that Georgiana was very grateful,
especially in the close atmosphere of the coach. Later, too,
at Lady Culpepper's house, she was glad of his company,
for the evening's gathering bore little resemblance to the
previous ball. This group was very small, with an atmosphere as intimate as was possible in the large, airy rooms.

It was only after Bertrand ambled off, leaving her alone
with her host that Georgiana began to once more regret
her attendance. Although ostensibly in Bath to help Lady
Culpepper, Savonierre did not appear particularly devoted
to her. He treated her with the same cool courtesy he
doled out to everyone, the sincerity of which Georgiana
still questioned. And when he turned that intense gaze
upon her, she nearly cringed.

"I was hoping that we could talk in private...about the
theft," he said. Taking her arm, he led her to the salon
where she had once questioned Lady Culpepper. The
room was deserted, and Georgiana hesitated on the threshold. She had fended off overzealous suitors before, and

she couldn't imagine Savonierre turning into one of those fumbling, heavy-breathing sorts, but still she knew that it was not wise to be alone with any gentleman.

Memories of Ashdowne and what the two of them had done together made her face flame. Surely Savonierre would not attempt such intimacies, she thought as he nudged her forward, but she knew a moment's alarm as he closed the door behind them.

"Please sit down," he said, gesturing to a medallion-backed chair. Stiffly Georgiana took a seat, and was glad when he chose the chair opposite and not one of the sofas. Although the arrangement was not conducive to seduction, she still felt a tinge of anxiety at the poorly lit surroundings.

"Now perhaps we can discuss the robbery more openly. I can't help but believe you are constrained in the presence of…others," Savonierre said smoothly.

"Really, I have nothing to add," Georgiana said, avoiding his gaze, while she tried to form a question for him.

"Really?" he asked, looking so skeptical that Georgiana blushed. "I had thought you were more clever than that, Miss Bellewether."

Georgiana bristled at the thread of amusement in his tone. Was he making fun of her? It was nearly impossible for her to judge the sincerity of his words, such was his cool reserve. "I fear I am still trying to piece together the series of events," she said with a touch of asperity. "For instance, when exactly did *you* arrive, Mr. Savonierre?" Was that a flicker of surprise or humor in his dark eyes, Georgiana wondered, as his lips curled.

"Ah. Now you justify my opinion of you, Miss Bellewether, but surely you don't think I had anything to do with the theft?"

When Georgiana tossed her curls without comment, he laughed aloud, though it was not the same warm, infectious sound that she had come to know from her assistant.

"Oh, you are interesting. I can see why Ashdowne likes to keep you on a close tether," Savonierre said.

"Whatever do you mean?" Georgiana asked. Startled by his mention of the marquis, who was so much upon her mind, she sought his gaze, and the dark eyes met hers with a regard so intense they seemed to strip her bare. She had the uneasy sense that he was robbing her of her will, not in the sensual manner of Ashdowne, but through the sheer force of his dark personality.

Georgiana felt a frisson of fear that had nothing to do with seduction and everything to do with the very ownership of her soul. Was this man a demon? Being a devotee of facts, not fiction, she was not usually given to such whimsy, but something about his probing stare unnerved her. Finally, just as she felt her resolve give way, he released her gaze, and Georgiana's shoulders slumped with relief.

"Why, I meant nothing at all," said Savonierre, glancing about the dim room in a careless manner, as if he had not just held her prisoner of his will. When his face swung toward her again, she refused to look him in the eye. "Then, again, I'm certain you are clever enough to figure out just what I mean for yourself, if you think upon it. Alone."

Georgiana blinked, nearly overwhelmed by this man whose words seemed to hold some cryptic messages that she could not decipher. Frantically she tried to gather her wits, and she admitted to herself that Ashdowne might have been right. Savonierre was far too dangerous for her.

"Alas, I am at a loss, Miss Bellewether, for my Bow Street Runner is as dumbfounded about this burglary as you claim to be," he said, blithely turning the conversation back to the theft, just as though it had never veered away into ominous territory.

"I suppose some cases are difficult even for a professional," Georgiana murmured, marshaling all of her reserves just to keep up with this man.

"Perhaps," Savonierre acknowledged. "But you, Miss Bellewether, you disappoint me. I had thought surely *you* would have solved the theft by now."

Georgiana didn't know whether to be insulted or flattered by his professed faith in her. "Well, it is difficult for an outsider like myself to gain access to all the necessary information when I cannot question the servants or view the scene of the crime," she said in her own defense.

Something flickered across Savonierre's hard features. "You wish to see the room where the theft occurred?" he asked in a casual tone.

"Why, of course! It is what I wish above all!" Georgiana exclaimed, without considering her words.

Savonierre's lips curved in a smile that held no warmth. "My dear Miss Bellewether, had I but known of this burning desire of yours, I would have satisfied it immediately," he said.

Georgiana felt her face flame at his choice of words, although his expression had not changed from its polite inquiry. She sensed, with either an investigator's instincts or her heretofore unexercised woman's intuition, that the man had no real interest in her. Perhaps he was one of those rakes who preyed on all women for the sheer thrill of conquest. Or, he might well be toying with her only because of Ashdowne.

That suspicion felt so right that it brought clearness to her thoughts, and so Georgiana lifted her chin in a parody of his own politesse. "When can I see it?"

"Why, you may see it right now," Savonierre said. "I have kept the room closed up and guarded so that nothing has been disturbed. You will find it just as it was that night, following the theft."

Georgiana drew in a sharp breath as he rose to his feet and presented his arm. Although she too stood, she shook her head. "I think tomorrow would be soon enough. I can return first thing in the morning, if you will leave the instructions with a servant."

Feeling his gaze on her, she forced herself to remain impassive, and soon she heard a soft chuckle. "My dear Miss Bellewether, are you intimating that you don't trust me, a gentleman of the realm, to take you into Lady Culpepper's bedroom?"

When Georgiana did not comment, he laughed, a low sound that held no real humor. "Touché, my little investigator. Perhaps you are clever enough, after all, to unveil the thief," he said, his smile taunting her.

"Tomorrow, then, but make it around eleven," he said. "I will have Mr. Jeffries here to escort you to the scene in my stead. Surely, you will consider yourself safe enough with him?" Savonierre asked, pausing to send her an assessing look. When she nodded, he bowed his head slightly. "Very good. And perhaps the fool can learn something from your methods."

"Thank you," Georgiana managed to murmur, though he made no acknowledgment. When he opened the door of the salon, led her into the reception room and released her in the general vicinity of Bertrand, Georgiana breathed a sigh of relief, only to swallow it again as his attention returned to her once more.

His gaze was hard and intent as it found hers. "I shall put my faith in you, Miss Bellewether," he promised, as if that in itself was a threat. And then, with a small bow, he was gone.

Georgiana's legs felt unsteady, and she had to restrain herself from falling against her brother in reaction to her nerve-racking encounter. It was only when she had recovered herself sufficiently that she paused to consider what kind of game Savonierre was playing. What did he hope to gain by letting her see the scene? She shook her head, baffled but too overcome by anticipation to worry about his motives.

At last she would see the scene of the crime.

She almost told Ashdowne. Georgiana had a notion to go straight to his residence in the morning and take him with her to Lady Culpepper's house. Several things stopped her, however. First, she was not certain what time he normally rose and did not want to rouse him from his bed, especially since she might be tempted to join him there. And, of course, there was his warning never to visit his home, but Georgiana didn't take that too seriously.

More important, to her mind, was her desire not to become embroiled in a major dispute with Ashdowne when she had an appointment at eleven that she did not want to miss. Worse, yet, Savonierre, being no friend of Ashdowne's, might well retract his invitation if she showed up with her assistant in tow.

Coldhearted reasoning perhaps, but Georgiana knew a pressing need to conclude the business of the case before going on to the more ephemeral concerns of her heart. And though she was not normally prone to whims, she could not deny a certain desire to examine the site of the burglary alone, without prejudice of any kind. Sometimes Ashdowne didn't take things seriously enough, she told herself, even though she knew there was more to her wariness than that.

And so, Georgiana didn't tell him, but presented herself, alone, at Lady Culpepper's exactly at eleven. There, she was immediately ushered into the drawing room, where Jeffries stood waiting, looking much as he always did, rumpled and yet steady, a far more comforting presence than she would have expected.

"Good morning, Miss Bellewether," he said with a nod of his head. "I believe you would like a look at the lady's bedroom?" Georgiana opened her mouth to exclaim, only to shut it again as she noticed the twinkle in the Bow Street Runner's eye. He knew very well just how much she wanted to view the scene.

"Why, yes, I would," she said with a smile.

He returned the grin, and although she had anticipated some ill feelings because of what he might perceive as encroachment into his territory, Jeffries was as kind and polite as usual. Without further ado, he led her through the upper rooms to where a servant sat positioned near a closed door.

"Why do you think Mr. Savonierre has kept the room untouched?" she whispered to the Bow Street Runner as she glanced toward the silent servant.

Jeffries waited until they were inside, the door closed behind them, before he answered. Then he simply shrugged, as if he knew no better than she. "Mr. Savonierre is quite intent upon finding the thief. Perhaps he thinks some clue awaits fresh eyes."

With a nod, Georgiana turned her attention to the room. Heavy drapes that hung over the tall windows were pulled open, sending a spill of light across the thick carpet and the mixture of gilt and white furniture in the French style.

And there upon the vast expanse of the bed lay the famous jewelry case, still open.

Georgiana felt a prickle of excitement run up her spine, for here she was at last doing some real investigative work. She released a shuddering sigh of pleasure and then began to move slowly around the area. She was careful to disturb nothing and Jeffries, apparently satisfied that she would not, walked to the windows to stare out at the misty morning.

Georgiana studied every inch of the carpet beneath her feet before she took each step, gradually making her way toward a cluttered dressing table. Mentally cataloging its contents, she crouched low to look beneath it, but decided that no one could take shelter there without notice. Finally moving on, she stopped before a narrow door. "Where does this lead?" she asked.

"The dressing room," Jeffries answered, with a cursory glance over his shoulder. "It has no other outlet."

Georgiana eyed the door in speculation. "Is it possible that someone could have hidden inside before the ball?"

Jeffries shook his head, although he showed no scorn for her question. "No. The maids were in and out all day and her ladyship was in dressing all afternoon, I gather," he muttered, his tone making clear his impatience with such lengthy feminine trivialities.

Smiling, Georgiana walked toward the wall where he stood staring outside. "And the windows were open?"

He nodded. "Just as they are now, I'm told."

Georgiana braced her hands on the edge and stuck her head out. As she suspected, the wide arch of a curved pediment butted outward not far below. Turning her head, she saw another on her right, close enough to use as a foothold. Drawing in a deep breath, she forced herself to look downward, only to shudder in horror at the sight of the ground, too far below her.

Yes, it was possible that a man had gained entrance to this room by climbing from one pediment to another, but what kind of person would risk his life sneaking in here? Immediately, a picture of Savonierre appeared in her mind, taunting, dangerous, and playing a strange game of his own. Such a man would laugh at the danger, she suspected, *if he was not afraid of heights.*

Jerking her head back inside, Georgiana continued circling the perimeter of the room, only to halt at the sound of a low curse. She turned in time to see the Bow Street Runner imitating her previous stance and muttering about the type of fool who would scale the side of a building for a few gems.

"He could have used a grappling hook, but there aren't any marks," Jeffries said, more to himself than to her. Shaking her head, Georgiana kept silent, for she had no intention of sharing her own theories just yet. Walking slowly, she approached the bed, her eyes bright and alert for anything unusual. Keeping out of a direct path from the window, she bent low to examine the carpet all along the side of the massive piece of furniture.

Although Georgiana heard the low drone of Jeffries's voice behind her, she paid no heed, for she was too intent upon her own investigation. The carpet was gold, with swirls of red and green, and she had to look closely to see beyond the pattern. Perhaps if it had been a darker color, she would have never noticed the small bits of dirt. But she did and, reaching out, she picked up a piece, testing it with her fingers.

It was not the same consistency as the dust that had settled on the contents of the room in the past few days. Nor was it the kind of earth that could be found in the garden, making its way in on someone's shoe. It was a darker, richer kind of a soil, and Georgiana blinked in horror as she suddenly recognized it.

Although she was crouching close to the floor, she felt unsteady, as if the whole world tilted upon its axis, threatening to upend her. Overcome by dizziness, she struggled for breath, her lungs seemingly unable to draw in enough air to support her. Dimly, from behind her, Georgiana heard Jeffries's voice droning on, oblivious to her plight, but she could not call out. Her hands trembled, and she felt so ill that she feared she might faint, but in the end, the pain cut through her light-headedness, honing her senses to a razor sharpness.

And it was the pain that gave her the strength to rise to her feet, the tiny fragment still clutched in her fingers as a talisman of her betrayal. For she knew this piece of dirt. No ordinary bit of soil, it had come from the potted plant she had knocked over the night of the ball, the very same earth that had been crushed into her gown and dusted over the elegant waistcoat of one of the guests.

Ashdowne.

Chapter Fifteen

Blinking against the tears that threatened, Georgiana realized that her very own assistant, the man she *loved,* was the thief, and probably The Cat himself. Yet somehow she managed to make her way around the rest of the room. Thankfully, there was little enough to draw an investigator's attention, for she simply went through the motions of looking, seeing nothing but Ashdowne's treachery.

No matter how angry and hurt she was, Georgiana was not prepared to share her findings with the Bow Street Runner. She had to gain a moment alone first to think, to decide what to do, so in the meantime, she was forced to keep up appearances. It was the most difficult thing she had ever done, for she knew Jeffries was no fool, and if he looked too closely at her, he might well suspect something was amiss.

When he finally ceased muttering about the way the thief had entered, Georgiana told him she was ready to leave. Knowing she was probably pale, she stood in the shadows. She had learned from the very best—The Cat himself—how to cling to the darkness. And yet, her education had been incomplete, for she hadn't learned how to lie and cheat and steal. And betray.

With steely resolve, Georgiana kept those thoughts at bay while Jeffries showed her out. For once, the usually quiet Bow Street Runner seemed determined to discuss the case with her, but Georgiana claimed that she was wanted at home and could not linger. If Jeffries sensed her agitation, she hoped he thought it due to her disappointment in finding no clue at the scene.

How ironic that her distress was caused by the opposite, by the very thing she had always desired. At last she had the evidence that pointed, irrevocably, to the thief, and yet Georgiana said nothing to the official who kindly offered to walk her back to her home.

She shook her head in answer, for she had no intention of returning to the house where Ashdowne might find her. Even if he did not appear, her giggling sisters would quiz her about him. Her jovial father and her distracted mother would be no comfort, for she could not tell them the truth about the marquis or her feelings for him. She headed toward the Orange Grove, finding a quiet corner among the elms to brood over the man she had thought she knew better than any other, the man she didn't know at all.

Ashdowne. The Cat.

The nobleman who had held her and kissed her and touched her and laughed with her was nothing more than a thief. He was no different than any common criminal off the streets, Georgiana realized, the knowledge giving her a stomachache that seeped upward to lodge behind her breast. Pain swept through her, from the back of her eyes to her very toes, and she sank down upon a bench, unable to stand.

Had he simply been toying with her all along? It was too monstrous to be believed, yet why else would The Cat offer to help her solve the burglary he had committed? Georgiana realized that all the times he had listened attentively, as if he believed in her theories, had been just an act. How he must have laughed at her! Georgiana thought dismally. And she had loved his laughter, never realizing that it made a mockery of her.

That was bad enough, but Georgiana was well accustomed to scorn for her talents. It was the *other* that tore at her insides, the way he had kissed and caressed her as if he delighted in her, when all the while she was only a game to him. She shuddered, forcing back the tears that threatened. Well, she had learned something from the experience, she told herself. She had all but satisfied her curiosity about intimacy, so she would count Ashdowne's instruction as useful. It would certainly be the last such experimentation.

Never again would she allow herself to care so much for someone, for her great-uncle was wrong. People were not the key to happiness. They were baffling and full of guile, using others for their own ends. Georgiana had thought herself a good judge of character, yet she had fallen in love with an infamous burglar, hardly a wise decision! Better to confine herself to her books and papers and facts that she could understand. They had no power to hurt.

Although grief swamped her, Georgiana refused to cry, and her naturally optimistic nature began to rally. She was made of stronger stuff than Ashdowne had ever imagined. Just like everyone else, he had underestimated her, thinking her nothing but a bit of fluff, empty-headed with plenty of curves. Well, he was wrong! Georgiana looked down at the soil that still clung to her fingers, crushed by the force of her distress, and she remembered how Ashdowne had initially looked at her as if she were a bug.

In the end, he had shown himself to be little more than

an insect, a big, black spider spinning a vast web for his own amusement. And now she was going to squish him.

Finn had talked him into coming. The Irishman who had always referred to Georgiana as "that dizzy Belle-wether chit" was suddenly concerned about her well-being. Having followed her about this morning, he had rushed back to Camden Place with news of her mooning about the Orange Grove as if she had lost her best friend.

Ashdowne, who felt much the same way, found it hard to work up a lot of sympathy for her. She seemed to flout him at every turn, showing a total disregard for his wishes, his desires, his decrees. Maybe he had been a little over-bearing the other day, but that was no reason for her to run off with Savonierre!

Ashdowne scowled. He had never pegged Georgiana as the type of flirtatious creature who worked one admirer against another, but he was beginning to have his doubts, especially after last night. Dem, but he had apologized, a rare enough occurrence that warranted some sort of re-sponse. And for a moment, he had been most gratified as he received a long-awaited version of The Look.

But then she had run off with Savonierre. Again. Ash-downe didn't know whether to laugh in astonishment at her idiocy or strangle her for defying him. Savonierre was liable to destroy her without blinking an eye, he knew, and his urge to protect his own warred with the bitter complaints of his battered pride. Although he didn't con-sider himself conceited, never in his life had he worked so hard to win a woman. And he was still uncertain where he stood with the elusive Miss Bellewether.

It rankled. He was half tempted to take his annoying sister-in-law and return to the family seat, never to see Georgiana again. But who would protect her from Savonierre? From other men? From herself? Ashdowne struggled against a thrum of panic that began whenever he thought about giving her up for good. And so here he was, searching through a park for the allegedly woebegone woman who had thrown his feelings for her in his face, preferring instead the cold comfort of her "case."

When he found her, Ashdowne had to bite back a sharp rebuke, for she was sitting all alone in a secluded area, as if inviting some importunities from a passing rogue. But he said nothing, only coming to a halt before her, uncertain of his reception. And when she finally looked up, her eyes red rimmed and watery, he felt as if someone had kicked him in the gut. If Savonierre had done this to her, he would kill the bastard outright, without a thought to the consequences.

Since he didn't trust himself to speak, Ashdowne simply stood watching her as she rose slowly to her feet, a haughty expression coming over her usually open features. Obviously he was not going to be received warmly this afternoon, and he swallowed his disappointment.

"Ashdowne. I guess I'm glad you're here. I won't ask how you found me, since you have your ways," she said with a bitterness he had never heard before. What had Savonierre done? "You are a man of many talents, aren't you?"

Before he could respond to that baffling statement, she turned away. "I know who you are," she said with grim finality. "Don't bother to deny that you are The Cat."

Ashdowne halted in the act of turning toward her, stricken for a moment, before the casual reply came to his lips. "Ah, so now I am the villain, am I?"

"I found soil at the scene, Ashdowne. The same soil that came from the plant that I knocked over onto you," she said, her voice so dull and lifeless that it cut him to the quick.

He took a steadying breath. "I assume it was the very same soil that several servants cleaned up. Have you accused them, or are you singling me out for a reason?"

She turned, her blue gaze so wretched that he nearly flinched. "After all that you have put me through, the least you could do is to show me some honesty, at the last."

Ashdowne felt as if she had torn out his guts and stomped upon them in the grass. "Very well, but this is hardly the place—" he began only to be cut off by her swift gesture of impatience.

"I have no intention of going anywhere with you, so you may save your breath in that regard," she said, and he felt a slow surge of anger at her pious attitude. Although he had known this day would come, he had hoped it would not. From the beginning he had been aware of the obstacles that stood between them, yet he had continually put off any reckoning.

After all, The Cat had been gone a long time. Ashdowne had never dreamed that anyone would make the connection, but he should have known that Georgiana would. Too often he had dismissed her as a silly, imaginative creature, yet she possessed the acumen and drive to ferret out the truth. And she had done so.

"Are you going to kill me now?" Her soft question drew a startled glance from him. What the devil was she talking about? he wondered, choking back a startled sound.

"Well, now that I know your secret, I would think you would like to make sure that I don't tell anyone else," she said with a poise that shocked him.

Is that what she thought of him? That he had no more

regard for her than to do her *murder?* Ashdowne's nearly nonexistent temper flared, along with a sting of pain that he ignored. "That's a great leap, isn't it, from jewel theft to assassination?"

"What's the difference?" she asked with a toss of her beautiful curls. "Where do you draw the line? You could hang for what you've done. Surely it would be simpler just to do away with your accuser?"

Ashdowne felt himself flush with anger, his mouth tightening as he tried to speak evenly. Instead, his words came out in a low, heated rush. "I'm not going to hang because no one is going to believe you."

She blinked at him, flinching as if he had slapped her, and he groaned, reaching for her, but she stepped back. "Get away from me! I can't think when you get close to me, as I'm sure was your intention all along!"

Ashdowne stood there, helplessly hurting for her and for himself. For the first time in his life, he could form no glib answer or casual dismissal. His original efforts had been a seduction of necessity, so he framed no denial. "I never meant to hurt you," he said.

He heard her soft, choked laugh. "Oh, no. You simply lied to me from the beginning, laughing at me—"

"I never laughed at you!" Ashdowne protested. When she whirled to level him an accusing stare, he sputtered. "Well, not in the way you think. I laughed because I found you so delightful. I still do! Georgiana, don't let this thing—"

"How do you get in, past the locked doors?" she asked, her lovely features stiff and unyielding.

He lifted a brow. "A lock pick."

"Like the one you used at Mr. Hawkins's lodgings?"

Ashdowne shrugged. "And sometimes nothing at all. Not many want to admit to being careless, but they leave doors unlocked, jewels scattered on their dressing tables, windows open...'' he said. If that was all she wanted to hear, then he would oblige her.

''And in that case, you simply climb up the outside of the house?''

Ashdowne frowned. ''No. You were right, of course. I would never scale a building. Too much bother for too little,'' he said with a negligent glance. Although he knew he was not furthering his cause, he felt driven to tell her all, perhaps by the same instincts that had sent him to his doom. ''I climbed out the window of one room and crossed upon the pediments to the other.''

Georgiana blanched. ''You could have been killed!''

''Are you pretending concern? How affecting!'' he said with a bitter laugh.

She lifted her chin, her contempt evident. ''And all for naught but a pretty bauble!''

''Ah, but there you have it wrong,'' Ashdowne said smoothly. She jerked her head toward him, and he lifted a brow. ''Yes, even the great Georgiana Bellewether doesn't always have all of the facts,'' he said, unable to stop himself.

''Well, then?''

''Ah. You've a mind to listen, do you? Well, I'm not certain whether I shall explain myself,'' Ashdowne said. He had never shared his motivations with anyone, not even Finn, and yet now, faced with the judgment of a petite blonde, he felt like prostrating himself. Anything to change her mind, to undo what he had done, to regain her good opinion.

He stared off into the trees, seeing not their greenery but the images of the past. ''I was born a younger son of rather stodgy parents. Luckily, my brother was all they could wish for, while I was too...adventurous. I never quite fit in with their plans, having discovered early on that I didn't care for the usual avenues available to me as a near penniless nobleman—a career in the military, the church or the law,'' Ashdowne said with a bitter smile.

''I went off to London to seek my fame and fortune— or at least some pleasure. I made the usual rounds of clubs, ton parties and gambling hells, and got along well enough on the strength of my wit and rather dubious charm,'' he said, frowning at the memory of that scapegrace existence.

''However, I possessed a certain restlessness that seemed unsatisfied until I fell into my destined vocation— quite by accident, mind you. It was a harmless prank, really, a sleight of hand that I wanted to see if I could pull off, and when I did—'' Ashdowne shrugged ''—I discovered a taste for the danger and skill required to separate expensive jewels from the most wealthy and obnoxious of my peers.''

And deuced if he didn't enjoy it. At the height of his infamy, it had been exhilarating, like a fever in his blood that required constant feeding. He had to admit that it was a heady feeling to fool everyone from his friends and acquaintances to the authorities he thwarted at every turn.

''But all that changed when my staid brother died,'' he said. He had found it ironic at first that his elder sibling, who rarely roused himself beyond the occasional ride to the hounds, had been struck down by apoplexy, while he thrived on his own bouts with peril. But he soon discovered that being marquis was a little more taxing than he had thought. And even though he swore that he wouldn't turn into his brother, Finn had accused him more than once of becoming indistinguishable from that stodgy fellow.

Ashdowne sighed. "The Cat retired, and I turned my attention to more legal pursuits."

"And just what drew you out of this so-called retirement?" Georgiana asked, her tone as disdainful as before.

"Nothing so trivial as a thirst for danger, I can assure you. Whether I will it or not, the title consumes all of my energy and attention," he said curtly.

"It wouldn't have anything to do with your sister-in-law, would it?" Georgiana asked, and Ashdowne swung round to face her in amazement. He knew he had underestimated her before, but he was still stunned at the accuracy of her accusation.

"Forgive me for ever doubting your abilities," he said, with a bow of acknowledgment that Georgiana accepted stoically. He was beginning to realize that nothing he said made a difference, but he continued, having no other choice.

"As I mentioned before, Anne, though a truly gentle creature, has a tendency to become tiresome. After her mourning was over, I insisted that she go off to visit relatives in London. However, even I had no idea just how unworldy she was, traveling for the first time without my brother's protection, and it wasn't long after her arrival that she fell into Lady Culpepper's clutches, losing quite a bit of money to the woman, whose methods of gambling, by the way—"

"Are suspect," Georgiana said.

No longer surprised at her astuteness, Ashdowne simply bowed his head in acknowledgment once more. "Although I managed to pay her off, I am afraid the debt did not sit well with me, especially since the woman is notorious for preying upon young innocents. Not as young as some, Anne still qualifies on both counts, and I felt responsible for her misfortune, having sent her to London, only to have her return home to languish in disgrace, awash in guilt and misery.''

''But why could you not just win the money back at cards?'' Georgiana asked.

Ashdowne laughed at her naiveté. Although more clever than the Bow Street officers she so admired, Georgiana still possessed a guilelessness that called out for the protection she would not allow him to give her. ''Lady Culpepper knows better than to take up a challenge from me,'' he said simply. ''She chooses her victims carefully and even should I manage to enter a game with her, she would quickly bow out.''

''And what did your sister-in-law think of your revenge?'' Georgiana asked, causing Ashdowne to laugh again.

''Anne has no idea! Far from thanking me for it, she would probably faint dead away, if I told her I had stolen the jewels,'' he said, aware, not for the first time, that Georgiana was made of sterner stuff, and grateful for it. Perhaps there was still hope. ''So, you see, I only took the necklace to repay Lady Culpepper's own thievery.''

''Still, that doesn't justify your stealing,'' Georgiana said righteously.

''Only from the exceedingly rich and exceedingly annoying, who could well afford it,'' Ashdowne argued.

But he had lost her. He could see it in the lift of her chin, in the way her beautiful blue eyes met his own, not in dazed wonder, but with censure. Accusing. ''Your scruples are far different than mine, my lord,'' she said.

''Variety is what makes life interesting,'' Ashdowne said, but Georgiana only shook her head, and frustration surged through him. ''Shall your overactive conscience force you to turn me in to Mr. Jeffries, then?''

At the question, all her bravado seemed to fade, leaving

her looking shaken and bleak, and Ashdowne wanted nothing more than to comfort her. Yet he knew she would not welcome anything from him. "I don't know," she murmured, taking the last of his hope.

Ashdowne didn't fear the gallows, for he suspected that even Georgiana couldn't convince Bow Street of his guilt, now that he held the title, but her indecision twisted inside him like a knife. How could she even consider it? Did she despise him so much that she longed for his death?

"Why, Georgiana?" he asked in helpless fury. "The Cat is past. Over and done with."

"You're wrong," she whispered. Rising to her feet, she wrapped her arms around her in a protective gesture that both enraged and pained Ashdowne. "I'm looking at him."

She turned and fled, and Ashdowne didn't attempt to go after her, for this time the often unintelligible Georgiana had made herself perfectly clear.

Ashdowne went through the motions. He returned to Camden Place, where he changed for the evening, and he escorted his sister-in-law to one of Bath's rather provincial dances. Anne seemed eager to speak with him, for once, but when he turned his attention toward her, she took one look at him and stammered some nonsense about the weather before hurriedly excusing herself.

All through the interminable hours that followed, Ashdowne thought about leaving, not the dance, but Bath itself. Georgiana had trampled his pride, and the remnants of it urged him to return to Ashdowne Manor, take up the reins of his life and dismiss her from his thoughts forever. But he rarely turned aside a challenge. He had done things that others called miraculous simply by examining a problem from all angles and using his skills and dexterity.

Could he still win Georgiana, despite all that had happened? More importantly, did he want to? All Ashdowne's instincts screamed that he should count himself fortunate to have escaped marriage to such a dizzy young woman, but his heart thundered with a more vital truth: he loved her. Never before had he been tempted to wed, yet now his mind, his heart, his body, all clamored that he make her his. Now and forever.

Well, that pretty much settled that. The question was would she have him? He had lied to her from the very beginning, used her, played at seducing her and become jealously possessive of her time and attention before falling for her completely, but he knew none of those dastardly deeds weighed as much with Georgiana as one thing: he was a thief.

During an evening spent cutting those who would approach him and dancing attendance on his jittery sister-in-law, Ashdowne had plenty of time to justify his past behavior to himself, but he could find no explanation that would suit Georgiana. He could tell himself that she was nothing but a green girl with a lot of useless morals that would garner her nothing but contempt in London, and yet her innocence and sterling character had won his reluctant admiration.

There was no getting around it. Long after the silent carriage ride home and his curt dismissal of Finn, Ashdowne pondered his past and future, a bottle of port at his side. Whether because of the wine or the depressing bent of his thoughts, he became increasingly morose as the night wore on. For the first time in his life he wanted something he couldn't have, and all his skill and wit and determination might not obtain it.

Frustration burned inside him like the fires of hell, for everything had always come easily to him. Unlike other younger sons, he had never taken up the sword or the book to earn a living. He had survived on his charm and his wits and called it work, but it had all been a lark, fueled by his arrogance.

His life as The Cat had been more than an adventure, but a way to prove, to himself at least, that he was just as good as his brother. Better even, for he had become successful on his own without a title or the Ashdowne inheritance. Yet, his relatives had never known of his accomplishments, and in the end, he had never really won their respect or affection.

And now that he had the title and the wealth and the heritage, what good did it do him? His existence seemed empty and purposeless and…lonely. Oh, he had friends and acquaintances, but none except Finn really knew him. How could they, when he had lived a lie? Suddenly, standing in the garish room he hated, awash in moonlight, Ashdowne was struck by a desperate yearning for a family, for a wife who knew who he really was and who could rekindle his sense of adventure, his joy in life.

Georgiana.

Little did he suspect, when he arrived in Bath, that a petite young woman he had once dismissed as empty-headed would become the focus of his being. And yet had he put forth more than a minimal effort to win her? Ashdowne groaned out a denial. He had treated her with the same selfishness that marked every facet of his life.

The admission startled him, for Ashdowne had never thought of himself as excessively selfish, but now he had to concede that it had been a hallmark of his existence. Always he had done what he pleased, when he pleased and how he pleased, with little regard for anyone else, and the knowledge didn't sit well upon his shoulders.

Only someone with unmitigated conceit would set himself up as an arbiter of the fortunes of others, and Ashdowne's casual dismissal of his victims as too rich and obnoxious to matter seemed the height of heedlessness. He had claimed to possess a sense of honor, yet now he saw himself as practically devoid of it. Yes, Lady Culpepper deserved to have her necklace stolen after what she had done to Anne, but who was he to decide—and to mete out his choice of revenge?

Setting down his glass, Ashdowne suddenly knew what he must do. It was a small thing, really, but a step in the right direction, or at least that's what Georgiana would say. The thought gave him hope, and he surged to his feet only to hesitate. Unfortunately, he could attempt nothing now, for his wits were too dull after the long hours of drinking and painful introspection.

Ashdowne frowned, impatient, before realizing with a smile that there was *something* he could do.

Chapter Sixteen

Despite his less than perfect equilibrium, Ashdowne easily obtained entry, his stealth second nature as he stepped through long windows into the bedroom. It was small, and she did not share it with her sisters, a fact he had made it his business to find out before this evening and for which he was infinitely grateful. For a long moment, he simply stood there watching her sleep, bathed in moonlight, her blond curls spread upon her pillow, one pale hand resting beside them.

Being Georgiana, she did not awaken slowly to rub her eyes and yawn. Instead, her lashes lifted, and she looked directly at him with intelligence all the more startling for its package. He saw a flicker of alarm pass across her lovely features before she sat up, pulling a blanket to her chest.

"How did you get in here?" she demanded in a whisper.

"Oh, we depraved criminals have our ways," Ashdowne said from his position in the shadows. She blinked at him, and he wondered if she was sleepier than she looked. And suddenly the wonder that had filled him at the sight of her turned to something else. Her locks were tousled, her cheeks pink, and he could just imagine the warmth of her skin. He took a step forward.

"Don't come any closer!" she warned, holding up one hand while clutching the bedding with another. It served as poor covering, for he could see the lacy bodice of her nightgown and his desire became as a living thing, fierce and undeniable.

"I can change," he whispered, moving to the side of the bed.

"What?" she asked, her expression dazed.

"I have changed, Georgiana, but I can change more." He sat down beside her, and the delicate waft of her scent was nearly his undoing. While he still could think, he bent over her, trapping her delectable form between his outstretched arms. "And to prove it to you, I'm going to return the necklace," he whispered.

"Don't!" she cried. "I mean, yes, *do* return it. That is a wonderful idea, but don't come any closer to me because then I can't think."

"Good," Ashdowne answered, the word holding a wealth of meanings. "I want you to stop thinking and simply feel. I want Georgiana, the incurable romantic tonight, not the hardheaded investigator. Give me another chance, Georgiana. Please." His plea was barely a whisper as he leaned forward, and whatever answer she might have made was lost when he took her mouth with his own.

She tasted drowsy and sweet and heavenly, and Ashdowne deepened the kiss, taking all that she would give him. Needy, desperate, begging for more, he hardly recognized himself, but it didn't matter. Nothing mattered when he felt the tentative touch of her tongue, innocent yet eager, and growing bolder as it entwined with his.

Her arms came up to enfold him, and Ashdowne lay down beside her, unwilling to pause even to remove his boots. He was well aware that at any moment she might come to her senses, but in the meantime he would revel in her passion. It rose like a tide, and when she arched upward to press herself against him, Ashdowne jerked away the blanket that stood between them.

Her nightgown was a frilly white concoction that reflected her mother's taste, and he could well imagine her in simple silk instead, but the lacy bodice caressed Georgiana's creamy skin along her abundant curves, and through the thin material, he saw the dark outline of her nipples. Ashdowne felt the blood rush to his head, then downward, in a great, dizzying spiral. He remembered the episode in the baths and gritted his teeth.

Those stolen moments seemed to have occurred aeons ago, in a time of delight and surprise when he hadn't been in the grips of such desperation. *When he hadn't been in love.* The thought acted as a douse of cold water on his careening senses, and Ashdowne struggled to rein in his rampant lust. He loved her, and for once, he wasn't going to be selfish.

Where he found the strength, Ashdowne would never know, but for a long while he simply looked at her, then he stroked her beautiful body, his hands working over the material of her gown, playing with it, using it to heighten her pleasure until she was breathless and panting. And then, finally, he stripped it from her and began all over again, learning her body as he would a lock whose secrets he must discover slowly and carefully.

But Georgiana was not content to lie prone, and she tugged at his coat until he removed it and his waistcoat and his shirt. Sitting up on the edge of the bed, he yanked off his boots, only to find her draped over his back, her bounteous breasts pressed against him, and his head fell backward on a groan. Apparently encouraged by the sound, she rubbed against him, making little purring noises while she kissed the back of his neck and nipped at his shoulders.

His erection straining painfully at his breeches, Ashdowne turned and tossed her onto the bed, climbing after her in a moment's weakness. And seeing her lying there all pink and tousled, her legs parted to reveal a tantalizing thatch of blond curls, was almost too much for him. He hesitated a moment, drawing on resources he didn't know existed, before picking up the foot nearest him and licking her toes.

By the time Ashdowne reached the tender skin at the very top of her inner thigh, she was whimpering, and he was smiling when he finally kissed her moist heat, tasting her sweetness, reveling in her essence. Being Georgiana, she didn't squawk or protest, but opened her mind and her legs to his unique explorations until she was tearing his hair out of his head in her enthusiasm.

When she bucked and cried out her pleasure, Ashdowne gently untangled her fingers from his strained locks and gazed down at the panting woman before him, the very picture of sated bliss. And he knew it would be so easy to finish what he had started, to indulge his own need for release by spilling his seed inside her.

By taking her maidenhead, perhaps even getting her with child, he could bind her to him, and the temptation was so great that Ashdowne shuddered with the force of it. But that kind of behavior would be the careless, heedless, *easy* way, and his developing scruples told him that way would be wrong. And, in truth, Ashdowne wanted more. He wanted all of her, not just the passion he could rouse in her body, but her clever mind and her romantic heart. He wanted her to love him, and so he drew a deep breath and rose from the bed.

His erection was so painful that he stifled a groan when he bent to pull on his boots. He had been too long in his monkish existence as marquis, buried at the family seat. He had always loved beautiful things, including women, and though he had chosen his lovers with a discerning eye, he could no longer remember their faces. Now only one face came to mind, one soft body taunted him with the memory of pale skin and soft curves. Ashdowne grimaced, his arousal making the task of getting dressed an odd business and he grunted as he bent over Georgiana, kissing her dampened forehead in farewell.

Scruples were a lot more painful than he had ever imagined.

Georgiana stood in the Pump Room, unsure what to believe. After Ashdowne's appearance in her bedroom last night, she had been ready to forgive him anything, but a restless dawn had brought the gradual return of her wits and now she wondered. Was he really capable of changing, or was he just trying to distract her from his guilt and betrayal? Worse yet, had he been trying to win her over for more nefarious reasons?

Georgiana knew she couldn't really turn him in to the Bow Street Runner, even though she felt a hollow sense of disappointment that the case she had worked so hard to solve would remained unexplained. All her dreams of glory were gone, but they no longer seemed so important now, after what had happened with Ashdowne. Maybe he was right, she thought dismally, and she was more romantic than pragmatic, after all.

Heaving a mighty sigh, Georgiana thought it hardly fitting that someone who devoted her life to the investigation and uncovering of wrongdoing should fall in love with a criminal, and yet hadn't she often marveled about her worthy opponent? At last, she had found someone clever enough to be her match, but could he put his past behind him? Could she?

Georgiana was just as confused as she had been after waking from a few hours of restless sleep, and she would rather have remained in her room trying to sort out her situation, but her family had insisted that she join them in a morning visit to the Pump Room. Although tempted to plead a headache, she was wary of even the smallest lie, and so agreed reluctantly.

At the best of times, Georgiana was not enthusiastic about socializing, so today she kept to herself even more than usual. For once, she didn't have the slightest interest in the conversations going on around her, and as for Ashdowne...she wasn't even sure she wanted to see him.

Lost in the dismals, Georgiana didn't notice the approach of an elegantly dressed woman until she heard the soft clearing of a feminine throat. She turned only to blink at the sight of the marchioness of Ashdowne. "My lady!" she said in surprise.

"Please call me Anne," Ashdowne's sister-in-law said as she reached for Georgiana's hand. "I have heard so much about you that I feel we are old friends."

Georgiana blinked again. "You've heard about *me?*" she asked, amazed.

Anne's delicate mouth curved into a beautiful smile. "Oh, yes, of course! According to Johnathon you are the most intelligent and clever and beautiful and brave of women!"

Georgiana gaped. She could imagine Ashdowne muttering imprecations about her, but extolling her virtues? And to this paragon of femininity?

Anne sighed, and continued, "I must admit to being a bit envious at first, for I fear that I am sorely lacking in all those attributes. But just hearing about you has made me vow to be more courageous.''

Georgiana felt her mouth drop open. The woman responsible for her fierce bout of jealousy was striving to be more like her?

"Yes, I know it is presumptuous of me,'' Anne said, obviously misinterpreting her reaction, "but I feel as if you have given me strength.'' She leaned close. "You see I came to Bath on a mission. However, Johnathon so intimidates me that I have failed in it! Oh, I have tried often to tell him my news, but every time I think I shall succeed, my heart quails,'' she said, a hand to her throat.

The gesture made Georgiana see how Ashdowne might react to his sister-in-law, for he was too arrogant and blunt for such theatrics. Yet, Anne was so sweet that Georgiana reined in her own impatience. "I'm sure Ashdowne would never scold *you,*'' she said.

"Oh, he doesn't scold exactly, but he gets that look upon his face as if he can hardly bear the sight of me,'' Anne confided.

"No! I'm sure that isn't true,'' Georgiana protested.

"Oh, you are too kind, as I knew you would be. May I be so bold as to confide in you?'' At Georgiana's nod, Anne leaned close once more. "You see, I have come to know a gentleman,'' she said, a gentle blush tinting her cheeks as she cast her eyes downward. "I met him during my ill-fated visit to London, the only good to come of that dreadful trip, I assure you. But he is wonderful, and he has asked me to become his wife!''

Georgiana blinked. Her jealousy now seemed doubly foolish, for not only were Anne and Ashdowne totally incompatible, but Anne's feelings were engaged elsewhere. What a goose she had been! Smiling with genuine pleasure, she squeezed Anne's gloved hand. "This is wonderful news!"

"Yes," Anne agreed, blushing again. "However, since Johnathon is now the head of the family, I feel that I must gain his permission, and I fear that he will not approve as the gentleman in question is not of a similar rank."

Georgiana felt a momentary qualm. Had Anne fallen for someone unsuitable, just as she had done?

"Oh, he is of genteel birth, and he is devoted to me," Anne said, obviously noticing her concern, "but my dear William, God rest his soul, would never have approved, for Mr. Dawson is in trade, you see."

A tradesman? Georgiana wondered.

"As one of the many younger sons of Viscount Salsbury, he had no title and no expectations, and so he went into speculation and made a fortune in the production of agricultural implements. Not quite the thing, the ton would say, but he is the most kind and gentle of men and I...I..." Her words trailed off as she flushed once more.

Glancing up to see Ashdowne approaching, Georgiana felt her own blush rising, for he had said not a word to her since doing all those extraordinary things to her in her bed. And she was fairly sure that he had left her room unsatisfied, another question that had kept her tossing and turning, and one which she could hardly put to him now.

All her mixed emotions concerning this man who had so lied to her rushed to the fore, unresolved, but for Anne's sake, she knew she must put her own feelings aside for the moment. With grim determination, she stepped forward to intercept him, tugging on his sleeve to pull him close. "Isn't it wonderful?" she said, smiling up at him. "Anne is getting married!"

Ashdowne, who looked startled enough by Georgiana's greeting, now swung his rather intimidating gaze toward his sister-in-law, who immediately looked down at her toes, as if afraid to speak.

"Mr. Dawson is the younger son of Viscount Salsbury," Georgiana explained. "And rich as a nabob!"

Anne glanced up at that, her sensibilities no doubt offended by the bluntness of the remark, but Georgiana continued blithely. "Naturally, you will approve, won't you, of giving Anne away?" Georgiana asked, pinching him through his coat sleeve.

"What? Uh, yes, of course!" Ashdowne said. He looked wary and wan and unhappy, and Georgiana wondered if the man she had thought impervious to everything had somehow been hurt. *By her?* The notion gave her a funny feeling deep inside, where she was already being affected by his mere presence.

"You mean, you will give us your blessing?" Anne asked, her expression sweetly hopeful.

"Certainly," Ashdowne answered. "I have no objections to the match."

For a moment Anne was silent, then she bit her lip in a nervous gesture. "He is in trade," she said in a forthright manner that Georgiana could only admire.

"I'm sure Ashdowne won't care, being a younger brother himself and having to earn his living as...best he could," Georgiana said, garnering a dark look from her companion. "Unless, of course, it bothers you," she added, turning once more to Anne.

Her face flushed, Ashdowne's sister-in-law lifted her dark gaze to Georgiana, her lovely face somber. "No. You see, I am very proud of him," she said.

The soft but sure affirmation from a woman who admitted to her own temerity struck Georgiana quite forcefully, as if Anne were somehow more courageous than herself. She not only believed in the man she loved, but stood up for him, and suddenly Georgiana's feelings for Ashdowne returned in a rush, becoming all mixed up in Anne's testimonial.

Maybe she had been a self-righteous prig to pass judgment on Ashdowne's deeds when deep down inside she felt a certain reluctant admiration for his cleverness and skills and daring. Not many men could have accomplished such feats, Georgiana reminded herself. No one else had ever come close to such a career, while managing to elude everyone—except herself.

"And he's going to pay my debt," Anne murmured, drawing Georgiana from her thoughts.

"Really, Anne, there's no need for—" Ashdowne began.

"No. The loss was due to my own folly, and I won't have you responsible for it. Dear Mr. Dawson says it is the least he can do since my visit to London brought me into his life."

"Very well," Ashdowne said, slanting Georgiana a glance, and she suspected he wanted to speak to her privately. Had he already returned the necklace? If not, he could do so now, without even taking a loss, and she knew a burgeoning sense of euphoria that belied all her doubts about him.

"Georgie!" The great boom of her father's voice made Georgiana wince, for she was not in the mood for his good-natured teasing, especially when it probably would involve Ashdowne. And sure enough, his next words were a hearty greeting to the marquis.

"Lord Ashdowne! Why, we haven't seen you since Georgie returned. Thought you'd abandoned us," he said, winking at the man in a manner that made Georgiana want to flee. Unfortunately, she saw no escape, for her mother was not far behind, with her giggly sisters in tow, while Anne stood waiting for an introduction.

Georgiana was just wondering how the morning could turn any worse when she spotted Jeffries heading toward them with a grim expression. *What now?* she wondered, glancing furtively at Ashdowne. His blue eyes flickered in warning before he donned his usual posture of cool, collected nobleman, and, for his sake, Georgiana tried to remain calm. However, she knew he had no idea that she had once tendered his name as a suspect to the Bow Street Runner. And now was probably not a good time to tell him.

"My lord, Miss Bellewether, ladies," Jeffries said. He nodded his head in a gesture of respect, but he was unusually somber, and for the first time, he looked as if he might actually be qualified for his position. Georgiana felt a shiver of foreboding dance up her spine, but she lifted her chin, determined to reveal nothing of what she knew.

Ashdowne might be a criminal, but she would never send him to the gallows. *Never.* Although the pain of his lies still lingered, his explanation yesterday had not left her unaffected, and last night…Georgiana's body hummed with the memory of his touch, of caresses that she, even in her innocence, sensed had been more than a ploy.

Ashdowne was right. The past was over; it was time to look to the future. And in that moment, Georgiana knew that no matter what he had done, she still loved him, and every experience that had made him the man he was now contributed to that love. She tried to still her telltale trembling at the nearly overwhelming rush of emotion that came with the realization, for she knew that she needed to keep her wits about her while Jeffries stood before them.

"If I could have a word with you in private, my lord," the Bow Street Runner said to Ashdowne, his tone ominous.

"As you can see, I am engaged at the moment," the marquis replied, with just a hint of hauteur that Georgiana had to admire.

"I'm afraid it can't wait, my lord," Jeffries mumbled. He looked chagrined, and Georgiana took heart. The Bow Street Runner couldn't possibly be convinced of Ashdowne's guilt, or he wouldn't look so apologetic, would he? Had Ashdowne had a chance to return the necklace yet? Georgiana wondered again. If so, then Jeffries's suspicions didn't matter, but if not...

"Well, then, say what you will," Ashdowne replied. "I'm sure I have no secrets from this company, especially the lovely Miss Bellewether." Only Georgiana caught the slight inflection in his tone that spoke to her alone, and she didn't know whether to laugh or weep at his bold gesture.

"Very well, then," Jeffries said, looking unhappy. "Some questions have been raised, my lord. And, uh, well, it seems that I must ask you exactly where you were during the time of the theft."

Georgiana started in surprise. Why would the Bow Street Runner suddenly turn his attention to Ashdowne when he had dismissed the marquis in the past? As gasps rose from those who surrounded them, she sent a horrified glance toward Ashdowne, but he evidenced no alarm, only a certain arrogant amusement.

"Really, Jeffries, haven't you got something better to do with your time?" he drawled, one dark brow lifted.

"I beg your pardon, my lord, but it has been brought to my attention that you are one of the few gentleman at the party whose whereabouts I can't account for. So if you will just be so kind as to inform me of them, then I'll be on my way," Jeffries said.

Although Georgiana sensed that the Bow Street Runner was hopeful of that very outcome, he seemed determined to stick to his guns, and she felt a shiver of panic run up her spine.

"Well, if you must know, I was in the garden enjoying a breath of evening air," Ashdowne said with an air of dismissal.

Jeffries's face hardened into a dour but determined expression. "And might there be anyone who could verify that, my lord?"

Ashdowne smiled slightly. "Yes, of course."

"And who might that be?"

Ashdowne eyed the Bow Street Runner with a show of affront. "You really can't expect me to say, Jeffries, for a lady is involved, and I consider myself a gentleman, despite our visit to the garden."

Georgiana was aware of her father's snort of laughter, followed by the nervous giggles of her sisters, while beside her Anne was wide-eyed, pale and dumbstruck. Obviously Ashdowne was hoping to dismiss the Bow Street Runner's insinuation, but Georgiana sensed that Jeffries was not going to be fobbed off so easily.

And before she had even formed the idea in her mind, she stepped forward. "This is really all unnecessary, Mr. Jeffries," she said. He swung toward her with a tired look that warned her not to expound upon her theories, and so she did not. Drawing in a sharp breath, she lifted her chin, intent upon her course. "I was the one with his lordship in the garden. I can vouch for his whereabouts all during the time in question, for he was with me."

Every eye in the vicinity turned to stare at her, and Georgiana heard her mother's horrified gasp as the poor woman swooned into her startled father's arms. Her sisters giggled, Anne blanched, and Jeffries appeared only slightly mollified. Since she had once mentioned Ashdowne as a suspect, the Bow Street Runner probably wondered why she had done so, especially after trysting with him during the theft.

Well, let him wonder, Georgiana thought, for no one but Ashdowne could dispute her claim, and he...she glanced at him, fearful for a moment that he might do just that, yet when she met his gaze, all her fears fled. He was looking at her with a kind of dazed wonder, along with something else that made her heart swell with happiness.

Then he turned toward Jeffries. "I hardly think you a gentleman to bully my fiancée into speech, but I trust you are satisfied now?" he asked, one dark brow lifted.

"Yes, of course, my lord," the Bow Street Runner mumbled. "My apologies, and, uh, congratulations," he added with a grin.

"Thank you," Ashdowne said. "Well, I can see that my secret is no longer safe," he said, with a glance of tender regard toward Georgiana. He reached for her hand and, taking her gloved fingers in her own, faced her parents. Her distraught mother, who was being fanned by both of her sisters, was still supported by her bewildered-looking father, and all of them stared at Ashdowne.

"I fear the situation has forced us to reveal our plans earlier than intended, and I apologize for not speaking with you first about the matter, Mr. Bellewether, but I would accept your best wishes for my upcoming nuptials," Ashdowne said. Lifting their entwined hands, he swung round, his deep voice rising over the murmuring voices of the crowd. "Miss Bellewether and I are to be married."

Her mother, having just been revived by Eustacia and

Araminta, swooned once more, while her sisters' mouths gaped open, and Anne smiled beatifically. For her part, Georgiana, stunned speechless by the announcement, could only blink stupidly as congratulations erupted all around them.

Chapter Seventeen

Amid the flurry of well wishes, Georgiana remained dazed. Her first reaction to Ashdowne's startling announcement had been shock, followed swiftly by a euphoria so intense she thought her knees would give way, and she had been grateful for his supporting arm.

But as her wits began to function once more, Georgiana realized that his sudden proposal had been prompted, not by any overwhelming affection for her, but as a means of salvaging her reputation. She had exonerated him, and a grateful Ashdowne had sought to remedy the injury she had wrought herself in doing so.

Yet Georgiana sought no repayment. She had spoken up out of love for him, and because of that love she wanted his happiness, not a marriage of sacrifice to the daughter of a country squire. Allowing herself no wonderful fancies of a future sharing Ashdowne's company, his conversation, his laughter and his bed, Georgiana tried to concentrate upon the facts of the matter. Unfortunately, the most glaring fact was that she would not make him a suitable marchioness.

And so, even though she wanted to wed Ashdowne more than anything in the world, Georgiana made a solemn vow to do so only if his feelings were engaged. If not, she would put it about that they had a falling out sometime before the end of the summer, so that she might return with her family to their country home, the amazing experiences of Bath behind her. Although the thought was wrenching, Georgiana knew what was right.

She must talk to Ashdowne privately.

Unfortunately, the people who crowded around them in the Pump Room left her little hope of that, and it seemed a full hour before they had finally managed to move through the gathering to the doors. There Georgiana tugged on Ashdowne's sleeve, in a hurry to escape her family and everyone else.

Although Ashdowne's deft maneuvers assured them their exit, once outside, Georgiana kept walking until they reached a secluded spot under a large oak that dipped its branches toward the street. Then she turned toward Ashdowne and blurted out her thoughts without preamble.

"You don't have to marry me," she said. Although anxious to study his face, she didn't trust herself to look at him, so she stared at his elegant neck cloth in an effort to keep her wits about her.

"Oh, but you're wrong, my clever investigator," Ashdowne said, and Georgiana glanced up at him in surprise. "You've discovered the nefarious Lord Whalsey's plans, Mr. Hawkins's unsavory doings, and the identity of The Cat, some very important accomplishments, I must admit. But all along, you have failed to see one very significant truth," he said, stepping closer.

Georgiana looked up at him, puzzled, and his lovely mouth curved into a tender smile. "I want you to be my wife, Georgiana. I wanted you long before your selfless heroism. I've been trying to broach the subject of marriage for some time, but something always seems to interrupt me.''

"But you said nothing the other night...in my room,'' Georgiana protested, a blush rising at the memory.

Ashdowne's smile faded as he studied her soberly. "No, for too much stood between us then. You were quite put out with me, if you remember, and I was certain that you thought me beyond redemption." He paused, his blue eyes glittering with emotion. "It wasn't until this morning that I realized you might care for me, in spite of everything, for why else would you lie to save a thief?"

"Why else, indeed?'' Georgiana whispered as his gaze took on the dark intensity that she had come to recognize.

"I want you, Georgiana, so badly I think I shall die if I don't have you," Ashdowne said, and Georgiana felt the bottom drop out of her stomach. Lifting a hand to her face, he brushed a curl back from her cheek. "I also happen to need you. Ever since I took the title, I've faced a life of drudgery and boredom that no one except you has been able to alleviate. And, just in case you might have forgotten, I am sadly in need of reformation, which only someone of your high moral character could possibly attempt.''

Georgiana smiled as his thumb stroked her cheek, scattering most of the reservations she had harbored about marrying a marquis and a former thief. And with his next words, he eradicated the last of them.

"Most significant of all, I love you. I love your beauty and your intelligence, the logical side of you that somehow coexists with your romantic streak, and the sense of adventure you bring to everything you do. I simply must have you beside me, entertaining and delighting me for the rest of my life. In return, I promise to do my best to avoid criminal activities, protect you in all your wild en-

deavors and—'' Ashdowne paused, his voice dipping low
''—to entertain you as best I can.''

Georgiana blushed as she imagined just how this man
of many talents planned to keep her amused, and she
wished they were really, truly alone, instead of standing
beneath a tree on a public street.

''What say you, Georgiana? Will you take a chance on
me?''

''Oh, Ashdowne!'' Heedless of their location, Georgiana threw her arms around him, burying her face against
his broad chest. ''I love you.''

''Is that a *yes?*'' he asked, his voice a low rumble.

''Yes,'' Georgiana whispered, leaning her head back to
look up at him. He smiled down at her, his gaze moving
from her eyes to her mouth and then to the pale breasts
that were pressed against his chest.

He cleared his throat. ''But, first of all, I promise to
buy you a new wardrobe.''

''That's not necessary, really,'' Georgiana muttered,
her skin heating under his perusal as her thoughts wandered far from fashion.

One dark brow lifted as Ashdowne gave her an amused
look and put her from him gently. ''Wouldn't you like to
get out of those flounces?''

''Uh, yes! Of course!'' Georgiana answered, gathering
her wits once more.

''I've often thought about dressing you,'' Ashdowne
said, as he placed her hand on his arm and led her from
beneath the canopy of leaves. Georgiana's fingers trembled at his words, and she tried not to think about the
night of their wedding—a wedding that she owed, in part,
to the persistent questioning of a certain Bow Street Runner. The thought made her pause, and she squeezed her
companion's arm with sudden urgency.

"Ashdowne. I was thinking—" Georgiana began, ignoring his ensuing groan. "Doesn't it seem strange to you that Jeffries made such a point of targeting you this morning?"

"Yes," he answered, his tone serious once more.

"I mean when I first suggested your name to him—" Georgiana began, only to be cut off by Ashdowne's sudden stop. He swung round to stare at her in horror, but she waved his reaction away with an airy gesture. "Oh, that was way back when I first met him, before you became my assistant," she explained.

When Ashdowne continued to scowl at her, Georgiana made a face. "The point is that Jeffries dismissed my suspicions as ridiculous. And since I've not spoken of you since, except in terms of being my assistant, why the sudden interest in you? Is there someone in Bath, besides me, of course," Georgiana said, flashing him an apologetic smile, "who would suggest your name to Jeffries, indeed, *demand* that he question you?"

They looked at each other, their thoughts coinciding as they spoke at once. "Savonierre."

"He's the only one with enough influence to force Jeffries's hand," Ashdowne muttered.

"And make him confront a marquis," Georgiana added. "And you have no idea why he dislikes you so? He must have some reason to accuse you, for why else would a so-called gentleman of the ton try to send a marquis to the gallows over a piece of jewelry?"

When Ashdowne did not answer, Georgiana frowned. "There has to be more involved than just this incident, for it is all too well contrived. It's almost as if he set you up, but how? Unless…" She turned to stare, dumbstruck, at Ashdowne. "He knows who you are."

"Impossible! No one knows," Ashdowne muttered with his usual arrogance.

"But what if he suspects, and it's The Cat he's seeking revenge against?" Georgiana asked. She swung on Ashdowne accusingly. "Did you steal something from him?"

Ashdowne lifted a dark brow in derision. "Although my actions might have been a bit daring at times, I was never that reckless," he said with a wry grimace before he paused thoughtfully. "However, there was that diamond necklace of Lady Godbey's..."

"What has that to do with Savonierre?" Georgiana asked.

Ashdowne gave her one of his jaded looks. "Rumor has it that Savonierre gifted her the necklace as a gesture of his...affection."

"I see," Georgiana said, ignoring the proprieties to consider the ramifications. "But why would he care after the fact—when the jewelry was no longer his?"

Ashdown shrugged slightly. "He's a very powerful man and doesn't like to be crossed—even indirectly, I suppose. The irony of the whole thing is that the necklace turned out to be paste."

"Paste?"

"Yes. I suspect that Lady Godbey was not so devoted to him as he would have liked. She either sold the original for cash or gave it to a younger, more impoverished fellow, an artist, with whom her name had been linked."

Georgiana shivered, shocked that anyone would trifle so with Savonierre, for she could well imagine his displeasure. Indeed, it was hard to picture him being duped by anyone, even a paramour. "Perhaps he gave her a fake and didn't want the duplicity discovered," she mused.

Ashdowne's mouth curved into an indulgent smile.

"Perhaps, but I suspect that Lady Godbey knows her jewels better than the average silversmith," he said dryly.

"Oh," Georgiana said, discarding that theory. "So he gives her a diamond necklace in good faith, unaware that she soon trades it in for a paste copy, and when The Cat strikes, taking that particular piece of jewelry, he's angry. Perhaps he even sees it as a personal insult and vows to discover the identity of the thief and see him punished."

Georgiana paused, her pulse thrumming, as everything started to come together in her mind. "But you retired, thwarting him rather effectively, and he's not a man to accept defeat. So he has to find a way to draw you out, for one last appearance," she said, her voice rising with her excitement. "He knows that you don't need the money, and so he has to concoct something special to lure you back into the game. What better way than through Anne? He's connected to Lady Culpepper, so it would be easy for him to gain her cooperation."

Ashdowne eyed her skeptically. "I don't know, Georgiana. It sounds like a rather elaborate, convoluted way to gain revenge when he could simply call me out."

"Yes, but Savonierre is complex and convoluted," Georgiana argued. "I have the feeling that he can't do anything straightforward, but must be hatching schemes, if only to entertain himself."

Ashdowne still looked dubious, but he deferred to her, and Georgiana could have kissed him for it. The thought of a lifetime spent kissing this man made her giddy, and she had to force her attention back to the case.

"Very well. Say you're right. Now what?" he asked.

Trying not to focus on his mouth, Georgiana dropped her gaze to his broad chest and swallowed hard as she considered the implications of her theory. "Of course, I can't tell you exactly what he'll do next, but I'm fairly sure of one thing.''

"What?'' Ashdowne said.

"He won't give up,'' Georgiana said, shuddering at the thought. "Ever.''

After she returned home, Georgiana was plagued with questions and more congratulations from her family, and though she loved them, she couldn't help wishing she could run off with Ashdowne immediately. Unfortunately, her mother was already planning the wedding, an event which, in itself, held little interest for Georgiana.

And so when the invitation arrived, Georgiana counted it a welcome interruption—until she realized just who had sent it. Looking down at the elaborately penned note, she felt only foreboding, for why would Lady Culpepper throw an impromptu evening to celebrate her engagement?

All too well, Georgiana recognized Savonierre's fine hand in this, but what did he have planned? Would he try to prove that she had not been with Ashdowne during the theft? He couldn't, Georgiana told herself. But what if he claimed she and Ashdowne had worked together to steal the necklace? Shuddering in outrage, Georgiana nevertheless sent the young messenger away with her acceptance, for she could hardly refuse a party in her own honor. And neither could Ashdowne.

Savonierre had them neatly trapped. Ashdowne could not return the necklace until nightfall, and now whatever opportunity he might have had would be foiled by a houseful of guests and his watchful nemesis. Suppose he was caught in the act? Georgiana wanted desperately to talk to him, but there was no time, for her parents were already urging her to dress for the evening.

Her mind ran in circles while she hurried through her toilette, and it continued doing so during the carriage ride amid the incessant chatter of her sisters. But all her rumination led her to no simple solutions, and she entered Lady Culpepper's lavish home with a cold knot of dread in her stomach.

Lady Culpepper's warm welcome startled her, as did the greetings of the other guests—a far different experience than her last visit when she had entered quietly with Savonierre, a surly Bertrand in tow. Although elevated from country nobody to future marchioness, Georgiana found most of the attention annoying.

The only person she was interested in seeing was Ashdowne, and he was late, forcing her to endure several jests about his possible defection. Her mother, who had always viewed the marquis's company warily, wore a worried frown until Georgiana patted her hand in comfort.

"He will be here," she said with an encouraging smile. It never crossed her mind that Ashdowne would leave her in the lurch, and the realization struck her quite forcefully that he would never abandon her.

Although Ashdowne had broken the law in the past, he had a sense of honor and a character that not many of the august persons gathered around her could claim. Georgiana lifted her chin, feeling a bit like Anne when she defended her tradesman. No matter what had gone before, she believed in Ashdowne implicitly, and she was proud of him, for all the wits and skill that had made him the man he was today.

Savonierre was suggesting dryly that they send someone to fetch her intended when at last Ashdowne arrived, looking as elegant and unconcerned as ever. He claimed his coach had thrown a wheel, forcing him to walk, and Georgiana knew that the vehicle would be found not far away, with Finn making repairs—whether necessary or not.

Where had he *really* been? she wondered, but she did not have a chance to ask him, for well-wishers crowded around them both, followed by endless toasts, and then Lady Culpepper imperiously announced supper, and Georgiana was forced to make polite conversation with a garrulous retired army captain while Ashdowne sat across from her.

It was only after the group had once again adjourned to the reception rooms that Savonierre made his move. Idly twirling a glass of champagne, he approached them with a cool expression that Georgiana knew masked a malevolent intent. She was even more alarmed when she saw Mr. Jeffries appear not far behind, decidedly uncomfortable. Surely the Bow Street Runner was not here to make an arrest?

"So, Miss Bellewether, I assume that your engagement means the end of your investigation?" Savonierre asked, and Georgiana, less accustomed to hiding her emotions than Ashdowne, could barely form an answer.

"Of course not," she finally squeaked in a pathetic imitation of her usual manner.

"Really?" Savonierre asked, his lips curling into a sardonic smile. "Somehow, I find that difficult to believe," he murmured. "How about you, Jeffries?"

"I wouldn't know, sir," the Bow Street Runner said.

"Well, I, for one, agree with you," Ashdowne said, startling Georgiana so that she had to swallow a gurgle of surprise. "After all, the lady's going to be married, so she won't have time for such nonsense."

Georgiana bristled, even though she suspected Ashdowne had a reason for his words. Unfortunately, several older gentlemen nearby heard his words and wholeheartedly agreed with him concerning a woman's place. Georgiana listened, quietly fuming until, just when she was going to burst with outrage, he lifted a dark brow.

"Oh, it's not the investigating in itself that I'm against, just this little matter," Ashdowne said. "I mean, really, a theft such as this in Bath? Bandits crawling up the sides of buildings?" He gave a polite snort of disbelief that made the entire thing seem ludicrous.

"And what exactly do *you* think happened to the emeralds, Ashdowne?" Savonierre asked.

Ashdowne shrugged, as if disinterested. "You know how women are. I suspect that this is all much ado about nothing and that the lady simply misplaced her jewelry."

Savonierre gave a soft, humorless laugh. "I'm afraid you'll have to do better than that, Ashdowne, as my man here has searched the room for clues several times over. Haven't you, Jeffries?" he said over his shoulder, and the Bow Street Runner nodded grimly.

Ashdowne appeared unconcerned. "For clues to some heinous crime perhaps, but for the necklace itself?" His brow lifted in silent query. "Perhaps it became tangled in the bedcovers or fell underneath the furniture," he suggested.

Jeffries, moving in closer, shook his head, his expression sober. "I would have seen it, my lord."

"Well, then, perhaps Lady Culpepper mislaid it, in a drawer while pressed for time. Or maybe she put it away in a another jewel case? I am not suggesting any ill intentions on her part, mind you, but a simple case of carelessness. Ladies these days have so much jewelry, I don't know how they keep track of it all."

Jeffries, looking like a dog that had been thrown a bone, immediately turned toward Lady Culpepper. "Have you more than one place where you keep your gems, my lady?'' he asked.

"Of course, but—" she began only to be cut off by Jeffries's eager speech.

"Please show me," he said.

"I will not! Why, this is outrageous!" she protested, looking down her aristocratic nose at the Bow Street Runner.

"Is there a reason why you would refuse such a reasonable request?" Georgiana asked, only to have the older woman swing toward her, a wrathful expression on her wrinkled countenance.

"You!" she sputtered, as if ready to launch into a diatribe. But then she halted, red faced, for she could hardly attack Georgiana when this gathering had been held to celebrate her engagement. Pasting a smile on her face, she nodded curtly, then turned back to Jeffries. "Come along then, you, and be quick about it, for I don't intend to waste my evening in my room when I have a houseful of guests."

Several of those nearby lauded Lady Culpepper for her graciousness, while others muttered imprecations about the Bow Street Runner they saw as overstepping his limited bounds. Only Savonierre kept his gaze upon Ashdowne, his regard so intent that it made Georgiana shiver. Suddenly cold, she inched closer to the marquis and his warmth.

They did not have long to wait. Georgiana thought she heard a faint shriek, and then Jeffries hurried down the stairs, the necklace in hand, while Lady Culpepper followed behind. She did not look at all pleased to have recovered her favorite piece. She wore a grim expression and glanced toward Savonierre with what Georgiana suspected was trepidation. Without sparing her a glance, he drew close to examine the gems.

When he pronounced them genuine with a harsh murmur, the crowd surged forward, eager to garner a glimpse of the famous emeralds, all except Georgiana and Ashdowne. Suddenly her legs felt unsteady, and her fingers trembled with the force of her relief at this turn of events.

As she sagged against him, Georgiana realized that while everyone below was awaiting his arrival, Ashdowne had managed to return the gems to some other jewelry box, which meant that he could hardly be held accountable for this theft. And the others, being a year ago and more, seemed far too long past to worry about.

He was safe, and Georgiana took his arm, her fingers squeezing his solid muscles as if to reassure herself of the truth. But when she flicked a glance toward Savonierre, she wondered if her joy was not a bit premature, for she could tell by one look at him that the powerful man was not finished with them. Indeed, the thought had barely crossed her mind, when he approached, and she had to force herself to keep her place, instead of backing away.

"May I have a word with you both?" he asked, tilting his head toward the salon where he had once questioned Georgiana.

"Certainly," Ashdowne said with his usual grace. Georgiana did not feel as sanguine, but clung to his side as Savonierre led them into the dim room. Once they were seated, their host shut the door behind him and walked to the center of the room, where he bowed his head in a gesture of acknowledgment.

"Touché, Miss Bellewether, Ashdowne. In this instance, I must concede my defeat," he said. Waving away Ashdowne's show of puzzlement with a deliberate move of his hand, he stood facing them. "No. Let me explain myself," he said.

"At one time I conducted a liaison with a certain lady of the ton, to whom I gave, as a token of my appreciation, a diamond necklace of some value. Although my interest in the lady did not last, you can imagine my annoyance when the piece of jewelry I gifted her was stolen by a rather infamous burglar of the time whom the papers had dubbed The Cat."

Savonierre paused, his lips curling as if to show contempt for that title, but Ashdowne did not react. He evidenced only a polite interest that drew Georgiana's admiration. For her part, it was all she could do not to reveal the stark terror that had struck her the moment Savonierre began to speak.

"In my irritation, I decided that I would put a stop to this fellow's thievery. Mind you, I had always found his exploits mildly amusing until he dared take what was mine." Savonierre's hard face made Georgiana stifle a shudder, and she gripped her hands together to contain her agitation.

"It took me several months to reach a conclusion concerning the robber's identity, but to my dismay, he had come into some good fortune, which precluded the continuation of his criminal activities. However, I was fairly confident that I could draw him out for one last theft," Savonierre said, pausing to eye Ashdowne intently. "You see I understood his desire for danger, for the thrill of duping the idle ton. I could even admire the fellow's cleverness, if only he had not dared to take what was mine."

"Really, Mr. Savonierre," Georgiana protested, alarmed by the direction of his speech, but he cut her off with a cool smile.

"A moment more of your indulgence, please," he said,

turning once more toward Ashdowne. "Unwilling to let the matter lie, I began setting traps for him, but to my frustration, The Cat was too busy or too disinterested to fall for the bait. Taking all the information that I had, I finally decided that, given his current situation, the thief would only make an appearance if I got personal, as he had with me. So I did." He smiled, a twist of his mouth that made Georgiana tremble.

"But I underestimated him," Savonierre said. Although his expression did not show it, she could hear the bitterness in his voice. "I had set the scene to perfection, but The Cat made sure that someone drew me away just long enough for him to steal the bait, so I could not catch him in the act, as I had intended. However, I was certain that I could still expose him."

Savonierre paused to frown consideringly. "Unfortunately, the Bow Street Runner I hired proved incompetent, and though I had high hopes for your abilities, Miss Belle-wether," he said, turning to face her, "I had not taken into account that the thief might use his seductive powers to persuade you to abandon your efforts."

"That's enough, Savonierre," Ashdowne said, rising from his seat, his own expression hard. "I have no idea what you're implying, but I won't let you malign Georgiana."

Did a flicker of surprise appear in Savonierre's fathomless eyes? Georgiana wasn't certain, but he inclined his head in polite concession. "I beg your pardon."

Ashdowne scowled, as if unwilling to accept the smooth apology that rang false, but when, if ever, was Savonierre sincere? Georgiana wondered.

"You are free to go, of course, but be advised that I won't rest until I have—" Savonierre began, only to be cut off by Ashdowne's harsh exclamation.

"No! You be advised, Savonierre," he muttered in a low tone that held its own threat. "Be advised that the necklace was paste, and if I were you, I wouldn't waste time chasing after a man who stole a fake from your ex-mistress. Instead, you might ask her just what she did with the real jewelry."

Although little enough showed on Savonierre's face, Georgiana trembled with the force of his reaction. He seemed to fill the room with a surge of energy, as if the struggle to maintain his polite civility was nearly too much for him. And then, as swiftly as it had come, the powerful sensation was gone, and Georgiana was left wondering what Savonierre would do now.

Would he take Ashdowne's words as an admission of guilt? Have them both thrown in prison, or demand satisfaction? To her surprise, he did none of those things, but simply inclined his head in a gesture of acknowledgment.

"If you are right, then I must extend my apologies. I will, of course, take your advice." With a slight smile of deprecation, he appeared to concede the game he had been playing, leaving Georgiana and Ashdowne to stare after him in mute surprise.

Chapter Eighteen

It seemed to Ashdowne as if all of Bath had turned out for the wedding, whether out of curiosity or as the final celebration of a summer spent in the picturesque city. Although Georgiana's mother had been heard to term the swift preparations for the event "scandalous," her father simply had claimed that Ashdowne knew his own mind and the sooner they were wed the better, in his opinion.

Ashdowne agreed heartily, for during the past weeks he had often been tempted to carry Georgiana off to Gretna Green in an impulsive and primitive act of possession. But he wanted no furtive whispers about their union and so the nuptials had been hurriedly planned and finally held this morning at the old abbey, with a breakfast following at the house in Camden Place.

And tonight, at last, Georgiana would be his. Ashdowne drew in a breath in an effort to restrain the passion that had been building in him for months. Slanting a glance at his bride in her deceptively simple blue silk gown, he thought about stripping the elegant creation from her gorgeous body and knew a sharp urge to throw her over his shoulder and march upstairs right now, the guests be damned.

Only his resolve to cause his wife no further distress kept him at her side, smiling and mumbling inanities to the seemingly endless number of well-wishers. Of course, not everyone they had met during the eventful summer was here. The much maligned Lord Whalsey reportedly had eloped with a spinster heiress who adored his balding pate, while Mr. Hawkins had been escorted out of town by a jealous husband, with Ashdowne's prompting.

As he stood surveying the crowd, Ashdowne noticed Jeffries moving toward them, and for the first time, he felt no unease at the Bow Street Runner's arrival. Having come from London especially for the festivities, Jeffries headed toward an oblivious Georgiana.

"Miss? I mean, my lady?" he said, trying to garner Georgiana's attention. Unfortunately, she was turned the other way and abruptly swung round, the reticule she was holding arcing fiercely toward Ashdowne's chest. Well accustomed to such threats, Ashdowne simply caught the missile in one hand, while snaking his other arm around his wife's waist in order to keep her perfectly balanced. He was rewarded with Georgiana's blink of surprise and a grateful smile that was an abbreviated version of The Look. He nearly sighed in bliss.

"Very neatly done, my lord," Jeffries said, breaking into a grin.

"Thank you," Ashdowne said dryly.

"I'm thinking you are her keeper, after all, and a good job you're doing of it," the Bow Street Runner said.

"And it's just as well since I've taken on the job permanently," Ashdowne said, slanting a fond look toward his wife. "It's a difficult task, but with such attractive benefits," he murmured, enjoying the sight of his wife's blush. As if she had put up with enough of his teasing,

Georgiana donned her most businesslike expression and nodded at the Bow Street Runner.

"Thank you for coming, Mr. Jeffries," she said. "You left Bath so abruptly that I never had a chance to say goodbye and to thank you for your collaboration."

"Well, once the necklace was found, there was no reason for me to stay, but I enjoyed our little talks, miss, I mean, my lady. You're the most unusual female I've ever met, if you pardon my saying so," Jeffries said.

"My thoughts exactly," Ashdowne muttered, but as Jeffries made his farewells, he felt a nagging twinge of guilt. Although he'd been avoiding it for weeks, it kept returning, reminding him that Jeffries had no idea Georgiana had solved the Bath case on her own. No one knew, for the theft wasn't even a theft anymore. Although the return of the emeralds had absolved Ashdowne of all possible suspicions, it had also dashed Georgiana's dreams. And that was something he couldn't forget—or forgive.

Suddenly aware of his own scowl, Ashdowne shook off his grim mood to greet Georgiana's great-uncle, a small, scholarly looking gentleman who studied him through thick glasses.

"So you're Ashdowne," Silas said, peering at him as if he were a scientific specimen.

Grateful that Georgiana had never gone to London with this fellow, Ashdowne smiled.

Silas nodded slowly, apparently satisfied with the inspection. "If Georgiana picked you, I expect you'll do, but just remember, my boy, geniuses are a bit eccentric. You have to give them the chance to pursue their studies, and every once in a while you have to indulge them."

Ashdowne tried to remember how long it had been since anyone had had the audacity to call him a boy, but he schooled his expression to sober agreement. "Well, I know it, sir. And I have every intention of keeping this one busy for a long time to come,'' he said, tilting his head toward Georgiana with a pride he did not attempt to disguise.

Obviously pleased with Ashdowne's reply, Silas moved off with a chuckle, but Ashdowne's uneasiness returned, along with his guilt, until he could no longer contain it. Taking Georgiana's hands in his own, he pulled her into a small alcove for a moment's privacy. When she gazed up at him expectantly, he felt his throat tighten.

"I've had so much to apologize for that I never told you...I'm sorry that I deprived you of your rightful recognition," he whispered. "But I meant all I said about London. Whenever you want to go, we will, and I'll introduce you to the most brilliant minds, so that you may shine among your own."

Georgiana gazed up at him in surprise. "I'm married to the most brilliant mind I've ever met, so what do I need with others?" she asked, giving him her *why are you being so obtuse* look. "I know I once craved fame, but I'm perfectly content with an admiring audience of one as long as *you* are that one, and maybe that's what I was looking for all along."

Uncertain of his composure, Ashdowne squeezed her hands with his own. "If you say so. Of course, at my estate there are hundreds of people, staff and tenants and villagers, who might be in need of your expertise." And if they weren't, Ashdowne had every intention of manufacturing something—anything—to engage her interest, for he planned to spend his lifetime trying to make her happy.

"That sounds wonderful, for you know that I do love a good mystery," Georgiana said. "But, do you know something else, Ashdowne? I think love is the greatest mystery of all, and I wouldn't mind working on solving it. Indeed, I'm ready for a new adventure…tonight.''

Her husky whisper made Ashdowne's body leap to life, and he groaned as he leaned toward her only to pull back. ''When are the guests leaving?'' he asked, lifting one dark brow in inquiry.

Not soon enough.

It was well into afternoon when Georgiana's relatives finally bade her goodbye. They were under the impression that the couple would be traveling to his family seat, but Ashdowne was rapidly reconsidering that plan. With Georgiana here, the Camden Place house didn't seem nearly so objectionable, and he had the uneasy suspicion that unless his wife wanted to be deflowered in a coach, they might as well stay here, for the night at least.

And so, in the hazy light of a golden Bath afternoon, Ashdowne led his countess to the garish bedroom, softened by her very presence, and began stripping off her elegant wedding gown, as he had so longed to do all day. And, as before, when they were together like this everything seemed to move more slowly, as if time itself was suspended. Like the night in the baths and in her bedroom, Ashdowne felt dazed, his blood thickening in his veins as he touched her.

He had not done so during the weeks before their wedding, for he had not trusted himself, and now he was glad of the wait, for a new poignancy colored each intention. Shuddering at his first caress of her bare skin, Ashdowne felt emotions swell within him. ''I love you, Georgiana,'' he murmured as he dipped his head to kiss her shoulder.

It was far smoother than the fine silk of her gown, and he let the garment fall to the floor as he explored each pale inch of her arms and her throat before turning his attention to the curves visible above her white shift. ''All of you, Georgiana. I want all of you, your mind, your heart, your body,'' he murmured as his palms covered her breasts.

She whimpered in agreement as he stroked, grazing the silk against her in wide circles that gradually narrowed down to the hard tips. But as delightful as this play was, he wanted to taste her nipples, free and unadorned, and so he reached for the hem of the undergarment, slowly lifting it as he stroked the backs of her legs, her buttocks, her shoulders. And then it was gone, and she stood before him in stockings and slippers, her body gilded by the late afternoon light that flooded through the tall windows.

''You are so beautiful,'' Ashdowne whispered. When she accepted his compliment with a grimace, he laughed and pointed to her heart. ''Here and here, too,'' he added, touching her forehead.

''Thank you. So are you,'' Georgiana murmured, and the way her gaze traveled up and down his body made Ashdowne want to rip off all his clothes in a heated frenzy. But there was no need. Georgiana stepped forward and tugged off his coat with a boldness that didn't surprise him.

Then she unbuttoned his waistcoat and slid off his shirt, her tiny hands exploring his chest in a manner that made him throw back his head in ecstasy. His innocent bride didn't stop there, but ran her palms down his hips to his groin. The feel of her touching him, even through the cloth, was almost too much, and for a moment he thought he might spill himself into his clothes.

''No, Georgiana sweet. Not yet,'' he whispered hoarsely, pushing her hand away. But Georgiana was nothing if not persistent, and she returned to struggle with his buttons and tug his garments down to his ankles. Instead of removing them entirely, she seemed distracted by his legs, for Ashdowne felt her gentle fingers slide upward, and he groaned.

Suddenly she paused, and when he looked down, he saw her kneeling before him, her blond curls a bright frame to the beautiful face that was poised within inches of his hardness. He sucked in a breath, warning her with his glance, but she rarely heeded him, and leaning forward, she pressed a kiss to the tip.

Where had innocent Georgiana learned such a thing? Ashdowne wondered, as he shuddered so forcefully that he came up against the bed and sat down hard on the soft surface.

As if divining his startled expression, she whispered, "Just like in the book."

Ashdowne had a fleeting memory of the erotic drawings they had viewed in the baths before Georgiana climbed onto his lap, and all thoughts fled as he frantically kicked off the restraints of his clothing and his boots.

Fully aware of the need to slow down, Ashdowne tried to restrain his own urgency, but his passion had been too long denied and Georgiana was straddling him. Stroking her hair, her face and her shoulders, he drew her close, his member throbbing insistently beneath her. When it touched her own moist heat, he released a harsh groan.

"Georgiana—" Ashdowne meant to warn her, but she was rubbing against him, and his restraint was gone. Gently gripping her hips, he lowered her and thrust upward into her slick heat. He heard her soft cry, and then he was home, so high inside her that he shuddered with the need to spill his seed. He stayed there, painfully still, as he stroked her back, his face buried in her hair until he felt her hands on his jaw, turning him toward her.

"It's all right. I want to give you pleasure," she said, softly. And when her mouth met his, open and giving,

Ashdowne's caution fled. Gripping her tightly, he thrust upward, slowly at first, and then with a frantic pace that had him grunting and groaning, his body sleek with sweat, his mind focused only on the hot pressure of need that drove him on until he exploded with a hoarse shout. His violent shudders gradually faded, and at last he fell back across the bed, Georgiana still in his arms only to realize just what he had done.

"It wasn't supposed to be like that," he muttered aloud. He had planned a tender, romantic initiation for his virgin bride, but somewhere along the line she had *distracted* him. With a frown, Ashdowne opened his eyes to see Georgiana sprawled on top of him, her chin resting in one hand. As he watched, she blew a curl from her forehead.

"Why not?" she asked. "It was your turn."

"My *turn?*" Ashdowne echoed.

"The last time, in my bedroom, I know that you went away without…" Her words dissolved into a pink blush, and Ashdowne felt a new rush of emotion at her selflessness.

"Oh, Georgiana sweet, that doesn't mean your first experience had to be like this. I should have taken my time," he muttered, reaching up to cup her cheek.

She shrugged, the action bobbing her breasts against his chest, and Ashdowne drew in a harsh breath. "But we have all the time in the world to do whatever we want, even all those things in the book," she whispered with a smile that was somehow both shy and provocative.

That book! Ashdowne wondered if it would be the death of him, and his body hardened in enthusiastic response. Rolling Georgiana beneath him, he smiled down at her luscious form, bound to him forever. She was right, for they were just beginning, Ashdowne thought, and he lowered his mouth to her breast, determined to discover all of her secrets. Soon he more than made up for his wife's previous lack, as he found those pleasure spots that most enthralled her, along with a certain movement that wrung new cries of ecstacy from her.

When at last they curled up together, too exhausted to move, moonlight was splashing over the disheveled covers of the bed, and Georgiana gave him a new version of The Look that left him blissful as she whispered to him. "As I said before, Ashdowne, you're a man of many talents."

They spent the next few days in the bedroom, Georgiana finally dragging him from the house so that the maids could clean and that they might take the air. Enjoying the first brisk breeze of the coming fall, Ashdowne walked along the familiar streets of Bath and began to wonder if they ought not to return next summer. Perhaps to a more comfortable residence, he thought, only to have his musings interrupted when Georgiana pulled him to a halt and tugged on his sleeve.

"Look at that," she whispered in a tone he had not heard for some time.

"What?" Ashdowne scanned the area, seeing nothing out of the ordinary, but he didn't have Georgiana's particular sensibilities. He glanced toward her in question.

"Over there. Don't you see anything suspicious about that man in the blue coat?" Without waiting for his answer, Georgiana continued, a bit breathlessly, "It looks as though he's following that woman!"

"Really?" Ashdowne asked, grinning in delight.

"See! There he goes, right after her. Do you think we ought to follow him?" Georgiana asked.

Gazing down at his wife, Ashdowne gave in to his next adventure, the first of many more, he knew, and he shrugged with careless abandon. ''Why not?''

*   *   *   *   *

Take a trip to Merry Old England
with four exciting stories from

In January 2000, look for
THE GENTLEMAN THIEF
by **Deborah Simmons**
(England, 1818)
and
MY LADY RELUCTANT
by **Laurie Grant**
(England, 1141)

In February 2000, look for
THE ROGUE
The second book of
KNIGHTS OF THE BLACK ROSE
by **Ana Seymour**
(England, 1222)
and
ANGEL OF THE KNIGHT
by **Diana Hall**
(England, 1154)

Harlequin Historicals
The way the past *should* have been.

Available at your favorite retail outlet.

If you enjoyed what you just read,
then we've got an offer you can't resist!

Take 2 bestselling love stories FREE!

Plus get a FREE surprise gift!

Clip this page and mail it to Harlequin Reader Service®

IN U.S.A.
3010 Walden Ave.
P.O. Box 1867
Buffalo, N.Y. 14240-1867

IN CANADA
P.O. Box 609
Fort Erie, Ontario
L2A 5X3

YES! Please send me 2 free Harlequin Historical™ novels and my free surprise gift. Then send me 6 brand-new novels every month, which I will receive months before they're available in stores. In the U.S.A., bill me at the bargain price of $3.94 plus 25¢ delivery per book and applicable sales tax, if any*. In Canada, bill me at the bargain price of $4.19 plus 25¢ delivery per book and applicable taxes**. That's the complete price and a savings of over 10% off the cover prices—what a great deal! I understand that accepting the 2 free books and gift places me under no obligation ever to buy any books. I can always return a shipment and cancel at any time. Even if I never buy another book from Harlequin, the 2 free books and gift are mine to keep forever. So why not take us up on our invitation. You'll be glad you did!

246 HEN CNE2
349 HEN CNE4

Name	(PLEASE PRINT)	
Address	Apt.#	
City	State/Prov.	Zip/Postal Code

* Terms and prices subject to change without notice. Sales tax applicable in N.Y.
** Canadian residents will be charged applicable provincial taxes and GST.
   All orders subject to approval. Offer limited to one per household.
   ® are registered trademarks of Harlequin Enterprises Limited.

HIST99   ©1998 Harlequin Enterprises Limited

COMING NEXT MONTH FROM

HARLEQUIN HISTORICALS

- **THE ROGUE**
  by **Ana Seymour,** author of LORD OF LYONSBRIDGE
  In the second book of the *Knights of the Black Rose* series, a
  knight returns from the Crusades to learn he has a young son,
  and finds himself involved in a battle of the heart with the
  woman who has been raising his child.
  HH #499 ISBN# 29099-3 $4.99 U.S./$5.99 CAN.

- **WRITTEN IN THE HEART**
  by **Judith Stacy,** author of THE DREAMMAKER
  When a wealthy, uptight businessman hires a marriage-shy
  handwriting analyst to solve his company's capers, he discovers
  the mystery of love beneath his hardened heart.
  HH #500 ISBN# 29100-0 $4.99 U.S./$5.99 CAN.

- **ANGEL OF THE KNIGHT**
  by **Diana Hall,** author of BRANDED HEARTS
  In the sequel to WARRIOR'S DECEPTION, a lucky knight
  loses his heart to his betrothed, but finds he must help free her
  from a family curse before they can ever have a future together.
  HH #501 ISBN# 29101-9 $4.99 U.S./$5.99 CAN.

- **A BRIDE FOR McCAIN**
  by **Mary Burton**
  A mining millionaire falls in love with an heiress masquerading
  as the town's schoolteacher, and they enter into a marriage of
  convenience to protect her from the dangers of the West.
  HH #502 ISBN# 29102-7 $4.99 U.S./$5.99 CAN.

DON'T MISS ANY OF
THESE TERRIFIC NEW TITLES!

CNM0200